LOCKED

LOCKED: Book Two of The Golden Trilogy
Copyright © 2017 by K.M. Robinson.

Published by Crescent Sea Publishing.
www.crescentseapublishing.com

Cover designed by Reading Transforms.
Image copyright © K.M. Robinson Photography.
Interior graphics by Millennium Genesis.

LOCKED

BOOK TWO OF THE GOLDEN TRILOGY

K.M. ROBINSON

DEDICATION

*To those who fight for what is right, even when it costs them.
It's not easy to put yourself last in order to take care of others.
Well done. I'm proud of you. Keep going!*

My story continues like this:

Goldilocks, having been separated from her love, the young Baer, is forced to work with her enemy to fight her way back to her people and country. She must decide who to trust and just how far she is willing to go to get back to where she belongs. Goldilocks was supposed to have a simple story, but that couldn't be further from the truth.

The stories never mention the war we had to fight, both in our country and on the other side of the wall. People neglect to talk about how enemies had to choose to unite or work to tear each other apart and destroy any hope of survival. They always ignore the part where I found myself trapped on the far side of the wall and what it took for me to return. They never talk about how many lives would be lost along the way.

My name is Auluria, and I won't stop until I've found out whether or not the Baers are still alive and I've brought the Society to its knees.

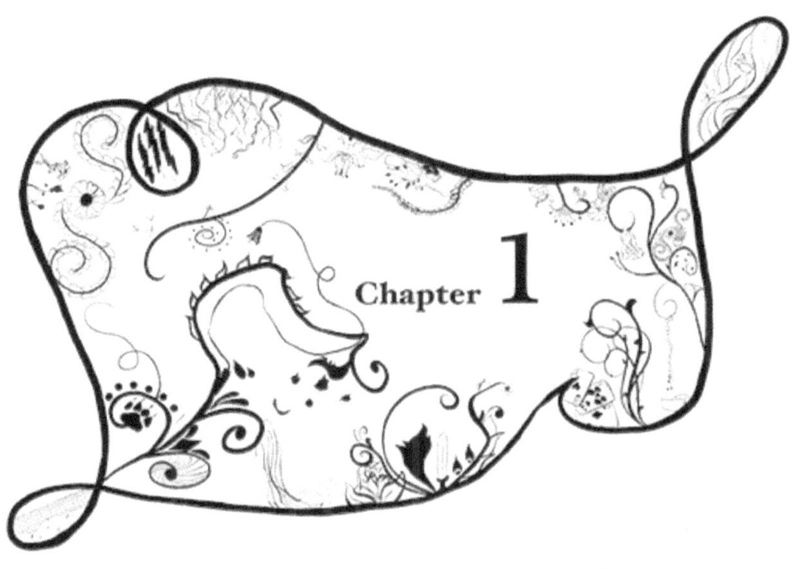

Chapter 1

THE MOMENTS BETWEEN *KNOWING* THE PAIN IS COMING and actually *feeling* it are the most agonizing. As soon as I heard it—the low, vicious growl—I stopped moving. I held in my gasp, as I had been trained to do.

Before I could turn to confront my attacker, I heard the collision as body met body. The wolf that had been crouching behind me flailed in the grass. It hissed and snarled as it tried to attack Shadoe.

He held the beast back, trying to strangle it. Without thinking, I picked up a large branch and brought it down on the gray wolf's head, silencing it. Shadoe made sure the job was done.

It had been a week since Shadoe and I escaped over

the wall. Dov, the man I cared for, was still trapped somewhere in the Society. He gave himself up to save me, as he had been doing since the day I met him all those months ago.

Shadoe, my former handler, and I had been traveling together since that day. I didn't trust him, but we still work as well together as the day we started training. I relaxed enough to work with him without fearing for my life.

The day we escaped, I learned a great deal of information from Shadoe as he attempted to convince me not to run. Every day since, he tried to show me he was not a threat. We both worked for my older cousin Lowell, following his every command. His mission was to take down the Society by framing Dov Baer, his older brother Berwyn, and Berwyn's wife, Eden, along with their entire group. Knowing I could never be a part of that once I met Dov, I betrayed Lowell.

Shadoe remained loyal to Lowell, despite the fact that he was gone. Just before our escape, the government was going to hang us. In an effort to save Lowell, his men unintentionally gave us the opportunity to escape. When the soldiers finally caught up with us, we split up. Silas and Eden ran toward the woods. Dov and I ran toward the town. Shadoe found us at the wall and helped Dov to save me. The last thing I saw was the soldiers capturing the man who stayed behind to protect me.

Shadoe and I had rabbit meat, having saved our meal from the wolf. A meal of anything more than tiny birds was more than I could ask for. My former handler and I set up camp in the wastelands that lie between our nation and the foreign nations that attacked our people. With our camp being only a few miles outside of the closest foreign town, we had the perfect opportunity to spy on them while staying far enough away to keep from being discovered.

Each day, we crept toward the city. Each day, we got a little closer, pushing our luck and challenging them to notice our approach. The next day we planned to go into the city. I prayed it wouldn't be our last.

"Are you ready Lur?" Shadoe asked me.

I tucked the last bit of my long, golden hair under my wrap and nodded to him.

Shadoe and I carried sacks of food we had gathered to trade. We decided the best thing we could do was disguise ourselves as traders to get around the city without much notice. Some of the rabbit meat was tucked away in our bags, ready to be bartered for supplies. I was grateful we could hunt in the wastelands.

"What do you have, dearie?" A woman clutched my arm and held up several strings of beads.

The glittering crystals caught my eye as they shimmered. For a moment I was lost in their beauty.

"They're beautiful, but not today, thank you." I shook her off.

"We need more weapons." Shadoe muttered.

Shadoe had always been practical. For as long as I'd known him, he always made the dependable choice. Shadoe had been assigned to me since the day my cousin brought me into his fold. He had been my trainer, my partner, and even the man I was supposed to marry. Together, we were to lead as Lowell's next in command.

I glanced around, looking at the goods for sale. This town was much freer than where Shadoe and I came from. People came and went as they pleased. There was still an oppressive feeling over the town, but the fear was not as great. I concluded it must be because they were so far away from the people controlling them.

"Shadoe… " I nodded to a nearby man.

He eyed the short man before stepping over to speak with him. I stood near, my back to his. I pretended to scan the area for trades, but really, I was watching for oncoming attacks.

I imagined they must have been hunting us by now. The Society was furious with me. They may not know Shadoe, but *I* had escaped. They would be coming for me.

Over the years I worked with Shadoe, he had trained me well; our reactions to each other came instinctively.

We walked away with several knives, having traded for the rabbit meat and several small birds. I put a knife in each crumbling boot, grateful to have it securely against my skin. My hand brushed over the knife in my belt.

I watched as children ran through the streets. They reminded me of the little ones from the storehouse. I hoped they were all safe under Berwyn's watch.

I still didn't know of Berwyn's fate. He had been poisoned during our plan to show the government it was Lowell who had attacked them, rather than the Baers. I still hadn't worked up the courage to ask Shadoe what he dosed Berwyn with. My sight bounced to Shadoe's hip where the dangerous metal claw hung, just out of sight under his shirt.

Shadoe nudged me and I looked away from the children's game. Just inside a small doorway sat a row of boots, ready for sale. We cautiously approached the illuminated doorway, warm with candlelight, even in the day.

"Welcome. Welcome." An older man eyed us. "Freshly made boots, perfect for long journeys and hard labor."

His eyes swept from my wrapped hair all the way down to my boots. He grimaced at the sight of them. They were the same boots I had had when I started

Lowell's mission all those months ago. Somehow they survived every attack and murder attempt. They served me well, but I was in desperate need of a new pair.

"What do you have?" he asked, and Shadoe showed him the remainder of our trade items. "Not enough, but for the pretty lady, I'll take it."

I shook my head at Shadoe. It was way too much and we hadn't finished gathering our supplies yet. I started to walk away when I heard the man speak again.

"Which pair would you like?"

I turned to see Shadoe handing everything we had left to the man.

"No." I shook my head again.

"Be practical, Lur. You need this. We can come back another day."

I tipped my head at him, trying to read him. On one hand, I couldn't imagine Shadoe ever paying such a steep price for something as simple as everyday boots. On the other hand, I really needed them. I hadn't complained, but I knew he could tell that it was getting too bad for me to continue in them.

Sighing, I reached down to inspect them. I tried several on before selecting a pair. I used my skirt to block my knives as I tested them. The man never knew I had them safely hidden around my ankles.

"Thank you," I said as we left.

"You needed them," was all he said.

Shadoe had always been a man of few words…at least to me.

We hunted again that afternoon. I never had the stomach for killing, so I helped Shadoe track, but allowed him to take them down. It made me sick each time, but I knew it was the only reason we were able to survive.

The sky was dark that night. The clouds blocked the moon, allowing us slivers of passing light as we lay on the ground next to the fire. On our journey we had seen several nomadic groups roaming about, so we felt safe enough to have the flames at night.

The days were growing short and the air was getting cooler as summer slipped into fall. The leaves dropped off of the trees and swirled around our feet.

"Tomorrow we'll go back again. We need to be seen. The more familiar they become with us, the more they will let their guard down." Shadoe said absent-mindedly.

"Shadoe?" I asked. "What's the plan?"

He looked at me as if I was crazy. "The plan is to get information, Lur, you know that."

"I mean the long-term plan. We escaped, but all those people are still back there. What are we going to do?"

"Auluria." He demanded my full attention. "We're not

going to *do* anything. You're safe. Now we just have to survive."

Now it was my turn to look shocked.

"Shadoe, I'm not just leaving them there. I'm going back for them, whether you help me or not. It's just a matter of when and how."

I couldn't read his expression as he gave me a strange look.

"The guards took him, Lur. If they didn't kill him on the spot, they have surely hung him by this point."

I felt like I had been punched in the gut. Not even the pain of the torture I had received only weeks earlier compared to the notion of Dov being dead.

"He's not dead. He can't be." I said quietly.

Shadoe sighed at me and rolled over, ending the discussion.

But I didn't care. I would find a way back. I'd save Dov and Eden, Silas and Berwyn. I'd save all of the Baers' group. I wouldn't give up on them.

I brushed my hair back with my cold hand and forced the tears back into their deep wells.

Chapter 2

BY MORNING I HAD A PLAN. I'D LEARN MY WAY AROUND THE city. I would find alliances if I could. I'd find a way to provide for myself, and then, if need be, I'd slip away from Shadoe and run. I knew it was very likely that he'd find me and drag me back away from the wall, but I had to try.

The town was full of people again. They bumped and jostled into each other as they walked. I watched carefully for every move they made.

"Hello again, dearie," an old lady said—the woman with the beads.

This time she carried a small cart behind her. "Help an

old woman, dearie, and I'll let you have one of these." She held up a sparkling necklace.

"What do you need?" I asked kindly.

"I need to be across town." She looked down to her cart, heavy with bottles, jars and crates.

I nodded to Shadoe, indicating he should let me be. He branched off and went to trade. I picked up the handles and followed behind the woman.

"What's your name, dearie?" she questioned me.

"Au… " I caught myself. "Lur. My name is Lur."

"That's an unusual name, dearie. *Lur.*" She grinned as she tried out my name. "I'm Necesta. As you can see, I'm a bit of a medicine woman. Nothing other-worldly, mind you, but herbs and natural remedies. And the beads, of course." She chuckled to herself.

"You seem to be quite experienced." I remarked, trying to keep the conversation going.

"Oh yes, dearie. I've been doing this since before your parents were even born."

"Where are you taking all this?" I asked.

"Across town where I set up shop once a month. If people need me, they find me, but I try to make myself available in different locations when I can," she croaked, still chuckling.

I could tell as she walked that she was stronger than she appeared to be. I had no doubt she had been about to haul the load by herself. It made me wary.

Once we arrived, she asked me to help set up. It was almost like a small shack, similar the ones the Baers had in back of their house—only this was missing a side. The front had been removed, leaving it open to the world. There were several chairs and a table waiting.

She set out a few things but left most of her work in her cart.

"Sit, dearie, you could learn a thing or two." She winked at me.

I obliged out of curiosity, but my hand sat on the knife in my belt as I leaned away from her.

Almost immediately people started making their way toward the shack. Necesta called out ingredients for me to fetch for her. I examined each one before handing it to her. Watching, I waited as she set a young boy's broken arm. I helped her as she wrapped the hand of a man who had lost a finger, barely stomaching the blood.

Within a few hours, I felt strangely at peace around the woman.

"Necesta, thank you for letting me help you today. I've truly enjoyed it." I said. "Let me help you take your cart back."

I stood and picked up the handles. She nodded and we walked together back to her side of the city. Most of the cart's contents were gone, making the trip lighter.

"Where's that friend of yours, dearie?" she asked as we drew close to the street we met on. "Is he your lover?"

Her question nearly pulled me to a halt, but I caught myself and continued with only a slight hesitation in my step.

"No, he's not. He's a friend."

"I thought so. You didn't seem too worried when he left your side. *Him*, on the other hand, *he likes you*."

I gathered that Necesta was a woman of many talents. She was very perceptive, even if she was a little off.

"You'll both come to dinner, and then I'll pay you for your help."

"Oh no, Necesta, you don't have to pay me, I enjoyed it. And we don't want to impose… "

"Oh, nonsense, dearie. Go find your companion and let's get on with it," she demanded, scuttling into a small house.

Shadoe appeared, as if on cue.

"You were watching," I said without turning to him.

"Of course," he grumbled.

"Did you get anything accomplished today?" I asked.

"Yes." He seemed cross. "I stayed close in case you needed me, but I didn't watch you all day. You're trained well enough to take care of yourself. I just wanted to be sure you were all right; this *is* a new place, after all."

"Necesta wants us to stay."

He raised his eyebrows at me.

"She's feeding us. Just don't be rude." I said stomping off toward Necesta's door.

Shadoe followed me. The house was small, but the warmth of the fire was like heaven. She pointed to the table where she had already started setting out food.

"So, young man," Necesta started. "I have already met *Goldilocks* here, but I haven't had the pleasure of meeting her *young male* companion yet."

"I'm Shadoe, ma'am." He introduced himself as she bustled about the room.

"Ma'am," she mocked. *"Ma'am.* I may be an old grandma, young man, but you will call me Necesta, understood?"

"Yes," Shadoe confirmed rigidly.

"Yes?" she prompted, hands on hips.

"Yes, Necesta."

"That's better." She proclaimed, "Now, tell me. Where are you two from? It's not around here, that's for sure. And it's not from *our* country... Now don't worry," she said glancing at us, "no one else knows that. I'm just a perceptive old lady who's been around long enough to know who's from here and who ain't."

Shadoe and I were both horrified but managed to keep straight faces. I felt him stiffen, preparing to run if needed.

"Relax, young man, I'm not telling anyone. I'm only saying if you and your pretty lady friend were to have come from over that wall"—

She pointed in the direction of the wall—"then I'd just

be obliged to tell you that there are those of us who wouldn't mind it. That's all. *Apple?*"

I sat stunned for a moment before reaching for the red apple in her hand. *How had she known? Did she know who I really was?*

"You aren't the first to run, dearie," she said, eyeing me.

"*You... ?*" I couldn't stop myself in time.

"Yes, dearie. I was once just like you. I jumped the wall and escaped. I found refuge here, though hardly anyone knows it. Don't worry; I'm on your side. Tell me, how has it been?"

"How did you survive?" Shadoe interrupted, unwilling to give her any information.

"Same as you will. I made friends. I learned to blend in. I made myself important." She nodded as she started to eat. "You'll find this place, while still controlled by violence and fear, to be a much easier place to live. Only, though, because we're so far removed from the capitol. Once they want something from us, which is still often, it can be very deadly. On days like today, when there is no oversight, we're free." She smiled thoughtfully.

I was beginning to like this woman. She was a no-nonsense, down-to-business, incredibly perceptive person. I had no doubt she was a good person to know in this town.

We finished our meal without upsetting Shadoe any

further. We thanked Necesta and walked back to our campsite. Shadoe checked behind us every few steps the entire way back.

"I like her," I announced. "I think she's going to be helpful to us."

I touched the necklace around my throat. I insisted Necesta keep it, but she forced me to try it on and then pushed me out the door. I took it off and put it in my pocket.

"Keep it on, dearie," she had said, "so they know you're one of my friends. It will keep you safe here."

The next day when we went back to the town, I would wear it for her to see. Its jewels sparkled in the firelight before I dropped them into my pocket.

"We'll be careful," I said, "but I think we can trust her."

Chapter 3

SLEEP NEVER CAME EASY. FACES FLITTED THROUGH MY dreams, vanishing and reappearing. I watched as Dov was murdered a hundred different ways. I woke up screaming, Shadoe at my side. He said nothing, but watched over me as I tried to shed the tension in my body.

I stared at Eden's hollow eyes as the Society dragged her away time after time. I saw Berwyn crumpling under the force of the poison. I watched Silas being carved apart. I even saw myself being forced to watch their torture.

At times, I pictured Reyla and the girls I met in the storehouse. Reyla's face fell in my dreams as it did the day

I told her that her beloved Peter was dead. Other times, I saw little Jaseleen and the other children, terrified, as we all went off to war.

Gone were the times I dreamed of happy memories from the past few months. Only the unanswered questions haunted me. Had any of us survived?

I dreamed of Dov that night. My precious Dov, who sacrificed his life for me, who saved me and protected me. My Dov, who took a beating to protect the lives of his people and his enemies. My darling Dov, who right now was with the people who hated us most… if he was alive at all. I would have given anything to just know what became of him after he chased me to safety that day.

I dreamed he was sitting in his cell—the same awful cell we had been forced into weeks earlier after our capture. In my twisted nightmare, the skin hung off his arm, even worse than the very real torture he had endured in my presence. I saw him covered with knife wounds and blood was everywhere. He blinked but he couldn't see me.

In my dream, I stood, just out of reach, screaming to him, but he never heard me. Suddenly Berwyn, Eden, Silas, Reyla, Gloria, and the others were standing there.

They blamed me. They screamed and accused and mocked me.

Lowell stepped out from the crowd, grinning at me. "At least I paid you back, *Missy*."

Shadoe stepped from behind him in my dream. "He was never yours anyway."

Marty, my vicious attacker, moved forward. "Not a golden boy anymore, is he? Nice work, golden girl." He laughed.

I tried to push past them, attempting to get to Dov. I screamed his name. When he finally turned to me, it wasn't his deep blue eyes I loved, but murky, dead eyes. His head lolled to the side as I slipped in his blood and fell at his feet.

The crowd behind me whispered, "You."

Somehow, even though I knew it couldn't happen, I found his dead hand grasping mine.

As I had each night before, I woke up screaming. Shadoe shushed me. He kept watch as I cried. Under normal circumstances, Shadoe would have never tolerated me showing this kind of emotion. I suppose I didn't give him much of a choice.

"Dearie, dearie!" I heard the old woman cry as Shadoe and I walked down the streets the next morning. He stiffened next to me but didn't hold me back as I walked toward Necesta.

She embraced me tightly, an action I wasn't expecting. I saw Shadoe reach for his weapon, but he held steady as the old woman pulled away. She grabbed my arm and pulled me toward her house. I glanced back to Shadoe, and he followed us through the streets.

She swung the door open and I saw several people sitting around the table we had occupied the night before.

"*There*, dearie, are your friends," she explained. "They escaped, too."

They all nodded and said hello. I could tell Shadoe wasn't happy.

"Come, sit. Sit." She demanded kindly.

"What is all this Necesta?" I asked.

"This, dearie, is what you've been looking for." She grinned at me.

"And what have I been looking for?" I played along. Maybe she was a bit more unstable than I thought.

"Oh, dearie, you've been looking for a way out. And

we're it." She spread her arms wide, motioning at the people in the room.

I must have looked confused because one of the men jumped in to explain.

"I'm Raselin," a stocky, brown-haired man said. He had to have been at least twenty years older than I was. "What Necesta is trying to say is that we all know what it's like over the wall. We came looking for freedom too. While we found oppression, it's slightly better here. But not one of us *wouldn't* choose to go back if we thought we could fix the Society.

"There are groups over there, working to fix things— we know this as fact. We also know that the majority of this town would jump the fence to be rid of this place if there was some promise of life over there.

"Necesta says you want to go back. So do we." He motioned around the room. "And we think, if we can band the town together, we can help overthrow the Society and start again."

"We'll need training, of course." A woman who looked to be a bit younger than Raselin said.

"And that's where you come in, dearies." Necesta concluded. "And don't even try to tell me you haven't been trained. I may be old, but I'm not blind," she said. Dropping her voice she added, "And even if I was, I could fix that."

She had tenacity.

"And what do you want from us?" Shadoe said gruffly.

"Train us. Turn us into an army," the woman said. "We'll fight."

"We are strong in numbers," Raselin added. "We, ourselves, can overtake the Society. If we can get the resistance groups to join us, there's no way the Society will survive."

"I need a word." I stood to my feet so quickly I actually may have scared Shadoe.

I pulled him into another room before turning on him.

"Shadoe, this could be our chance."

"Lur, this could be a trap. We don't know these people," he argued.

"They want to go back. They want to fight," I insisted.

"They want to use us. And who knows, they may actually know about us and want to collect the reward. Lur, this is insane."

"Maybe it *is* insane." I would not stop. "But who cares? This is our chance to set things right. This is our chance to fix what Lowell did."

He paled and his face became taut.

"We can undo this mess. We can help save both of our groups and save the innocent people who got caught up in all this." I formulated a plan with every syllable I spoke.

I would lead these people. I would train them if Shadoe didn't. I knew enough. We'd cross the wall and take out the guards. We'd head straight for the center city and take out the leadership. Once we took over, I'd personally see to the agonizing pain of Magistrate Canton for what he did to us. We'd set the camps free. The people would be able to take care of themselves again.

There would be bloodshed, but there would also be freedom.

"We're doing this," I announced.

Without waiting for him to answer, I slipped under his arm and ran back to the group waiting for me. Shadoe clutched at my arm but I shook him off.

"I'll do it." I clamored. "I'll train you and we'll fight the Society together."

Their faces radiated with elation. I knew I had made the right choice.

"Now, how can we tell who is on our side?" I asked.

"Give us a few days, Goldilocks." Necesta said smiling, "We'll get them ready for you."

I was ready.

"Move over, Raselin, give Goldilocks some room. She has a lot to plan and her boyfriend is none too happy about it." She pointed a finger at Shadoe.

"*Clearly* not her boyfriend," Shadoe said under his breath. I almost didn't hear him.

I kept my eyes on Necesta, refusing to look at Shadoe.

I didn't care what he was thinking or feeling. He could sit there and sulk for all I cared.

A chorus of screams rose up from the streets. Raselin was the first to the door, Necesta at his heels. I heard a loud crash as I ran to the window to see. I pulled the curtains away just in time to see several men who looked to be in uniform pushing several carts on their sides and rolling them over.

"Stay back, dearie." Necesta hissed at me when she caught sight of me at the window.

I ducked low, but held the curtain back just enough that I could still see out. Shadoe was crouched by my side, his hand near my foot. He sighed, shifting the curtains slightly.

"This can't be good." He huffed in a whisper.

The men in uniform jumped up on the overturned carts and started addressing the crowd. We had to strain to hear the men at the end of the street.

"…time… you all will… no one… by order of… " I made out a few words from the speech.

I watched as Necesta closed her eyes, clearly worried. She brushed back her graying hair, her other hand grasping the doorframe.

"Heavens." She breathed.

We waited for the men to leave, the minutes stretching on until my legs started to cramp. Necesta swayed back, rocking onto her heels when they finally moved on.

Her slight nod prompted us to stand, knowing it was clear of the uniformed men.

"Well, this changes things," Raselin said as soon as he shut the door.

"What happened? I rushed toward him, eager to find out what I had missed.

"The government is changing how they do things." Raselin explained. "They are now demanding even more of our people to go fight for them. We have one month before they are coming back for the selected. They're posting names in the city center now."

"Guess it's not too much different than home, now is it?" Shadoe remarked.

"At least they have the decency to warn their people first," I muttered.

"I imagine that will add a few people to our list," Necesta quipped, almost looking happy.

I gave her a look and she just winked back at me. I knew in that instant that I would never truly figure out Necesta.

"Well, off with you all now." Necesta waved us off. "You clearly have a lot to do."

She escorted us all out of the house and shut the door behind her.

"Come back tomorrow," Raselin whispered to me

before branching off in a different direction. "We'll be ready for you."

"Shadoe, this is a good thing," I tried convincing him.

He walked several paces ahead of me, not even stopping to trade. As soon as we left Necesta's house he stormed off toward our campsite.

"Can we just talk about this?" I asked.

"Talk about what?" He fumed. "Auluria, I did not pull you over that wall and get you this far just to go back."

"I thought you would want to go back." I shot back at him, "The rest of Lowell's team is still there, and who knows what has happened to them?"

"They'll be fine on their own," he said spitefully. "They're trained to survive."

"Well maybe you don't have people you care about, but I do!" I said forcefully. I felt the anger in me rising. "How could you not care about them?"

He cut me off. "I *do* care, *Lur*. You think I don't care? If I didn't care, I never would have saved you. I would have saved Lowell, or if I couldn't, I'd have stayed behind and run the group. Instead, I came after *you*. You're my… partner." He faltered, then added slowly, "I had to make sure you were all right."

So, Shadoe, who never seemed to actually care about me a day in his life, had formed an attachment to me.

"If you care about me, then help me. We're partners. I'd like to be in this together." I said softly.

"It's not a good idea." He tried to persuade me. When I wouldn't relent, he gave in. "Fine."

I felt a smile tugging at the corner of my lips. I nodded my head instead.

"Thank you."

Chapter 4

Necesta and Raselin greeted us alone in her house the next day.

"Where is everyone?" I asked.

Raselin motioned us forward. Without saying a word we followed our two new friends down the streets, winding around people and buildings. The wind blew my hair out of my face as we walked and I arched up into the breeze. I allowed my eyes to slip closed for just a moment and Dov's face flashed through my mind. An aching stab clenched my chest, but I refused to let it hold me back.

When we reached our destination, we found ourselves in the woods. I felt Shadoe come alive as we entered the bark-covered fortress, both our bodies humming in anticipation. The woods gave us safety.

We wandered a bit into the depths of the trees. I watched as Shadoe's eyes swept across the terrain. He pointed just before Raselin held back a tangled clump of vines.

Of course he noticed.

Shadoe and I slipped in after Raselin and Necesta. The opening to the hidden place was small, good for deterring unwanted guests. Once we got passed the tight opening, we found ourselves in a spacious cave. I decided we must be mostly underground, not having seen much space on the surface.

A large crowd greeted us, turning in unison as we approached. Many of them nodded to us.

"This is Lur and Shadoe," Raselin announced. "They're here to help train us. Do everything they say."

Everyone nodded, eager to begin.

"We'll split into groups. You'll all work with one of us and we'll rotate often. Be ready, this will not be easy. Once we finish our training, we not only have to breech the wall, but we also have to defeat the Society from our neighboring country. Some of us come from there and are familiar with the cities and towns. For those of you that aren't, we'll do our best to prepare you." The crowd watched intently as Raselin addressed them.

"Anything is better than staying here!" a voice

shouted.

"It's going to be dangerous there." Raselin said. "But if we succeed, and help take control of the Society there, we have a chance at a better life."

They cheered.

"We will work hard and learn to fight. We'll succeed in our mission and give good lives to our children. Now, break up into your groups."

They started splitting up as Raselin turned back to us. "Lur, you'll go over there, and Shadoe, you'll…"

Shadoe stopped him. "No, we're staying together."

"We need smaller groups and more leaders. You can be near each other, but you each need to train people."

"That's fine," I said before Shadoe could object.

"For the first few days we'll work on fighting. After that, we can make a plan to rotate and teach them the other skills they will need," he said. "As you can see, we already have some trained fighters, just not quite as finessed as you both."

"We can work on that." I assured him.

Stepping to my left, I found a small group of older men and women. I waved my hand toward another group —made of mostly young people—that Shadoe should focus on.

He positioned himself so he could see my every move and began. His sharp tone did nothing to encourage the youths, but my glare softened his words.

We spent the next few hours training our different groups. Raselin rotated them out, allowing each group time to practice while we worked with a new group.

I walked around the men and women, watching for the correct positioning. Repositioning elbows, I gave strength. Moving feet into the proper stance, I gave power.

Shadoe watched as I demonstrated proper techniques to the group, working hard not to overwhelm them on their first day. Some were better than I anticipated, others stronger than they looked.

I ignored Shadoe as I worked, talking to the group I was overseeing. Soon, I blocked him out entirely and focused on the sound of elbows striking flesh as the fighters practiced.

By the end of the day I felt certain that with the proper training and planning, we could accomplish our goal. Raselin motioned for us to join him when he dismissed the people for the day, and I quickly joined him standing by Necesta.

"You didn't train with me today," I said to the older women, sad she hadn't worked with me.

"No dearie, that's coming." She nodded to me, eyes searching the length of Shadoe as he approached slowly.

"What did you think?" Raselin asked us.

"I think they have potential," I started to say.

"I think this is a suicide mission," Shadoe muttered under his breath, just loud enough for me to hear him.

Raselin shot him a look, but obviously missed what Shadoe had said.

"Lur, you seem to be the sensible one, how do you want to proceed with this?"

"I think you're right. Spend a few days exclusively on fighting and then we can start adding in the other elements. We have to move quickly, but we still need to assess where they stand."

"Good, I'm glad you feel that way." He nodded to me.

"Lur and I will work on a plan and we'll have it ready for you tomorrow," Shadoe said.

"Excellent," Raselin said.

"So you can go now." Shadoe dismissed him.

I gaped at him, but Raselin only held a hand up, telling me not to start a fight.

Raselin and Necesta turned and left.

"Shadoe!" I scolded. "They're trying to help us get our home back, you have no right to speak to them—"

"*Save it*, Lur. We have too much to do to argue over manners."

Before I realized what he was doing, his hand slammed into my arm, and I stumbled back. Readying myself, I attacked in retaliation and we locked in a battle of wills.

"I'll take charge of the physical training," Shadoe said

as he attempted to kick my knee out from under me. "You oversee the spy training and manipulation lessons."

"Of course," I said sarcastically as I slammed my fist into the side of his head.

We spent several minutes arguing over what to teach them and when to teach it, but by the end of our sparring match we had a plan, and we were both exhausted. Collapsing on the ground, we tried to catch our breath. I may not have liked Shadoe, but he certainly was a good trainer.

"Lur?" he said quietly. "You know this is going to get us both killed, don't you?"

"Yeah." I sighed. "I'm pretty sure it will."

The bells jingled as the young girl reached into the test pocket.

"Like this." I showed her again how to use two fingers to slide into the pocket I was pretending to pick. She gave an exasperated sigh when I pulled my fingers back in silence.

"Like this, dear." Necesta brushed past her and reached for the pocket. She deftly reached inside and pulled out the coin.

I smiled at the older woman. Her eyes glittered

mischievously.

"Don't look at me like that, Goldilocks. I know my way around the spy world." She chuckled.

"I see that. Why don't you take over here and I'll move on to my other group?"

She nodded and I walked quickly to my team a few feet away. I watched as they practice the flirtation techniques I described to them. Brittella had trained me well when Lowell had put me in her charge so very long ago. It was strange to think of her now after all this time has passed since my training with her.

I had no doubt she had survived whatever the Society had thrown at her since I had last seen her.

"Very good. Now, let's try something else," I said, entering the circle.

I described ways of being seen without really being noticed and sent them off to practice observing quietly around the room, an art only the best could master. Shadoe continued to push the trainees to their limits, giving them the same coldness he had once offered to me. His face softened when he saw me watching him, but only enough that someone who knew him very well could tell.

Shadoe started walking toward me and I met him halfway.

"It's been three weeks, Lur. How much more time can we spare?" he asked, glancing around the room.

"Not long, but we can't risk sending them in too early. We just have to see this through," I said.

He nodded gruffly.

"Go spar with him. I need to see what he's doing wrong."

I looked as a man about our age stood in the center of Shadoe's training space. He was much larger than me as I stepped up to him.

"Lur's going to help us for a moment; I need to see how you do against someone of her level."

I waited for the boy to make the first strike. When he didn't, I moved first, kicking his leg out from under him. Before he could stand up, a voice sounded from behind us.

"You're not pitting them against Lur, are you?" Raselin asked. "Shouldn't you partner her with someone more matched to her skills?"

"Like you?" Shadoe said skeptically. He waves his hand dismissively, gesturing toward me. "If you want to fight her… go ahead."

Raselin eyed me, asking for permission. At my nod, he stepped forward as the boy on the floor scrambled out of the way. I noticed the other groups eyeing us as we size each other up. They moved so slowly, but it seemed they were at our side so quickly. Everyone gathered around to watch.

He circled around me and I matched his steps,

keeping on the opposite side of our invisible circle. Shadoe's eyes lingered on me as I moved deftly around the ring created by the people we were training. We both seemed to be waiting for the other to begin the sparring match.

When he finally ran at me, I flipped him over my back. Raselin slammed into the ground, air rushing from his lungs. I quickly met him on the floor as he kicked me so hard in retaliation, I was convinced something had broken. Raselin rolled on top of me, attempting to pin me down, but I managed to slip my leg under him, pushing to throw him off balance.

We were on our feet at the same time, fists swinging in calculated motions. I held back my yelp as he connected with the side of my face. Shouts went up all around us and I blocked out the noise, focusing only on my opponent. Soon, I no longer even saw Shadoe in the crowd.

Dov's face filled my thoughts, distracting me momentarily. *Where was he? Was he alive?*

The searing pain stretching from my jaw to my ear brought me back to life. With a few quick swings, I connected and sent Raselin to the floor, ending the match. He reached out his hand and I helped him up.

"That, ladies and gentlemen, is how we will win this." He grinned at me.

Shaking my hand, he turned to challenge someone

else. For a moment I'm worried he had slipped into thinking it was something fun, but I realized he was only keeping morale up. Turning it into something less terrifying than it really was made it easier for everyone to cope.

"That was amusing," Shadoe grumbled as he slipped to my side.

"You've been wanting to hit him for days… Here I thought you'd be happy," I mumbled back as I watched Raselin begin his next match.

"I *am* happy you hit him. Wish it could have been me. But this spectacle… this is ridiculous." His eyes glanced around the room, unappreciative of the hard work we had been putting in the last few weeks.

"It's better than what you did to me, Shadoe," I snipped before I realized what I was saying.

Instead of lecturing me, he stalked back to his group. I went to check on the group I had been training.

Two hours later I noticed someone run into the training room. The young man whispered something to Raselin who immediately looked concerned. When he glanced up at me, I knew whatever it was couldn't be good. He had the same look on his face that Berwyn had in the storehouse when he found out about our people being captured. *Our people.* I wasn't sure when I had considered the Baers as mine, but I knew how right that thought was.

Raselin swung around to face me.

"Okay, everyone, that's enough for today. Go home. Eat something and rest. Meet back here tomorrow." He announced, holding my gaze.

When the room cleared, Raselin walked over to a table set up on the side of the room. Only the leadership remained after training. Pulling out the table, we sat, waiting for an update.

Necesta set out the food for us. I knew I needed to eat after everything that day, but I couldn't think of anything but the information our spy had brought back to us.

I waited for him to speak but he took his time, thanking Necesta for all her hard work with the food.

"Our spy has just returned from the other side of the wall." Raselin started. "He arrived with much news. It seems the government has been spending their time and resources tracking several large resistance groups throughout the country."

I looked to Shadoe. We both knew who they were. The Baers... Lowell's men... Marty and Jake's group. *We* were the people they were tracking.

"You know something," Raselin started to say, eyeing us.

"We have an idea of who they are," Shadoe replied. "Keep going."

"They're focused on finding these groups and exterminating them. I'd almost guess that they're willing to remove the older men and women and send the younger ones to the camps. Trouble within their borders makes it harder to fight the monsters outside."

"Are we the monsters outside?" Necesta laughed darkly.

"For now." Raselin glanced at her. "But not for long. We'll be over the wall soon, and then we'll be the monsters inside… One more group for them to fight against. Hopefully with being pulled in so many directions, they won't notice us until it's too late."

"What else did Devin say, Raselin?" I asked, redirecting the conversation. "Do we know what groups they are going after or why?"

"I'm afraid I don't have much news on that front. Devin went into the heart of the Society, so he only learned what the townspeople could tell him, and even then, they didn't have much information."

"We learned never to talk," Shadoe muttered.

"Which is why we only have a vague idea of what was happening with these groups. As far as we can tell, they all want to destroy the Society. Can you confirm this?"

"Yes, basically," I answer before Shadoe can.

"So we can get them on our side."

"Of course we can. Goldilocks can be very convincing when she wants to be, can't you, dearie?" Necesta turned to me and cupped my chin in her hand.

She watched me for a moment, as if trying to tell me

something. Backing away, she let her hand fall as she turned back to Raselin.

"What else? Give us all the details." Her voice settled into a hum as she sat beside me.

"The man in charge, at least in charge of that area, is Magistrate Canton."

"We know him," I interrupted, shuddering.

The group's eyes swung toward me, waiting for an explanation.

"He captured Lur for a time," Shadoe supplied, unwilling to give details to the group.

He held Raselin's gaze, challenging him to push for answers. I slowly lowered my eyelids in a signal that was blocked from Shadoe's sight by my hair flowing in front of me. I would give details later, without the entire leadership group watching.

"From what Devin gathered," Raselin continued, "Canton is working on something big."

Just then Devin stepped back into the room, as if on cue, his arm in a sling that hadn't been there earlier.

"Devin, come tell the team what you learned."

Devin settled on the bench across the table, his injured arm resting on the table as Necesta pushed her plate toward him.

"I was in the town, talking to people, trying to find answers. I met a few men who weren't bright enough to know not to talk to me, fortunately.

"Magistrate Canton, the man in charge, is searching for survivors from rebel groups he is trying to dismantle. I hear that not too long ago, he took out key leaders of two of these groups, but I also hear there was an escape attempt and not everyone was killed. From what I could tell, it seems like the Society hasn't been able to locate some of these leaders and it's believed that they are creating an even stronger resistance group.

"I also heard that Canton has some kind of a plan. He managed to get a few hostages and is holding them to try to manipulate the leaders of the groups he is searching for."

Shadoe elbowed me and my gasp turned into a grimace.

"I've been told that one of the people Canton is holding is a woman. No further details," he said, slipping into a militaristic recount of what he had learned. "A man is being held. He's older and they aren't sure how he is connected, but he's being held on suspicion. Based on the conversations I overheard, 'being held on suspicion' is code for being submitted to torture.

"I know there is someone else they are holding, too. A younger man; a leader. They confirmed his identity as one of the men who runs one of the main groups they are fighting with.

"While I was there, they paraded him out in front of the crowds of people forced to watched. His clothes were torn and he looked like he had been dragged off of the front lines of the war.

"The soldiers shouted about his crimes and warned the people that their fate would be the same if they tried to rebel against the Society. They beat him in front of everyone and told the people to spread the word that if his family surrendered, they'd let him live," Devin said, his hand moving toward the sling his damaged arm rested in on the table, suddenly uncomfortable as he picked at the fabric.

"Devin, you saw this man?" I asked.

"Yes." His eyes swept up from their mark on the table in front of his arm. "From a distance."

"What did he look like?" I held my breath.

Shadoe straightened his back, waiting for the answer.

"He was tall, but it was hard to see his features after the beating he had obviously taken before they brought him out in public. They shoved him into the middle of a stage, surrounded by what looked to be places where they could set up gallows."

"But what did he *look* like, Devin?" I erupted in a rush of words, causing the entire table to look to me.

"Oh, my dear." Necesta said in a low, breathy voice. "It's him, isn't it? The one you left."

How Necesta could have guessed that there was a man in my life besides Shadoe was beyond me, but she had figured it out.

"Devin," she said quietly when she noticed the tears forming in my eyes, "Go on."

"He was tall…" he said quietly, unsure of himself. Tears always made men unsure of themselves—Brittella had taught me that—though this was by no means an attempt to elicit information by crying. I fought to stop.

"He was tall," he said again. "He had dark hair and the soldiers were calling him an animal. I think it must be his group's symbol or something."

"What was it?" Shadoe asked, his voice filled with loathing, already knowing the answer.

"He said to tell the bears they had their cub."

I closed my eyes so hard it hurt. Dov was alive, or had been when Devin was there.

I knew the Society had him—there had been no way for him to escape them once he sent me over the wall—but the confirmation of his capture made it real. Until that point, I could have at least hoped that Dov hadn't been hurt, but Devin's account confirmed otherwise.

"Your young man?" Necesta asked.

"You have a… Never mind." Raselin caught his curiosity.

"Not bear the animal," I choked, "Baer the last name. And his first name is Dov, and yes, he is mine. He sent me over the wall to protect me and they captured him."

"He's still alive," Devin said quickly, trying to silence the tears I was keeping at bay.

"Canton is trying to call the Baers out." Shadoe mused.

"But why is he targeting them?" I turned to Shadoe and dropped my voice. The group casually looked away to give us a moment, as if they couldn't hear everything we were saying.

"Is it just because they have Dov and they don't have any of Lowell's men, or is there a reason?"

"I don't know," he answered, tipping his head toward me, adding to the illusion of privacy.

"We need to get him out of there."

"We need to find out why they're keeping him and not executing him," Shadoe countered, confronting me with the deadly reality of the situation.

If Canton and his men had Dov and hadn't killed him yet, there was a reason.

Whatever the reason was, he was using Dov to get to someone—*me? Eden?* Had Eden survived? Did he have her too? Could she be the woman Devin was talking about?

"Who is he targeting?" I wondered out loud.

"We'll find out, I suppose," Shadoe said reluctantly.

"We need to find out why Canton has Dov." I turned back to the group, their attention immediately on me. I saw Necesta's eyes light up at the mention of Dov's name. I would likely regret giving her that information.

"He tried to kill us once. If he's holding Dov, there is a reason."

"Canton has a plan. He always has a plan. But we're smarter than him. We'll figure it out and beat him at his own game," Shadoe announced.

"It's time," Raselin said, ignoring the conversation. "We need to start running missions over the wall. We need to test what we're up against. Small groups at first; a few men at a time. We need to know how quickly they will discover us."

"I'll go," I volunteered.

"No," Shadoe said next to me, leaning toward Raselin and nodding once. He was trying to intimidate the man.

Raselin raised an eyebrow at my former handler, deciding whether to challenge him or not. Shadoe and I had the upper hand, our training far outweighing his experience, but which of us would he side with?

"I'm going; they need people who know the land," I repeated.

"You will get too distracted. You'll try to run in and save your precious boyfriend and we can't afford that. You're not going."

"*You* trained me. Are you saying my training isn't good enough to stay focused?" I challenged him.

His face grew red, and I could see him fighting between the two options, wrestling with them privately before he answered. Pride won out.

"You will stay with me the entire time. You will not run off to help him. We stick to the plan."

"Is the team ready?" Devin asked, interrupting the impending battle.

"No," Shadoe and I answered together.

"But not everyone is going on the test missions," I added. "We'll only take those who are ready. The rest will continue to train here with Raselin."

"Oh, no." He raised a hand, stopping me. "I'm coming along too. There's no way I'm letting you out there with this one alone—he might not let you come back."

Shadoe scowled as the man nodded toward him. Pulling me out of the mission was a distinct possibility, especially if we managed to sneak back into the Society's side of the wall and could get back to Lowell's group. I was suddenly very grateful for Raselin's involvement in this mission.

"Fine." I practically jumped out of my seat to ensure Shadoe wouldn't resist. "When do we leave?"

"We spend tomorrow preparing," Shadoe said, taking the lead on the mission. "We'll leave the next day. We'll be back within two weeks."

He stood up and swung his leg over the bench we sat on at the table. I took a deep breath, knowing this wouldn't be pleasant.

"Should we discuss who you're taking with you?" Necesta asked politely, waiting for Shadoe to sit down.

Had anyone but the older woman asked, Shadoe would have walked away. By some miracle, he sat down next to me, locking eyes with me. He waited for me to give him a name.

"Well, Devin is injured," I said, glancing at the man. "It's probably wise that he stays here and heals. Besides, the town just saw him. It might not help our cause if they see him with us lurking around."

Necesta reached over the table and fussed with the sling. Standing, she walked away from the group as Devin watched curiously.

"What about Fitch?" Raselin suggested. "He seems to be doing very well during training. And I trust him with my life."

"Fitch would be a good asset to have. His strength might be helpful," I said, thinking of the way he nearly put Devin's brother, Justin, through a wall two days ago during a sparring match.

"Send Justin," Devin interjected, obviously reading my mind.

"Justin is acceptable." Shadoe nodded. "Reed, too."

"Here, try this," Necesta interrupted, bringing a cup to Devin's place at the table. "This will reduce the swelling."

Devin glanced at the cup, taking a quick breath, and lifted it to his lips.

"Thank you, ma'am," he said after swallowing. Another drink and the cup was empty.

She pressed something into his injured hand.

"For later." She winked at him and returned to her seat. "You're taking Nian, right?"

"I think that's a good choice." Raselin waited for more suggestions.

Several minutes later we had completed our team. Devin was sent to gather the men while we discussed what we would need to do to prepare and who would be in charge while we were gone.

"Lydia can help Necesta while we're gone. Fitch has been training her to fight since before we started her training and she's got a good handle on things," I suggest.

"Lydia is a good girl. She'll be missing her husband while he's with you on the mission, so this will give her something to do." Necesta smiled conspiratorially at me.

"You summoned?" Nian asked as he walked back into the training room. Reed followed behind him, joining him where Devin sat earlier.

"We're going on a mission," Raselin informed them. He looked to the door, indicating that we were waiting for more members before we gave out details.

Fitch sauntered in a moment later, with Devin and Justin in his wake. It always struck me how similar Justin and Devin looked, despite their age difference. It reminded me of how similar Dov and Berwyn were.

The men stood behind the benches and waited for directions. Raselin stood at the head of the table to address them.

"Men, we're going on a mission. We need to test our limits over the wall. Devin just arrived back with valuable information for us and it's time that we start to make our move. The team as a whole isn't ready yet, which is why we're taking a select group of you over the wall with us to run a few test missions.

"We need to know the Society's response time. Our job will be to map the area, figure out how they respond to things, and determine what their goals are." He turned to face our side of the table. "Lur…?"

I stared blankly at him, unsure of how to respond.

"Would you like to tell them what you know?"

I continued to stare.

"About your friend?" he waited for me to catch on.

"Oh." I caught on. "The man in charge, Magistrate Canton, has our friend. He captured him when he helped us to escape. He gave himself up to save us."

I motioned to Shadoe as he glared at me. In his opinion, Dov had never saved him. I knew the truth, but Shadoe would never accept that Dov sacrificed for him too.

"The point, gentlemen, is that Canton would never let this man live if there wasn't a reason," Raselin added, making me realize I had trailed off while trying to decipher Shadoe's resistance to the fact that Dov had saved us.

"He had sentenced us all to hang. Actually, that's how

we escaped." I glanced around the group, noting their reactions. "It's a long story. But Dov wouldn't be alive if Canton didn't have some purpose. Devin said he was using him as bait. We just have to figure out who he's using him against and what his plan is once he gets what he wants from them."

"This is a rescue mission?" Reed asked.

"No; this is a scouting mission. If we find an opportunity to help people along the way, we will. It would be in our best interest to recover this boy. If Canton wants him, he's valuable to have with us."

"I also imagine it will motivate Goldilocks a bit more, too," Necesta prattled and rocked forward to look at me. She played the frail, meddling, old woman well, but I knew she was very direct in her methods.

"I don't mind saving the kid," Fitch said, shrugging a shoulder.

"I heard he wasn't someone you wanted to mess with while I was over there," Devin added, grinning at me. "Tough guy."

Why Devin decided to show me this small mercy, I didn't know, but I'd happily accept any hope he could give me of Dov's resilience.

"We'll see if we get that close," Raselin said, glancing at Shadoe. "Now, let's talk about tomorrow and what we need to do."

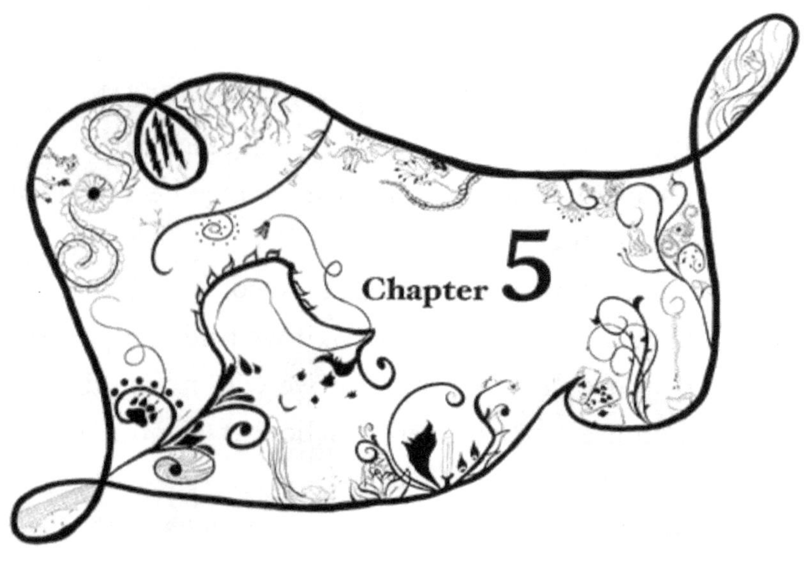

Chapter 5

"Lur?" Shadoe called into the room.

"Back here," I replied, lifting the basket to my hip.

He eyed the woven container balanced between my body and hand. Walking forward, he glanced at the contents.

"Beads?" he asked.

"I'm moving them for Necesta. She's got something back there she said could help."

"What's that?"

"I don't know yet. Help me move the boards."

He lowered himself to the ground and reached forward to move the boards. For a moment, I braced myself for him to turn and attack like he did during my time training with him… I was never to let my guard down. The strike never came.

We were no longer in training.

I stepped backwards, setting the beads down carefully to avoid spilling them. When I turned around, the first board popped free of the wall.

"Careful, dearie," Necesta said, walking in the room. "That's fragile."

Shadoe cautiously reached inside the wall. When he drew back, he held two small vials. The clinking indicated there were more hidden in the recess.

Necesta brushed past me, her clothing catching against mine, creating friction against my arm. She took the glass from him and turned her back to Shadoe to face me.

"Take these with you." She handed me the vials, but pulled back suddenly. "No, not that one."

Bending down, she leaned into the hole in the wall and moved things softly. Her back bent low, unnaturally hunched over to reach what she was looking for. When she returned to her normal posture, she held a few small containers.

"Goldilocks," she said softly, waving her hand to indicate that I should join her on the floor.

Gathering my skirt in my hands, I settled myself on the ground next to her. Her glance at Shadoe was meant to dismiss him, but he waited, arms crossed across his chest, raising his shirt just enough for me to see the metallic claw that hung there.

Berwyn.

His face flashed in front of me again. I should ask Shadoe. I should know what became of my friend.

Friend. When Berwyn had become a friend, I didn't know, but there it was. I was worried about him for more than Dov's sake.

"Take these with you, Goldilocks. You might need them." The old woman handed me several vials. "Put them in that pouch of yours."

"What are these for, Necesta?"

Holding them up to inspect them, the first sparkled in the light as it passed through the clear liquid.

"That's for injury. But only use it if it's bad. You can't afford to waste that."

I nodded, setting it in my skirt to rest. The second vial was dark, filled with murky liquid that reminded me of the mud out in the woods I was trained in.

"That one is for poison." She touched my knee with the tips of her fingers, as if impressing great wisdom upon me. "It counteracts the effects of most poisons, dearie. Use it wisely."

She waited for me to make eye contact and nodded slightly.

Dov. This was for Dov.

Did she know something? Had Devin told her something he didn't tell the rest of us?

One side of her face hitched up into a half grin, her eyelids lowering just slightly in sympathy. She was guessing what might have been happening to Dov; she would tell me if she knew.

She placed a few other vials in my hands, explaining how to use each one before pointing a long finger at the pouch attached to my hip. I placed each container in, committing their uses to memory.

"Don't mix them up."

Her warning prompted Shadoe into action.

"She won't." He grabbed my elbow and lifted me up. "We need to go."

"You're coming back with us, right, Necesta?" I asked as I scrambled to pull my feet under me to alleviate the pressure on my arm.

"Yes, dearie. We just needed to collect the things from the house."

She waited on the floor for me to reach down and help her up. The woman was surprisingly solid for how tiny she looked—another of her quiet deceptions.

Shadoe reached out to steady her as she stood, offering his arm to the woman. Necesta looped her arm around his elbow once she was on her feet, refusing to relinquish it. Shadoe grumbled, but stopped trying to pull away once he realized she wouldn't let go. She let him lead her the entire way back to the training facility, leaning heavily on him for support that she didn't actually need.

I followed along side of them and she prattled on as she had the day I helped her with her cart: an act for the town. Once we reached the hidden door, Shadoe allowed her to go first, casting me a look when she stepped ahead of him. I rolled my eyes, which annoyed him even more.

Underground was cooler than outside, the shade from the sun making it easier to work in. I hadn't realized it when I was in the storehouse with the Baers, but thinking back, that had been cooler too, despite the large number of people staying there during our time in hiding from Lowell's men.

Glancing around the room, I notice Lydia helping Fitch packing a bag. Talley, the woman I had met in Necesta's house the day I met Raselin, stood nearby, talking to Justin and Devin.

They glanced up as I approached.

"Hello, Lur." Justin nodded to me. "You ready to go?"

I took a deep breath.

"Yes, I think so."

Rather than follow me, Shadoe walked over to Raselin.

"What's his deal?" Lydia asked, nodding to my former fiancé.

"Is he always like that?" Devin asked.

"From what I've seen." Talley's voice was low as she answered.

"It makes him a good soldier." Fitch responded, his deep voice hushed so that it didn't project around the room. "We don't need *feelings* on this mission; we need level headed people who can be practical in bad situations. Emotions have no place here."

He glanced at me.

"Did he cut you down when you escaped, Lur?" Talley said. "Sounds a little emotional to me."

"Being a decent human being, doesn't mean he's emotional, Talley." Necesta joined us. "He's fond of Goldilocks. That's not a bad thing. It means he will protect her… We need her more than we need the rest."

"How so?" Devin asked, a touch of resentment in his voice.

"She's connected to the one Canton has. Somewhere in all of this mess, that's going to be leverage." She stepped closer. "So you see, we need her. And if he's the one to protect her until that comes into play, then let him have his little attachment, and you lot stay out of it."

"You're important too, big brother." Justin reached over and patted Devin's uninjured shoulder.

"Shove off," Devin replied, grinning as he pushed his sibling's hand back.

"Don't make me separate you two," Talley added, joining in with them. They both rolled their eyes at her and grumbled to each other about how she always tried to mother them.

"Don't let the power go to your head while I'm gone, sis." Justin joked. He turned to instruct Devin. "If she gets a big ego while I'm gone, do something about it."

"And how is he supposed to do that with a bum arm?" She challenged her younger brothers.

"All right," Lydia interjected, "Enough. Devin, we're running the show, so no arguments, and Justin... Just don't die out there, okay?"

"Wow, such confidence." Fitch laughed.

"Now, Fitch, you know I didn't mean you. It's not *you* I'm worried about."

Justin's eyes grew wide until he caught her smile and realized she was teasing.

"Oh, don't worry, Lydia, I'll protect your man while we're gone." He glanced at the man twice his size. "I've got your back, buddy."

"I feel so safe." Fitch replied in a monotone voice, making everyone laugh.

Maybe this mission wouldn't be as serious as I thought. The banter made me miss Reyla and her group of friends. I wondered what they were doing to try to save Dov. I knew they'd never leave him in the hands of Magistrate Canton.

"All set?" Nian joined the group, dropping a bag of supplies at his feet.

"Almost," Necesta replied. "Goldilocks, join me for a moment."

We walked along the edge of the room, eyes roaming over the men and women continuing to train without us.

"They're doing well," she commented.

"They are," I agreed, wondering what she was up to.

"By the time you return, they might be ready."

"You'll have to work hard with them."

"Lydia and Talley will work hard with them." She slowed her steps. "Now, Goldilocks, there's something you must do for me."

I nod.

"Take this." She handed me a brass necklace, tarnished from years of ware.

"Necesta, I don't think it's wise to wear—"

"You must." She stopped me, closing my hands around the beads. "Just like you have your secrets locked inside that pretty golden head of yours, these beads hold secrets too. Look."

She guided me to turn to fully face her, using my long hair to block the beads from the sight of the room. She nodded and motioned for me to get on with it when I shot her a questioning look.

Bringing the necklace closer, I saw that each bead had the ability to open.

"Not yet, dearie." She placed her hand over mine. "Look here. You'll notice the tarnishing on each is a bit different. That's how you tell them apart. These three here are poison. Those four are antidote. These two heal."

She turned the necklace, explaining each of the beads' particular mixture of life, death, and power. I counted each with her, from left to right, start to finish.

"They match the ones I gave you earlier. The bottles, the colors, the liquids… They all match. Remember one, remember them both." She concludes. "Now, dearie, don't use these unless you don't have a choice. I've had these for a long time and have never had to resort to exposing the necklace. It's old and decaying, at least it looks that way, so no one should question you about it. Keep it under your clothing, though. Don't give them any reason to be suspicious."

"I will," I said, slipping it around my neck. I tucked it under my dress.

"Are you wearing that out?" She appraised my outfit.

"I fit into a crowd better in the dresses. I'll save the pants for when we're running." I smiled, knowing she already knew that.

"We best be getting you back to your young friend." She nodded toward Shadoe and Raselin as they start to walk toward the others.

Necesta and I walked over to join the group as they reached down to pick up their packs that had been resting on the floor. Shadoe handed one to me, barely waiting for me to take hold before he released it.

"Necesta, you are in charge of overseeing everything that happens here while we're gone. Lydia and Talley answer to you." Raselin turned to the younger women. "You ladies are in charge. Make sure they are prepared by the time we return. Do not come looking for us if something goes wrong. Keep the people protected, no matter what that means."

They nodded, Lydia slipping her arm through her husband's in their final moments together before we left for our trial mission. Talley glanced at her brothers, standing on either side of her. Devin would be safe, still in her care, but Justin would be with us. She glanced at Devin's sling before looking to her youngest brother.

"Am I clear, Devin?" Raselin asked. "You are not to come after us."

He opened his mouth to speak, but quickly closed it.

"Devin," Raselin warned, "You are not to come after us. Talley will need you here to help protect the people. Your obligation is to them, do you understand?"

"Yes, sir," he finally responded, refusing to make eye contact as a touch of red crept into his cheeks at being called out.

Raselin gave specific instructions on how things were to be run while we were gone, Shadoe adding a few harsh directions on training. When they were finished, we said our goodbyes.

Justin hugged his siblings, promising to return safely

and reminding his brother to keep Talley level headed. Lydia and Fitch stepped away for a private moment, while Nian and Reed said goodbye to their people as well.

"Take care of each other, dearies," Necesta said, turning to where I stood beside Shadoe. She winked at me, whispering, "Bring that young man of yours home."

Shadoe turned and walked away. I watched as he made his way to the door.

"He'll be fine," Necesta sang as she walked away from me, tossing her words over her shoulder. "So will you, Goldilocks. Take care."

Alone, I decided to follow Shadoe. Once through the tunnel, I stepped out into the fall air. The smell of slowly dying leaves permeated the breeze and floated around us in gentle waves.

"You know we likely won't make it out this time, don't you?" Shadoe said without turning to me, kicking a leaf out of his way. It was just beginning to turn yellow.

"I know."

"We probably won't even make it through this trial mission. You know Canton is looking for us. *Specifically* for us."

"You mean *for me.*" I corrected.

"Yes, for you. You're the one that escaped. He doesn't actually know about me. He never saw me, and the only ones that could have were too preoccupied with your boyfriend at the wall."

"And yet, we'll both probably die."

"Yes."

"What are you going to do when we get over the wall, Shadoe?" I asked, knowing he must have a plan.

"I don't know yet, truthfully." He looked up from the leaf he was moving with his boot and surveyed the land in front of us. "I'll have to see what we encounter when we get over there. From what Devin said, things have changed, Lur."

"You're going to help me save them, aren't you?" I asked tentatively.

Before he could answer, the rest of the team joined us, the sound of their boots announcing their arrival. Raselin stepped to my side and nodded to me and then to Shadoe.

Shadoe led the team without a word. We followed quietly behind until we reached the edge of the town.

One at a time, we slipped onto the crowded streets of merchants selling their wares, trying to survive on what little money they could make. Raselin went first, judging the atmosphere of the town he had known for years. The men followed behind, several minutes between each, until only Shadoe and I were left standing in the tall grass.

"Go," he said.

I thought about using the opportunity to talk to him, but when he pushed me out into the street, I had no choice but to move. Wandering through the area, I looked at packages of food and bolts of material.

A shout rose up a few yards away, claiming my attention. Someone had called Justin into the commotion, putting him on display.

"I really need to go," he said, attempting to step back.

"Justin!" a woman screeched, reaching for him over the table she stood behind.

The look on his face might have been hilarious, had we not been trying to keep a low profile as we made our way through the town. The woman was angry, obviously wanting Justin to return to her table. He glanced around, looking for escape when he caught sight of me. He leaned forward just enough for me to get the picture.

Walking toward them, I added a bounce to my step, acting oblivious to the chaos around us.

"There you are," I said as I approached. Looping my arm through his, I weaved our fingers together, making his breath catch. "I got separated from you. I'm sorry, darling. Did you find anything for my parents? We really need to find the perfect gift for them…"

I trailed off, pretending to wait for an answer. I locked eyes with him, willing him to not look away. I had stunned the woman into silence, but if he engaged with her again, I didn't know how I could slip away with him.

"Oh, you did!" I gushed before he could speak. "Show me!"

I pushed him back, turning Justin away from the rogue woman who was beginning to collect herself. As I moved him farther away, I uncoiled myself from his arm and moved closely against his hip, wrapping myself around his back to hold his hip, claiming him.

Her gasp told me I had succeeded, but I pressed on, forcing us forward. Three steps and I sped up. Another three steps and I quickened our pace again as he leaned in and whispered in my ear.

"You decided making her jealous was a good thing?" he teased.

"Was that a bad call?" I asked.

"No." He shrugged as he wound his arm around me possessively. "It gets her off *my* case. She used to have a thing for Devin, but when he ignored her, she moved on to me. Aren't I so lucky?"

"Clearly," I said, shrugging him off once we made it around a corner. "We need to move."

"Before she sends the soldiers after you?"

I stopped in my tracks, hair whipping me in the face as I turned to look at him.

"Relax, Lur. The soldiers won't be around for at least a few more days. By then, we'll be long gone." He laughed.

I blinked a few times, trying to decide if he was joking about her sending the soldiers or if she was the type that really would do that to someone she was mad at.

"Hurry, before Shadoe finds us." His words spurred

me into motion. "Besides, there were lots of witnesses. If anything happened to you, they could come forward and tell them it was her and not you."

"You really think they'd stand for me if it came down to it?" I questioned as we walked faster.

"You probably didn't notice this because you were so busy focusing on me," he grinned, "but all those men back there had their eyes glued to you. They'd step up to help the pretty girl."

"Would they now?"

He nodded.

"You'd have to marry one of them, but they'd certainly speak on your behalf." He grinned; reminding me of Gregory that night I played cards with the boys and Reyla's friends at the storehouse. If we made it over the wall and survived, my goal would be to find the Baers' group and see what had become of the others.

"Hurry." Justin's voice changed, his arm tugging at me, as the noise rose behind us.

We scurried down the alley, exiting behind the buildings onto another street. I held my hand up, motioning my companion to wait while I cleared the area. Tentatively I stepped out and swept my eyes around, looking for people in our way. When I found no one, I nodded to him.

A few minutes later, we arrived at the meeting point; the field on the opposite side of town that would lead us to the hill Shadoe and I camped on when we first approached the community. Shadoe arrived a moment later, making me wonder how much of our display he had seen.

"Lur," Shadoe said, taking his place next to me. He waited for me to respond to the wordless command he had given.

"Fine." I didn't bother to hide the exasperation in my voice. I didn't like him telling me what to do, even though I knew it was the smart move.

"Where are you going?" Raselin asked as I started to walk away.

"She shouldn't be traveling in a dress." Shadoe answered for me.

I slipped behind a tree even though I had my pants on under my skirt, prepared to make an easy switch. Dropping the skirt, I adjusted the waistband of the trousers and scooped up the fabric I had left on the ground. I rolled up the skirt and tucked it in my bag as I rejoined the group.

"That was fast." Nian looked shocked.

"I was prepared." I smiled demurely. I was going to enjoy surprising these men.

"Prepared to waste time?" Shadoe grumbled so only I could hear him, knowing I didn't actually need to step away to change.

We walked up the hill, away from the town. Each step

carried me closer to the wall where I had last seen Dov. I had to force myself to keep pace with the men and not run ahead. I would have run all the way to Canton's prisons if I could have.

I was exhausted by the time we stopped. We would arrive at the wall the next day if we kept pace, a point Reed brought up as we sat around the fire.

"We'll arrive by nightfall. Should we wait until morning to cross over into the Society?" Nian asked, brushing his hair out of his eyes.

My entire body screamed at the thought of waiting longer.

"No. Nightfall," Shadoe calmly answered instead. "The dark will be our cover."

"I agree. Our best shot at not being noticed is after dark. Do we know where to go once we breach the barrier?" Raselin looked to me.

"Toward the woods." Shadoe replied, dashing my hopes of attempting an immediate rescue. My judgment was being clouded; Lowell would have destroyed me for it.

I straightened at the thought and Shadoe stiffened beside me, wary of whatever had caused my change in posture. When he decided that I hadn't been alerted to a potential threat, he relaxed, letting his shoulders lean toward the fire. I nodded once to affirm nothing was wrong, and he continued to eat the bread we had brought with us.

"I asked if you were familiar with the woods." Fitch's voice grounded me.

"Yes, I know the woods," Shadoe said as if he hadn't ignored the man a moment earlier. "Lur will easily be able to navigate it as well. She's never had a problem finding her way around."

"And just what do we hope to get out of traipsing around in the woods?" Reed reached for his mug. "Shouldn't we go to the city?"

"We will have the upper hand in the woods," Shadoe said by way of explanation.

"We need to stay hidden. We can watch from the woods," I added, "set up our home base there. Then we can go into the towns and cities as needed. It's the best choice."

Raselin nodded, as did Fitch.

"Okay. Tomorrow we go to the wall and come evening, we make our way to the woods." Justin announced, looking around the circle. "I'll take first watch."

I prayed the woods would bring answers.

Chapter 6

IN THE DISTANCE, I COULD SEE THE WALL, AS DARK AND small as the first time I had laid eyes on it. The closer we walked, the further away it seemed. Eventually, it loomed above us, not nearly as tall as I remembered it.

Fitch was the first to climb it, just before we lost our light. He peered over, checking for signs of Society soldiers. Dropping down on the other side, he walked in both directions, checking for an ambush. Three taps gave us permission to join him.

Shadoe walked to the wall and readied himself for my approach. Once he was in position, I crouched and ran at him, letting him lift me off the ground, high into the air. My fingers grasped the edge and I realized how much work Shadoe had actually done to pull me up as Dov worked to ensure my safety.

I struggled to swing my leg up over the wall, my boot slipping against the divider. Using my arms, I pulled myself further over the barrier and tried to move my leg again, this time managing to perch on the top of the wall.

I dropped down into the dying grass on the Society side of the wall. *Home.*

Nian dropped to my left, stumbling a bit as he hit the ground. He caught himself, brushing his hair back, and straightened. Shadoe deftly landed to my right, immediately steering me toward the woods as if he were afraid I might run. I slapped his hand away and guided myself to the tree line.

"It's like we never even left," Raselin said, making me wonder if he meant here or there.

"Come on." Shadoe stepped in front of everyone. "Let's get an hour or two in and make camp."

The remaining bits of daylight in the far distance faded away under the covering of branches and leaves, leaving bits of moon to filter down to us. I caught sight of the stars when we came to a small clearing in the forest, the small dots sparkling and disappearing in the night sky.

My eyes grew heavy, having taken the last watch shift before we moved that morning. Each step left me more tired than the last and more committed to taking the next step, because each foot forward brought me closer to answers.

I inched closer to Raselin, knowing he'd be better support than Shadoe would as I felt my body slow. He noticed my forced movements and matched his to mine, slowing our rate.

"I give it another twenty minutes and we rest for the night." He looked at the group for approval. Shadoe nodded along with the others. Even someone with his strength needed to rest.

We made it another mile before we stopped to set up camp. Shadoe took his place near me as we slept, telling me he would wake me for my watch in a few hours. We had to be up with the sun, so we wouldn't get much rest.

I slept without dreaming, so deeply that Shadoe had to shake me awake.

"I'm not covering your shift, Lur," he said gruffly as I grasped consciousness.

Sitting up, I surveyed the area, familiarizing myself with the landscape. Once I was confident in its memorization in limited lighting, I looked up. The stars once again greeted me, darting in and out of the clouds.

Nian snored quietly across from the fire, his hair falling in his eyes again. I would have to encourage him to cut it back if it would interfere with our missions. The last thing we needed was for someone to die because their hair blocked their sight.

Shadoe fell asleep quickly. I watched his shoulders rise up and lower as he breathed evenly, as I had often watched Dov sleep from across the room. These men were nothing alike.

A noise caught my attention, a far off animal replying. Their game continued, moving further away as they spoke to one another.

I twisted my hair in my hands as they sat in my lap. Whenever I needed to move and couldn't, I twirled my hair through my fingers. The movement was so slight most people rarely noticed, as it calmed and focused me. I pulled my locks through my fingers over and over again, weaving it around my hand.

The crickets slowly stopped chirping, their chorus dying away so slowly I didn't notice until it was profoundly silent. My fingers found their way to the necklace tucked below my shirt. For as tarnished as they looked, they certainly didn't feel that way.

My eyes traced over the outline of the trees, searching for signs of Silas and Eden. I knew I wouldn't find evidence here, even if they had been through this area. The last time I saw them, they had been running toward the woods. I only hoped that Dov had drawn the soldiers away from his sister-in-law and best friend as much as he had drawn them away from me. Dov would want his capture to matter.

I hated his selfless streak as much as I adored it.

"Lur? You ready to switch?" Justin's voice made me jump.

"Is it time already?" I asked, trying to distinguish how long I had been lost in thought.

"I'm guessing so," he replied, dragging himself into an upright position. "You should rest."

"What is it like to have siblings?"

"What?" He adjusted his shirt and ran a hand through his hair.

I shrugged, unsure why I had asked.

Justin raised an eyebrow at me, weighing my words.

"It's not the worst thing in the world." He offered me a half smile. "But also not the best. Don't get me wrong, I love them, but that's part of the problem. It's hard to leave them like this, or worse, to have *them* leave. Devin came back injured, but it could have been worse. I worry.

"It's great because you always have people to rely on, but it gets a bit overwhelming at times, trying to protect them. I imagine it's worse for them, since they're older. I know they've spent a lot of time protecting me.

"Do you have siblings, Lur?"

"Auluria."

"What?" His eyes pinched together at the change in the direction of the conversation.

"My name. It's Auluria. And no, no siblings."

"But…"

"We didn't know you. It was safer. Only Shadoe calls me Lur, and I hate it."

"Auluria." He said my name gently, nodding.

"Good night, Justin." I turned to lie down, closing my eyes.

"Auluria is prettier anyway. It suits you," he murmured as I drifted back to sleep

"There's a stream over here, Auluria." Justin waved me over in the morning.

Raselin turned to face us, but said nothing. I walked toward Justin, looking forward to cleaning up. Down a small embankment ran a creek flowing to the brim with water.

Dropping to my knees, I dipped a hand into the cool water. I held in a gasp as my fingers penetrated the surface, a chill running through my body. I brushed the dirt off my hands, pulling the water up my arms until it met my sleeves.

It tasted amazing as I raised my hands to my lips. Justin dipped his container into the water alongside of me.

"Auluria, fill your canteen," Raselin reminded me, having caught on to the switch of names.

I reached behind me, waiting for him to hand his to me as well. When I felt it touch my dripping hands, I pulled back, dipping it in the water for him.

A gasp made me turn. Fitch pulled his face back from his hands where the cold water had hit his skin.

"A warning would have been nice," he commented, throwing us a look.

"It's fall, Fitch, what did you expect?" Raselin chastised him playfully.

We finished rinsing our visible skin off, the cold water terrorizing our systems. I raked my wet hands through my hair, pushing it back. It was as good as it was going to get.

Walking up the embankment, we found Shadoe dropping out of a tree. He joined us, telling us where we had ended up during the night.

"There's a town two miles from here. We can reach it within the hour and make a supply run," he announced, lifting his chin as if he'd won some kind of competition.

Nian's hair dripped in his eyes as he walked up beside me and cocked his head.

"So what's the plan?" he asked.

"We need to see what the town is like first, but two of us should probably go in and gather some more food and scout the area." Shadoe looked at me as I started to speak. "Not you."

The syllable I squeaked out before he narrowed his eyes to threaten me meant nothing. I considered kicking his leg out from under him, but I knew that would only result in an unnecessary beating for both of us as we battled wills.

"Auluria will stay behind for now." Fitch's deep voice ended the discussion. "Shadoe, are you going or staying?"

He was silent for a moment, weighing his options. "I'll go. Reed, you can come with me. You'll be the least likely to be remembered."

Reed's lips pursed at the veiled insult, but he didn't say anything. I considered stomping on Shadoe's foot.

We started walking in the direction of the town, Shadoe took the lead, Reed trailing behind him, unwilling to show his pride was wounded. Justin sidled up next to me, nodding toward Shadoe.

"Has a way with words, doesn't he?"

I sighed, knowing if I said anything at all, I'd tell him everything. He shrugs.

"When you get tired of him, just let me know and Dev and I will take him out for you," he volunteered, pulling away from me and continuing the journey a few feet from me.

A bird trilled in the distance when we reached a place where we could see the town on the horizon. Shadoe and

Reed left their packs with us, taking just a few things to trade in the town. Before they left, Shadoe checked to make sure Reed had his knives properly hidden in his boots, aggravating the man yet again.

I watched as they jogged toward the road. Once they reached the end of the trees, they slowed, ducking out into the quiet road. I turned my back once they were in public.

"Now what?" Justin asked.

"Now we work," Raselin said, grabbing his pack. "Nian, stay here. We'll be back before they are, but cover for us in case."

My grin was unintentional. I hadn't pegged Raselin for this much of a rule breaker, but I could work with it. Grabbing my pack, I jumped to my feet from where I was sitting on a giant tree root.

"Lead on."

The other men followed suit, tucking their packs behind them and turning from the town.

"Now we're talking," Fitch said. "Where are we going, boss?"

"We need to know what's here. Auluria?" His hand gestured for me to take the lead.

"Me?"

"No one knows these woods like you do, even Shadoe said so. Lead the way."

I took a tentative step forward. Somewhere along the

way I had forgotten the girl Shadoe had trained me to be while I was busy following his lead. I wasn't the girl Lowell had taken in after her aunt died. I wasn't Lur, the girl Shadoe had trained to destroy. I was Auluria, the woman who fought for the family she chose, who decided to love instead of go after revenge, who was going to save the man she cared for and her people. I wasn't just *a* leader; I was *their* leader.

After a few dozen yards, I announced over my shoulder that we would be splitting up to cover more ground.

"Raselin, you and Fitch go to the right. Justin and I will go to the left. Meet back in one hour. Check in with Nian if anything comes up."

Once we were far enough away, I turned to Justin.

"You ready to do some running?" I challenged.

"Oh, so *that's* why you brought me along instead of Raselin." He grinned, shrugging one shoulder. "I could run."

"Good." I took off.

"Are we looking for anything in particular?" he asked after a moment.

"Signs of life? I mean, my people are exceptional at covering their tracks. Well, both of my groups, actually. But some of the others aren't.

"Look for good places to shelter. Look for food. Just *look*."

"Should we split up?" Justin suggested.

"Not a bad idea, just stay within shouting distance. We can cover more ground this way." I split off from him and ran toward an embankment, dipping down below tree branches as I descended. Justin ran out of view, covering the higher ground.

I leapt over a small stream, barely worth the effort to jump. A branch hit me in the head as I attempted to duck mid-leap, the soft pine needles brushing against my cheek. I landed harder than I anticipated, but kept running, knowing I needed to keep up with Justin.

The sun filtering through the trees was blinding. A golden color settled around me, illuminating the area with a metallic tone. It glistened off of the bark and flashed off the water as I propelled my feet forward.

Sprinting around a large rock, I corrected my course. My eyes darted back and forth as I moved, looking for things I should take account of.

A branch behind me cracked, bringing me to a halt. Whipping around, I looked for Justin. He wasn't there.

I took a few steps backward, watching for movement in the bushes. I saw nothing, but I could sense it. Someone was there.

Turning, I ran, not worrying about kicking up the dirt and brush behind me. They knew I was there, they didn't need to track me, they would just follow me.

My arms pumped at my sides and fear coursed

through my body. I pushed myself faster, harder. I would escape. I needed to warn Justin. I attempted to control my breathing, trying to reserve enough air to yell out.

Crashing through the underbrush, I forced myself forward as a bird shrieked above us. No one followed me, but that gave me no security.

Ahead, I saw a bush. Going around it would take far too much time. Through was my only option. I lowered my stance, hoping to gain more power in my steps.

I didn't know what was on the other side of the bush, but it didn't matter; it was my escape. My hope waved its branches in front of me, beckoning me to enter its realm of protection. I accepted its offer and crashed into its greenery.

Far too late, I realized that it was a drop off. I plummeted downward, crashing into the short ledge the size of a tall man during my descent. Rocks embedded themselves into my arms. The exposed roots of plants tangled in my hair, ripping pieces out as I slid down in the dirt.

I righted myself once I hit the ground. Without checking for injuries, I pushed myself to my feet and took off. The trees reached out for me as I fled, demanding I stop and confront my unexpected company. I had to get to Justin, though, and I refused to stop.

"Justin!" I screamed his name, praying he could hear me, wherever he was.

I crashed past another set of trees and slammed into a

tall bush made mostly of tangled vine-like branches. My foot caught, forcing me to leap over the edge of the brush.

I saw the second stream before I landed, my foot getting caught on a rock as I tried to avoid tumbling into the water. Overshooting the water, I slammed into something else.

Arms wrapped around me, body heat enveloping me as we swung around together. I knocked the breath out of my captor and he grunted as our collision slowed. Throwing myself back, I tried to escape his grasp.

"Auluria?" a voice barked.

A flash of blue, then black jumped into my line of sight as I made eye contact with the man holding me. *Dov.*

No...Berwyn.

"You're alive?" I gasped, throwing myself at him, knocking him off balance once again. I couldn't stop my tears.

He roughly pushed me back.

"What are you doing here?" he asked, anger in his voice.

"You survived." My words frustrated him even more.

"Auluria! What are you doing here?" he shouted.

My eyes dragged the length of him, focusing on his arm that Shadoe cut with his claw-like blade.

"The poison didn't kill you," I concluded.

"No it didn't, now why are you here?" He shook me, trying to get me to focus.

"Where is Dov?" I demanded.

"Canton has him. He's using him as bait to try to get the rest of us," Berwyn confirmed. "Where is Eden?"

"You don't know?" I asked in horror.

"I haven't seen her since we split up. I had heard some of you made it over the wall. I was hoping she was with you."

I shook my head.

"Dov gave himself up so we could get away. Eden and Silas ran toward the woods."

"Why are you here if you made it over the wall?" he asked, looking for information.

"It's just as bad over there, Berwyn. We've come back to help bring down the Society once and for all."

"We?" He looked at me skeptically.

"I have a team, Berwyn. There are men and women. They are trained and ready to fight. Some of them are from here and escaped to look for a better life. Some just want freedom, but they're here Berwyn, and they're ready."

"And just where are they?" He nearly sounded like Lowell, casual, but searching for answers he didn't believe were there.

"Most of them are on the other side of the wall," I admit. "I came with a small team as a trial run. We've had spies here the last few weeks. We know Canton has Dov, or at least he did the last time our spy saw him."

"And just how many people do you have on this team?"

"There are seven of us." I said. "Berwyn, there's something you should know."

He waits for me to continue.

"Shadoe is with me." I cringe as I say it.

Berwyn flinches and my eyes dart to his arm, the wound still visible; a dark red color.

"He helped me escape." I tried to assuage his anger before it built up.

"Did he help *Dov* escape?" *Too late.*

"He did what Dov instructed him to do. He's stayed with me this entire time; he even trained the people from the other side of the wall."

"And you think he won't return to his group now that he's here?" Berwyn challenged.

"I don't know. He's loyal to Lowell; he always has been. If Lowell wants him back, he'll probably go."

"Lowell is dead, Auluria," he said bluntly. "He was the only one that didn't escape, I'm told."

"Shadoe thought that might have happened," I said, trying to digest the information. Lowell was really gone. I should have known if *Shadoe,* his most loyal follower, thought Lowell was dead, than he had to be gone.

"Shadoe was the one who cut me down." I glanced at

him, hoping that would win him some points with Berwyn.

He raised his eyebrows again, as if asking if that was supposed to be a good thing.

"If he hadn't cut me down, there wouldn't have been chaos, and Dov, Eden and Silas would have died too."

"You don't know that they haven't," Berwyn challenged. "*You* don't have Eden and Silas, *I* don't have Eden and Silas… And Dov is only partially alive, from what I hear."

"Have you seen him?" I asked, his words slapping me as I stepped closer.

"No. I haven't. I'm on my way to the city now. We're going to rescue him, but we need some information first."

We.

It was Berwyn's people that I had been running from.

"You brought a team."

I nodded.

Berwyn shook his head once, realizing his people were waiting.

"It's fine," he announced, with a flick of his wrist.

Several people stepped out. One man in particular caught my attention—the man who had interrogated me when I first joined Berwyn's group. He was the last man I wanted to see—other than Lowell, who would no longer be a problem.

"And *you* made me stop." The tall man turned to Berwyn when he realized I was there.

"It's not her fault, Arin." Berwyn silenced him. "She didn't do this to us, and even though she escaped, she came back to help us."

I fought to keep my face from twitching. *This was not the Berwyn Baer I knew.*

He turned back to me and glared.

Or maybe he was.

"Sir!" A voice interrupted, followed by the heavy footsteps of the man it belonged to.

The man joined us, his eyes widening and his brow dropping at the sight of me.

"You're back," he said to me. "You're not with them."

"With who?" Berwyn asked skeptically.

"Your wife, sir." The man turned to face Berwyn.

"You found her?" he asks, astonished, dropping the glare from his face as a hunger for information takes over.

"Yes, sir. She's alive, as is Silas." The man confirms quickly. "Wallace has her."

"Berwyn..." I turned back to him.

"What do you know?" He commanded me to speak, his voice a deep growl.

"Marty and Jake ambushed us while we were escaping. They wanted to capture us for the reward. We tied them up but..."

"But they must have found a way to untie themselves and captured Eden and Silas after you split up." He finished for me.

I nodded miserably.

A metallic thud sounded behind Berwyn. We both turned to find a knife bouncing in the dirt, settling a few feet behind him. I turned to see who had thrown it.

"Auluria, run!" Justin shouted.

"No, wait!" I moved toward the voice, trying to prevent him from actually hitting someone with the next knife. "It's safe! Stand down. It's safe."

I repeated my words until Justin stood, popping up slowly out of the bushes. He looked skeptically at me until I waved him forward.

Berwyn stood, weapon in hand, ready to assault the man approaching us. Arin and the others were poised for action.

"Everyone stand down. He's with us."

I knew Berwyn's men would never unnecessarily hurt someone—that wasn't who they were—but I rushed to Justin's side anyway, bringing him safely into the group.

"This is Justin. He's part of the team I brought here to run our trial mission. Justin, these are my people." I motioned around at the group.

He hesitated a moment before smiling.

"Nice to meet you all. I take it we'll be working together?"

Berwyn flinched.

"Maybe," he replied.

"Sir," the scout interrupted quietly. "We need more men, if you want to rescue Eden *and* Dov."

"He's right, Berwyn. The Society doesn't know about my team, but they're actively looking for your group. It gives us the ability to surprise them," I tried to encourage him.

"What else do we know about Eden?" Berwyn turned back to the scout.

"Nothing. I can only confirm that Wallace has them."

"Why hasn't he made this known yet?" Berwyn mumbled to himself.

"Maybe he doesn't want to tip his hand yet… Maybe he has a plan." I suggested.

"What is happening?" Justin finally asked in a clipped voice, prompting me to quickly explain what we had just learned.

"We need to get our people here." Justin said, confident that we could assist Berwyn. "We can help you, but you have to help us first. We need to get our people over the wall and we need to do it quickly."

"What are you proposing?" Berwyn crossed his arms, leveling a glare at Justin.

"If you want to save your wife and your brother, you need more backup that the Society doesn't know about. It seems like you've kept most of your group hidden from what I can tell, but the more people you have, the more likely you will be able to overtake the Society.

"If we can free your people, we can combine our forces and take out the Society once and for all. We can all live here, free of the threats we live under. If we can take out your government, then we can rally the entire country and take out the government on *our* side of the wall. Our countries can live in peace. We could even knock down the wall entirely and form a bigger, stronger nation to keep the others from coming after us."

Berwyn tipped his head, thinking through the implications of teaming up.

"Who exactly is in charge of your little band of men?" Berwyn asked.

"Auluria." Justin crossed his arms and tipped his chin up, mimicking Berwyn. "Auluria is in charge, along with Raselin, Necesta, and Shadoe."

"Shadoe?" Berwyn gapped before turning on me. "You let *Shadoe* have any say in—"

"Yes. Shadoe has a say." I cut him off. "He has just as much right as any of us, and he's the best trainer we have. He trained *me*—"

"Because that means so much," he snapped.

"When have I ever failed, Berwyn? I'm still alive, aren't I? I did every job you asked me to do, didn't I?"

"He tried to *kill* me, Auluria," he shouted, holding his scarred arm out to me. "He nearly did!"

Arin jumped into the conversation, yelling his distaste for me and for Shadoe. The scout tried to calm everyone, but no one listened.

"Are you sure this is a good idea?" Justin hissed in my ear, leaning close so I could hear him over the argument. "Maybe we should do this on our own."

"We are not doing this on our own!" I yell, swinging to face him as I disrupted the fight. "We are going to save Eden and Silas, then we are going to save Dov, and then we're going to bring the Society down once and for all, and the Baers are our best chance of making that happen and surviving it all."

I refused to back down.

"Berwyn, enough," I lectured. "This is happening. You are working with these men and women. You need help. We need help too. Canton won't kill Dov yet because he's too useful, so that means our first job is to get our people over the wall and go after Eden and Silas. We'll probably need them anyway. Then we go straight for Dov. Once we have him, we bring Canton down and use him to dismantle the Society. Now move!"

I turned on my heels and marched away, Justin following immediately behind me. I could sense Berwyn hesitate, but only because he wasn't in the lead. He knew my plan was the smart move.

He stomped behind me until he caught up with me. I kept a brisk pace, forcing everyone back toward our rendezvous point where I would introduce him to Raselin.

Eventually I broke the silence.

"What happened to you after we left?" I asked quietly, hoping the others wouldn't notice.

"I barely survived. The men got me back to the storehouse and by some miracle, they extracted some of the poison. They had almost given up on me when I started to pull out of it. Whatever they gave me counteracted the drugs.

"He meant to kill me, Auluria. How can you work with him?"

"He's been protecting me. He's done what I asked. He saved me from dying with a noose around my neck," I replied. "I don't trust him, not like I trust you, but I will work with him, because I'd rather have him on our team where I can watch him, than possibly working against us somewhere else.

"He could change, Berwyn. It's possible, especially now that Lowell is gone."

"You think he won't go back to them and take Lowell's place?" Berwyn scoffed. "I think that's exactly what he plans to do, and he'll probably try to drag you with him."

"I would never leave Dov," I said, trying once again to prove my loyalties.

"We'll see."

"We should go ahead and warn Nian and Raselin," Justin interrupted.

"Go ahead. I'll stay with the men to guide them." I nodded at him as he held my gaze. "Go."

Justin took off, running ahead to prepare our team.

"What's that all about?" Berwyn asked, nodding toward Justin's disappearing figure.

"He's a good guy, Berwyn. His family is a lot like yours. I think you'll like them."

He grumbled as we continued to walk.

"We just need to get them back." Berwyn finally said.

"We will," I insisted. "We'll save them. We'll get Eden and Silas, and then we'll go get Dov."

My voice cracked. I missed him.

Berwyn looked at me out of the corner of his eye but didn't comment.

"What do we have here?" Raselin greeted us, clearly having walked out to meet us away from the meeting point.

"Berwyn, this is Raselin. He's one of the leaders from the other side of the wall."

Raselin reached out to shake his hand. After a moment, Berwyn accepted it.

"I'm Berwyn Baer. I hear you want to take down the Society as badly as we do." He removed his hand and placed it on the knife on his belt, tightening his fingers around it.

"We do," Raselin confirmed. "And if Auluria trusts you, so do we. I hope you feel as though her confidence in us will allow you to trust us as well."

Berwyn appraised the man who was just a bit younger than his father, Griz, would have been, had he lived.

"Auluria says she trained you." He avoided the question.

"She did. She and Shadoe are strong leaders."

Berwyn tensed at Shadoe's name. I could tell he would blame Shadoe for what was happening to Eden. He needed a target, and for once, it couldn't be me. He needed me too much, and for Dov's sake, he had to accept me.

"We have a strong group of men and women who are ready to fight. We've spent many years on the outskirts of our government's reach because we were so close to the wall. We've lived more privileged lives than many of our countrymen, but it's getting worse.

"It's only a matter of time before they force us to work for them. In fact, it's already starting, though not nearly as bad as it is here. We want to preemptively strike back and end this before it gets out of hand."

"And you're willing to take down *our* government to do that?"

"Some of us started out here, Berwyn, but even those that didn't know how effective it will be to take down your government first. Ours is much stronger and we need your people to overtake our oppressors. If we help free you of your reign of tyranny, you can help us. We can have a country united, working for peace.

"Justin told me about your wife, and Auluria informed us about your brother. We were already planning on making him one of our priorities, hoping that he would bring his people to join us.

"Now that we have you on our team, our priority is to restore him to leadership in your group. The faster we have our people in place, the easier it will be to take them by surprise when we strike."

"Baer?" A dark, piercing voice filled the air, shattering the quiet I hadn't noticed until that point.

Berwyn looked beyond Raselin at Shadoe's approaching form.

"You should be dead," Shadoe threatened.

"Yet here I am." Berwyn scowled at him, the muscles in his arms tightening.

"Not as easy to kill as your father, I see." Shadoe sneered, looking eerily like Lowell.

Berwyn ran at him, stopping only because Raselin injected himself into his path, blocking him from murdering Shadoe.

I lurched forward, grabbing Berwyn's arm to pull him back. He turned on me, hand ready to strike as he had once struck Dov. Catching himself, he bit down, grinding his teeth in an effort to control his rage.

Rocking back, I saw him deflate slightly, and I released his elbow where my nails dug into his skin.

Turning, I marched over to Shadoe, his eyes tracking me as I moved. Every moment of anger I had felt toward Shadoe in the time since we scaled the wall built up in my steps. My hand flew from my side, wrapping in front of me. I brought my elbow back to his face with as much force as I could, intentionally aiming for his cheek and not his nose.

The sharp crack made the spectators gasp. Shadoe stumbled back, not having expected my attack, his hand on his face. His eyes flashed, rage turning them dark.

Berwyn marched up behind me, getting dangerously close. He stopped just behind my shoulder blade, leaning around my body.

"She was *never* yours." He hissed, echoing the words Dov had once said to Shadoe when my handler claimed me.

He must have told his brother about the encounter. What else had he told Berwyn?

He pulled away from me, the sudden force causing my hair to move in the breeze he created with his movements. Satisfied that he had won the conversation, he stalked back to his team, arms crossed, and waited.

Shadoe stared, wide-eyed at the scene. He glanced to me, but I had no intention of lending him my support. He deserved all that and more.

"Wallace has Eden and Silas. We're going to get them back," I announced, breaking the tense silence.

Raselin and Fitch stood back, watching, waiting for the moment they would have to intercede and quell whatever fight might break out. Reed looked worried one might, slowly reaching for his knife. Nian brushed his hair back, his amused smirk matching Justin's. Arin looked ready to kill on Berwyn's behalf.

"Wallace?" Shadoe grunted. "You had to go and involve him, didn't you, Baer?"

"If anyone is at fault here, it's you, leech."

"Leech?" Shadoe demanded.

"What else would you call someone who hung onto that wolf like you did?"

"Enough!" I shouted, stepping between them.

Shadoe lowered his hand and a nasty welt surrounded the bloody cut I had created. I turned to him.

"Berwyn will help us get our people across the wall and into the Society. We will help extract Eden and Silas before Wallace can hurt them and then we'll go after the Society."

"You think we can get them out of Wallace's hands before anything happens to them? He's probably already torturing them. You thought those boys who attacked you were bad, Lur? You have no idea what Wallace will do to them."

Arin's quick movement reminded Berwyn to restrain himself as he angled his shoulder in front of his leader.

"Then we'll have to move quickly, won't we?" I replied.

"Excuse me," Raselin interrupted, "but for those of us who don't know, what *exactly* is this Wallace capable of?"

Berwyn's scout gave him a brief outline of what he knew of Wallace's group, avoiding any discussion on what he might be doing to them. For all of Lowell's faults, he was far less reckless than Wallace. My cousin didn't destroy just for the fun of it.

"Bit of a wildcard, isn't he?" Raselin ventured.

"Which is why we need to move quickly." Berwyn confirmed. "Wallace knows how we operate. He will be watching for us."

"We need our people," Raselin said, motioning for us to start walking. "They'll have to be ready."

Chapter 7

"You've checked all of these people out?" Berwyn asked, slipping away from the group when we stopped at the stream.

"Yes, Berwyn. I trust them."

"You trusted Lowell once, too."

"So did you," I countered, reminding him that Lowell had once belonged to the Baers' group, working alongside Griz.

"And you trust the man we sent ahead? Fitch?" Berwyn ignored my comment.

"Yes, his wife is there. He wants to protect her." I tried giving him a reason to feel more secure. "He won't betray us."

"How do you propose we get them over the wall?" He asked, filling his canteen with water.

"I was hoping *you'd* have an idea." I squirmed under his watchful eyes. "It's not going to be easy getting that many people over the wall without being noticed."

"Well." He considered our options. "We could create a distraction. Send some of the boys to the town and draw the soldiers away. That should give us more time."

"Can we risk that?"

"I don't think we have much of a choice." We discussed our options.

Berwyn walked over to his men and instructed them where to go.

"We have a plan?" Raselin asked, walking up behind me.

"We do. Berwyn is going to send some of our men into the town to distract the soldiers. They will be tasked with leading the men away from the wall for a day or two. That should give our people enough time to get to the wall and climb over it."

"Why not just lead them away when it's time? Why have them go early?"

"The soldiers will be suspicious. They'll investigate when our men start causing problems. If they start early, the men will look into it and find nothing, so by the time we're actually doing something, they won't be watching as closely because they'll think the threat has passed."

"Interesting."

We watched as Berwyn's men branched off, taking a more direct route toward the town. One of his men walked back the way we came.

"He's going to the storehouse," Berwyn said as he approached. "Did you fill him in?"

"She did." Raselin answered. "Interesting plan. Now the question is how we're going to get everyone over."

"Most of them can climb the wall. A few people, like Necesta, will need help."

"Fitch will help with that," Justin said, joining the group. "I've seen him carry full grown men around when they're injured. Last fall he carried Reed's cousin clear across town when the soldier's ran him over as they marched through."

"I'm sure he's already thought about that." Raselin nodded. "He's had the entire journey back without anyone to talk to. I'm sure he's come up with at least a few solutions.

"Let's get moving, boys." Arin stomped into the circle, glancing at me. "We have a lot of ground to cover."

The stars were out when we finally arrived.

I woke up a few feet from Reed. Nian slept on my other side, hair once again in his eyes. During the night, I moved to the far side of the fire, instructing Raselin to stay between Berwyn and Shadoe as they fought over who should be watching out for me.

"Did you sleep well?" Reed whispered.

"Not at all." I raked my hands through my hair, pulling it out of my face. "You?"

"Kind of," he said, sitting up. "What's the plan for today?"

"Not much we *can* do. We can't move anyone until nightfall."

"So we're just going to wait around all day?"

"Are you volunteering to go back over the wall and wait for them to arrive?"

"Is that an option?" he asked casually.

"It is if you want it to be."

We let the others sleep, knowing it would be a long day and they'd need all the rest they could get. The sun cast shadows through the trees when they started to stir.

Reed slipped over the wall late that afternoon, after the entire team stared at the open space between the town and the wall for over an hour, watching for movement.

Once he disappeared beyond the barrier, we did our best to keep ourselves occupied. It was immediately clear that staying together was a bad choice given the impending fight between Shadoe and Berwyn.

Spacing out, we each moved off on our own. Shadoe sharpened his knives, gaze moving between where I paced and Berwyn's location a dozen yards away as he talked with Arin.

The minutes were agonizing. I stretched my arms above my head, bringing them down to my neck as I tried to work out a knot, succeeding only in tangling them in my hair. Flipping my head over, I let my hair fall in front of me. It fell to the ground, brushing over the grass as I massaged my neck.

"Wow, girl. That is some hair." Justin smirked, coming to sit on a log near me.

"It's taken you this long to notice?" I straightened and moved to take a seat by him.

"It's on the ground, Auluria. It didn't look that long when you were beating us in the training."

"Auluria, a word." Berwyn approached, waiting for Justin to leave. Mysteriously, Shadoe appeared behind him, glaring at Justin.

Justin glanced at me, assuming if both men were there to see me, it couldn't be good. I smiled tightly, telling him to go. The man stood and walked away, giving us space.

"Leave, Shadoe." Berwyn instructed.

"*You* leave, Baer."

"I'll leave," I volunteer, standing to make a quick exit.

"No," they respond in unison.

The men faced off once again, squaring their shoulders until Raselin called for Shadoe. I was grateful for his choice.

"What are you doing?" Berwyn whispered harshly once we were alone.

"What do you mean?"

"That boy."

"That *boy* is *your age,* Berwyn," I pointed out.

"Dov is being held captive and you're—"

"Whoa!" I cut him off, fist clenched, daring him to say another word.

We wait to see who will break first. He wins.

"I've known Justin for a few weeks. We didn't even talk much until this mission. He's a nice guy. He reminds me of Silas, actually, but that's all. So stop seeing things where nothing is there."

"That better be all it is." He cautioned me.

"Is that why Shadoe came over here too? Because of Justin?"

"I assume so." He glanced over his shoulder at his enemy. "He nearly beat me over here. Just one more time I bested him."

He grinned to himself.

"Shadoe isn't as clever as he thinks, and you'd do well to remember that, Auluria."

"I've known him a lot longer than you have, Berwyn."

Berwyn spent the next hour detailing the plan to break into Wallace's camp, partially to pass the time, but mainly to keep Shadoe away. If Dov couldn't be there to protect me, Berwyn was going to make it his mission to get between us.

I waited in the trees as the next group of people ran as quietly as they could through the tall grass.

"Keep going. One hundred yards and you'll find Nian. He's waiting with everyone else." I pointed in the direction they should run as people filed past me.

Finally, Shadoe, Berwyn, and Raselin reached my checkpoint.

"That's everyone," Raselin said, Necesta on his arm.

"Hello there, Goldilocks," She crooned, eyeing me.

Berwyn frowned, but I ignored him.

Lydia hung on Fitch's arm, Talley trailing behind her, head darting back and forth as she looked for Devin.

"He's already with Nian," I said as she neared.

Justin stayed close by to appease his sister's nervousness. He nodded as he walked by, but didn't try to speak to me after what had happened earlier.

Once we reached the group, Berwyn addressed them, informing them that we'd be going as far as we could during the night. We needed to move them away from the wall. We'd head straight for the storehouse. I was anxious to arrive.

We planned to regroup at Berwyn's hiding place, something he had been reluctant to give up in Shadoe's presence. The children and young people would be staying at the storehouse, along with the adults who weren't trained enough yet. Berwyn would select the best of the teenage boys to continue their training while we worked to free Eden and Silas.

The night dragged on well into the early morning hours before we broke for camp. I made sure to stay close to Berwyn from the time the new members joined us to show my trust for Berwyn and the Baers. If the people had to choose between Shadoe and Berwyn, I wanted the choice to be clear.

He chose when to stop. He chose when to go. I always yielded to Berwyn. By the time we rested, the group surrounding us was looking to him. Raselin's approval solidified their acceptance of this new leader.

"Auluria, are you ready for this?" Berwyn asked as we sat.

"I need you to promise me something, Berwyn." I tucked my hair behind my ear and focused on the fire's flames.

"What?"

"No matter what, you get Dov out," I requested,

knowing my chances of survival going up against Marty and Jake one more time. I had pushed grace too far with those two; this time I very well might not survive it.

He raised an eyebrow at me.

"We'll get Dov," he said, "but you don't get to die for my wife, Auluria. Not now."

I attempted to grin.

"Maybe I'll die for Silas."

"You keep trying that, from what you told me. It hasn't worked so far."

"Suddenly you care, Berwyn? I didn't know you had it in you," I teased, desperately wanting something more than the dread that was washing over me.

"I sent people to look for you too, Auluria," he said quietly.

"You did that for Dov."

"I did for *you*. I might not like you, but I still respect you. I don't want to see you hurt." He took a deep breath. "Besides, Dov would kill me if I didn't."

I tried to hide my smile. Dov would definitely kill him if he didn't step up while Dov couldn't.

"Seriously, Berwyn, promise me you'll get him out of there."

"I'm not going to abandon my brother, Auluria," he said tersely.

"I know, I just…"

"You'll be fine. *He'll* be fine. We'll make it through this.

We survived Lowell. We can survive Canton too. And now we have back up. So stop sulking and get your head in the right space," Berwyn snapped, reminding me of my little talks with his wife. Those two were definitely suited for each other.

He turned away and ended the conversation.

Definitely like Eden.

I just hoped Eden was still like Eden when we found her.

Shadoe claimed me as we walked the next morning, refusing to leave my side. I waved Berwyn away, knowing I needed to make sure I didn't isolate Shadoe. As long as he stayed on our side, we might actually survive this rescue attempt, but if he went out on his own, there was no telling what type of damage he would create.

His hatred of Berwyn was evident. I decided to play on his remaining loyalty to Lowell, working the Society's potential destruction into the conversation as much as I could while we walked. Convincing him that Berwyn could be useful in its downfall wasn't an easy task.

Shadoe remained quiet most of the walk, only speaking when he noticed people watching, an attempt to keep them from approaching us. My former fiancé had never been a man of many words. I knew the conversation must have been killing him by the way he ground his teeth each time I started a new branch of the conversation. Something about that knowledge delighted me.

"Enough, Lur." He finally tried silencing me. "I've heard you. Enough."

"So you'll put this nonsense behind you and work with the Baers?"

"I will do what we need to do to finish Lowell's mission. The Society will fall. Whatever it takes to accomplish that, I'll deal with."

"Good." I replied, only slightly satisfied that he had relented.

"There." Shadoe pointed ahead.

Once again he had selected the entrance to the hidden underground storehouse. The man had a knack for knowing these things. I was surprised he hadn't stumbled on any of the Baers' storehouses before.

The tunnel was cool, the temperature dropping as the earthy smell enveloped us in its embrace. I trailed my hands along the tunnel walls, momentarily forgetting they were made of dirt. I brushed my palms along my pants, knocking off the loose dirt.

The room brightened as we stepped out of the entrance and into the main room. It was filled with life.

People moved around the room, changing locations to create space for the newcomers.

"Auluria?" Katarina's surprised voice floated above the crowd.

"Auluria?" A second voice sounded from the other side of the room. *"Auluria!"*

Reyla slammed into me, knocking me into Shadoe as she wrapped her arms around me, tears in her eyes. Maylin followed closely behind her, throwing her arms around me as well.

Katarina quickly walked over to join us, swaying her hips as she moved. She commanded to be observed. Henry stepped up next to her, keeping pace, forcing several men to look away.

Sharone made her way through the crowd, finishing the group of girls surrounding me.

"You're alive," Reyla squealed. "We were so worried."

"We heard they hung you." Maylin informed me. "They thought you got away, but we weren't sure…"

"We escaped." I nodded, still holding on to them.

"They have Dov." Katarina said gently, as if she were unsure if I knew.

"I know. One of the men I met on the other side of the wall saw him. He was alive last we knew."

"We'll save him." Reyla said quietly.

"Well, look who is back!" Gregory bellowed, joining the group.

"The team is back together at last." Carter grinned.

"I don't see how any of you can celebrate." Gloria cast us a disparaging look. "Dov *and* Silas are still gone."

She curled her fingernails into her palms as she walked past us, looking Shadoe up and down. She blamed me for Dov's imprisonment, and she didn't trust Shadoe.

Just then, the group noticed my former mentor standing behind me, scowling. They turned in unison from him to me.

"This is Shadoe." I saw Reyla mouth his name as I spoke, making the connection before I told her. Her face paled.

"He is the man who trained me before I joined you all. He managed to cut me down when Canton took us to the gallows and has been helping me train the people from the other side of the wall." I tried to calm their tension.

Reyla dug her nails into my arm, questioning why I would let him anywhere near me. I appreciated her worry over my safety, but she had also never seen me on a mission. I had confided in her about my training, but she would be shocked to see just how capable I really was.

I pried her hand off of my arm.

"He's working with us to bring down the Society. Shadoe, these are—"

"It doesn't matter," Shadoe announced, walking away.

Everyone turned to look at me, eyes wide.

"He takes some getting used to?" I phrase it as a question.

"Are you '*used to*' him yet?" Gregory challenged with a smirk.

"More than I'm used to you, Gregory," I teased.

"Oh, please, you adore me." He acted offended, placing his hand over his heart. He winked at me, a low growl escaping as he jutted his chin at me.

"Go find some other girl to harass, Gregory." Reyla pushed him.

"Really, Gregory. Are you that desperate?" Katarina asked, winking at Henry.

"I wouldn't do that if I were you." Justin leaned into the conversation. "Shadoe will probably murder you in your sleep."

"Hilarious," Gregory said sarcastically. His face dropped when I didn't laugh along. "Seriously?"

"Probably." I thought about softening it with a smile or laugh, but when it came to Shadoe, they really needed to know the risks.

The boys tentatively took a step back.

"Okay."

"Got it."

"Distance is our friend." They chorused.

I sent them off to find me something to eat before we started on our new mission, leaving the girls by my side.

Reyla looped her arm through mine and leaned close as she stared at Shadoe across the room.

"You were really engaged to him?" she asked, her nose turned up a touch.

"You what?" Katarina asked, demanding a further explanation.

"Not by choice," I assured her. "My cousin came up with the idea."

"Did you… Kiss him?" She looked horrified, her face matching Sharone's.

"But what about Dov?" Maylin asked.

"I wasn't with Shadoe by choice. We were never a real couple. I'm with Dov. End of discussion," I replied.

"No wonder you came running to us," Reyla said, still watching Shadoe.

"I don't know. He's kind of cute, in that standoffish way," Sharone said.

"I guess I can see it," Katarina mused, "but I'm still Team Dov."

"Aren't we all?" I accidentally said out loud. The girls looked at me before breaking into laughter.

Together, we wandered over to where the boys had procured food and found a seat on the ground. In the few minutes we had to talk, I told them what I had been through since I left them, and they regaled me with tales of their heroics while I was gone. The girls attempted to keep Gregory's wild stories in check.

"Auluria, we need to talk," Berwyn interrupted.

I cast the group a look. This was goodbye again. Their faces fell as fast as mine had.

"Berwyn, I'm coming too." Reyla stood with me.

"No, you're not, Reyla." Berwyn turned to walk away.

"I am. Peter gave his life up to protect your brother, so the way I see it, you owe me. This is what I want," she said defiantly.

Berwyn continued to walk away. Reyla grabbed my arm and followed behind him. When we reached his inner circle, he didn't stop her.

Being in the inner circle without Dov and Silas felt wrong. I hesitated as I approached, but this was my place now. I was a leader. Raselin stepped up beside me. I felt Shadoe's presence behind me, but even *he* didn't have the gall to separate me from Reyla.

"We have a plan." Berwyn announced, turning to me. "You will be bait."

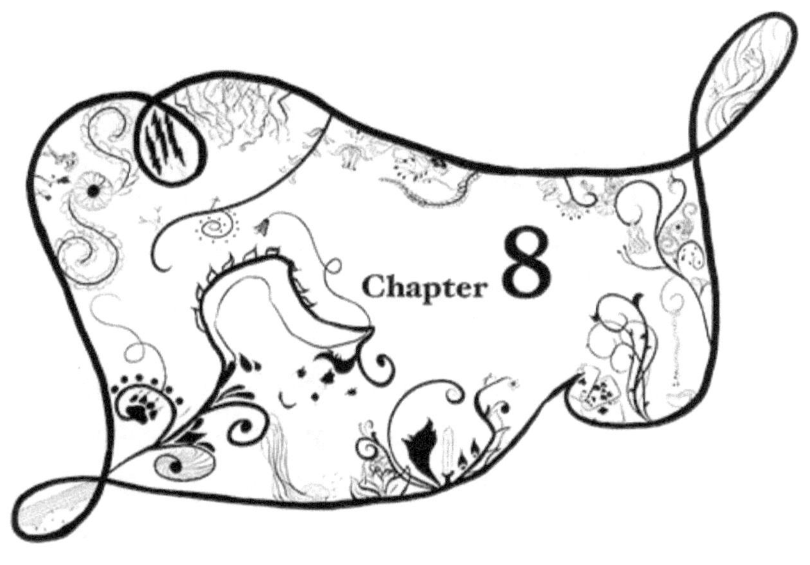

Chapter 8

MY EYES GREW WIDE. ONCE AGAIN BERWYN PLANNED TO dangle me in front of someone to get what he wanted.

Reyla swallowed hard. "And me. Where she goes, I go."

"Fine," Shadoe said, not giving Berwyn a chance to object. "Wallace will be thrilled to get his hands on them and I imagine Marty and Jake won't be too upset about it either."

I didn't like the idea of Reyla being anywhere near Marty or Jake after all of my accidental run-ins with them. I knew I couldn't convince her to stay any more than she had been able to convince me not to clean up Lowell's mess. Protecting her would be a distraction. Shadoe had to know that.

"We'll get as close as we can to Wallace's territory without being suspicious," Berwyn said. "He will likely take the girls to where Eden and Silas are being held. We'll track them there and finalize the plan from there based on the conditions we find them in.

"If we all strike at once, we should be able to over-whelm Wallace's people, especially if they don't see us coming." He ignored the part where things likely wouldn't go as planned.

Shadoe and I took turns adding to the plan, tweaking the Baers' mission until we were all satisfied it was the best of the choices we had. Reyla quietly stood next to me, taking it all in.

"This is going to be bad, isn't it?" she asked once the group broke apart, tucking her hair behind her nervously.

"You don't have to do this Reyla."

"The last time you went off on your own, you didn't come back, Auluria. That's not happening again."

"You're not trained, Reyla," I said. "Not well enough for this."

"I'll be fine. Peter used to teach me things. I know more than I let on." She tried putting on a brave face. "Silas is our friend, and Eden is our leader. We need them back, and like Shadoe said, two of us are better than one. Besides, would they really believe they captured *you*? You've escaped Marty how many times now?"

I tipped my head, wishing she would listen to me.

"If they catch us both, they'll actually believe it. They'll also assume they can use me as leverage. You'll have to listen to them to protect me."

"I want you to be safe," I protested.

"I know. But I'll be fine. Right now the priority is rescuing our people, so stop arguing and let's go. The faster we get moving, the better."

"Fine. Here," I said, bending down to show her how to hide a knife in her boot. "They're going to take this from you when they search us, but it will be more believable that way.

"You ladies ready?" Raselin asked, eyeing me as I stood up.

"Almost." I glanced down at my clothing. "This isn't going to do me any favors."

"I remember not too long ago we had to work to get you out of here in those," Reyla nodded to the trousers I was wearing. "Now look at you, trying to get out in a dress."

I couldn't stop a giggle from escaping my lips. We'd come full circle, and this time, Reyla was jumping in with me.

"There." I stiffened. "Get ready."

I continued to adjust the snare I was setting. Reyla calmly reached out for the one she was working on.

"Is this right?" she asked casually enough that even *I* was impressed.

I lifted my head, leaning over to see what she was doing. It was perfect, but I stood up as if I were going to help her adjust it. Before I made it to her, a fallen branch snapped loudly.

"Well, well. What do we have here?"

We both turned to face the man watching us.

"Are we in your way?" I asked tersely. There was no need to play coy. They would know who I was soon enough, and being polite would be out of character once Marty saw me after our capture.

"You are." He stepped closer.

"We can leave," Reyla said quickly, grabbing my arm as if to tug me away.

"No, I don't think you can, young lady. You see, this is our land." He gestured around him. "And when you enter our land, you answer to us."

"We don't answer to you." I glanced around, looking for a branch to use as a weapon. I spotted one a few feet away.

"No, you answer to my boss." He sneered. "Boys…"

Five men advanced from the bushes and trees, surrounding us. I dove for the branch, whipping it above my shoulder, ready to swing. As the first man came at me, I swung, connecting with his shoulder. I intentionally avoided his face. I had to make the fight look good, but not good enough that we could have escaped.

The man fell backward as Reyla screamed. One of the men plucked her off the ground, arms around her waist as she kicked. A sickening thud echoed off the trees as her heel connected with his knee, forcing him to drop her. She kicked at his other leg, knocking him to the ground and she scrambled to get up.

Hitting another man with my branch, I cracked it in half. I dropped it, knowing I would have to fight with my fists.

The man caught Reyla by the arm, whipping her around to face him. He backhanded her, sending her reeling to the ground once more, red cascading over her face.

Anger boiled inside me as I ran to her side. I lifted my leg up, drawing all my strength, and slammed into the man's knee from the side. He shrieked as badly as my friends and I had when Canton tortured us. I knew it would be the only injury I would be able to get away with during the attack, but I wasn't sad about wasting it on him after he hit Reyla like that.

The men converged on us, blocking us in a tight circle as the injured man pulled himself far enough back from the group that he wouldn't accidentally be stepped on as they captured us. Hands grasped my arms, wrenching them behind my back.

My skirt tangled around my ankles as they turned me to tie my hands, and I pitched forward. The men holding me kept me upright, the force straining my bones from their sockets. Before it could cause more than pain, they righted me and I stood on my own.

The ropes bit into my wrists as we walked, but none of the men recognized me. Reyla walked quietly beside me, the only tear stains on her cheeks from her eyes watering after being hit. She was brave, holding herself together after the attack, but the worst was yet to come.

When we arrived, we were pushed into the center of their camp. I watched for signs of our friends but found nothing. Noise fluttered all around us, the waves crashing and subsiding as we moved along.

"Where do you want them?" one of the men shouted, his unexpectedly loud voice making me jump.

"Take them to Wallace," someone shouted in the distance.

"Are we taking them to Wallace?" the man holding Reyla's bound wrists asked quietly.

"Might as well. He has to see them at some point anyway. We'll just have to drag them back out again if he doesn't see them now." The man behind me answered.

When we arrived, Wallace was sitting inside a large area with many tables that appeared to be a dining area.

Groups of people milled about, finishing their food and conversations.

"What is this?" He had the same presence Lowell had, but there was something far more reckless about him. His hair, while combed, was wild. His movements had an edge to them like a cornered animal.

He stood, walking over to appraise us.

"Who are you?" he asked us.

Reyla looked tentatively at me. I made eye contact before turning back to stare at Wallace. Aggravating him would be easy, though it would have been easier to play nice. That version of Auluria wouldn't be the one Marty and Jake had built up though. I had to stay true to the girl they believed I was and had likely told their people to explain why I had escaped so many times.

"Who are you?" Wallace demanded again.

The men behind us kicked the back of our legs down, bringing us to our knees. Reyla crouched low, ready to submit to their questioning, just as I had told her to do. The man behind me gripped my hair, pulling back, forcing me to look up.

"Who are you?" He bellowed one more time.

"It can't be!" a voice in the crowd said.

Jake.

He pushed his way through.

"Wallace, that's her. That's the one that was helping the Baers." He pointed an accusatory finger at me.

Wallace whipped his head back to look at me.

"Well, seems we caught another Baer." He walked forward until he was standing an arm's length in front of us. "You too?"

Reyla nodded slightly, looking miserable. She was better than I expected.

Wallace grinned gleefully.

"We have your friends. Would you like to see them?"

The men lifted us up, pulling once again on our shoulders painfully.

"I think it's about time we reached out to Berwyn Baer, don't you?" He bellowed for the crowd, as if it were a joke. They all laughed.

"We have his wife. Now we have the little one's woman. What more could we ask for?" He flicked his wrist, dismissing us. He lowered his voice so only the group surrounding him could hear. "I'll be by to talk to you soon. Eden and I need to have a little conversation anyway."

A body nearly slammed into me as we walked. He careened out of an alleyway into our path.

"So it's true," Marty said, astonished. He quickly collected himself. "The golden girl is back again."

He leaned as close as he dared, but with my hands tied behind my back, it was far too close. I felt his breath crawl over me as he tipped his head, watching me.

"Too bad your golden boy isn't here to save you." He baited me.

From my peripheral vision, Reyla looked ready to take him out. She would have shattered him in two if she could have, but she held back as Eden screamed my name.

Glancing beyond Marty, I saw Eden's hands wrapped around the bars of a holding cell. She was deep in the heart of a building, only visible because the main door was opened for us to enter. It glowed a yellow color as the sky itself dimmed for the show.

Eden looked horrified as she pulled on the bars, trying to escape. Silas was quickly by her side, slamming his open palm into the bars, yelling my name once along with her.

"Marty, don't you touch her!" He threatened from his cage.

He grinned at me.

"Reyla?" Silas noticed my companion.

"Oh no." Eden breathed out, suddenly aware that it wasn't just me she needed to worry about. "*Marty!*"

She screamed as she slammed her hands against the bars.

"Move." My captor commanded. "We don't have time for this."

"We're not done yet," Marty said roughly, sliding to the side so we could pass.

He argued that I couldn't be in the same cell as Silas and Eden, but the men didn't listen. One of the men stepped around us to unlock the door and I tried to signal Silas not to do anything stupid. I could see him preparing to run at the men as soon as the door was open. Reyla's gasp was the only thing that stopped him as the door swung open.

At her throat sat a knife: the controlling factor in our obedience. I was pushed into the cell, tripping into Eden.

"Slowly." The man cautioned as he eased Reyla forward. "That's it, slow."

Once they reached the door, he pulled back the knife before throwing Reyla inside and slamming the bars shut. They left as quickly as they could, forcing Marty away as well.

Eden turned to me, throwing herself around my shoulders. I could feel the bones through her skin. Hollow eyes looked back at me. Tears pricked at my eyes.

"Oh, Silas," Reyla said, looking over the damage.

He was in rough shape too, bruised from an obvious beating.

"Silas," I said, reaching for him.

"I'm fine." He brushed me off. "Why are you here?"

I grinned.

"A rescue, of course. We only have a few minutes." I turned to Eden. "Berwyn is fine. He's alive."

Her face crumbled as the news overwhelmed her.

"You've seen him?" she asked.

"I just left him."

"Dov?" Silas interrupted.

"Canton has him. He's using Dov against us, but once we get out of here, that's our next mission."

Crashing outside told me it was time to move.

"Listen carefully," I said as I darted to the door to try to open it. "I went over the wall. I brought back a team I trained. There will be people you don't know helping us."

Eden rushed to my side to try to help. We both knew it was useless. Silas would have found a way out a long time ago if there had been one.

"Shadoe is helping me," I confessed. Silas and Eden froze.

"What?" Confusion won out in Silas' voice.

"Excuse me?" Eden demanded.

"It's a long story, just don't kill him." Reyla snapped. "Now let's get moving and we can handle the rest later."

Chaos erupted outside. I was a bit surprised that Berwyn hadn't held back until it was later in the evening, but I'm sure he wanted to get Eden back to safety as quickly as possible.

The main door flew open, revealing a figure illuminated only by the lights outside the entrance. We waited for our savior to unlock the door and free us.

We all backed up to allow the door to swing open. The man's hand shot out, grabbing onto me as he pulled me out. The force moved me so quickly I stumbled out into his waiting arms. He pulled the door behind me shut, blocking the others.

Looking up, I saw not one of our men, but Marty.

"I told you we weren't done."

My friends yelled behind me, fighting against the door once more. Throwing myself toward Marty, I struggled to get the keys he held. We grappled, each trying to get the upper hand. I was thrown against the wall, slamming my head into the rock. I slid down, preparing myself for the next attack.

He yelped when I kicked him. The keys fell to the floor. Dirt crammed under my nails as I clawed at the keys, trying to beat him to them. Marty pulled me back, digging his fingers into my leg where I had been burned. If I didn't have scars before, he certainly would have created some.

Lifting my elbow back, I slammed into his face, making him reel back. I caught the keys as he tangled his fist in my hair, dragging me to my feet. I dangled in the air for a moment before he kicked my knees out, sending me back to the dirt, shrieking.

I made eye contact with Silas just long enough to

know my scream took him back to Canton's torture. He slammed into the door again, trying to free them.

Whipping my head back, I connected with Marty's chin, giving me just long enough to throw the keys. My opponent reached around my stomach, clutching me under his arm. I was off the ground and unable to get the leverage I needed to escape. Twirling, he threw me into the wall, making me dizzy enough to be unable to regain my balance.

He dragged me outside as the others fought to get the correct angle to get the key into the door. Marty forced me past people fighting; Berwyn's men taking on the people holding their leaders captive.

I raked my fingers down his arm, leaving bloody gashes that barely deterred him.

"I owe your golden boy for a few things," he hissed in my ear, throwing me face first into a tree as we neared a line of denser forest. "This time, he doesn't get to win."

"Canton has him, I hardly call that winning," I shouted back, throwing a fist at him.

The second he released me into the tree, I knew it was my only chance to fight. I swung, readying my elbow for his recourse. He came at me, but I ducked to the side, allowing him to overstep and hit the tree smeared with my blood.

He struck, landing a tight fist to my chin, snapping my head back. I moved my arm as if to jab him, but instead pulled back, and attacked with my foot. I slammed into his boot, wishing Wallace's men hadn't taken my knife when they tied us up.

In response, Marty brandished a knife from his belt, slashing it through the air at me. I attempted to take the cut on my arm rather than my face. I moved just enough that he missed, barely slicing my skin. When he swung again, I stepped just out of range. He crashed into another tree, arm high above his head as he collided into the bark.

Red rained from the sky as a scream so fierce I thought the world was ending rang out. Marty's knife toppled to the ground, still wrapped in his hand.

My scream nearly shattered the world.

Shadoe pulled Marty's trembling body away from the tree, turning him to look into his eyes. Shadoe used the entire force of his body to slam Marty into the tree.

"You will never touch her again, or next time, I won't let you live." Shadoe took his knife and slowly buried it into Marty's shoulder, slicing flat down his back, so that it missed the bones but separated the skin in an agonizing way. One more reminder of who held the power.

"Shadoe!" I screamed, hoping to deter him.

My eyes fixated on Marty's hand lying on the ground. Shadoe stooped to pick up the knife. He stood, wiping the blood from his blade on Marty's shirt as he shivered in shock against the pine.

Shadoe turned back as he started to leave. He picked up Marty's hand, avoiding the bloody stump. Opening the man's hand, he placed the missing one in it.

"Dov and I wish you a nice day." Shadoe leaned forward, growling. "*She is not yours.*"

With that final reminder, Shadoe turned back to me. I stood frozen, watching the scene before me. He gently turned my body away, making me walk back toward the cell.

"Do you want to save your friends or not?" he hissed, handing me Marty's knife as he shrieked in the background, writhing on the ground where he had slipped down when Shadoe walked away.

Another scream filled the air, this time far more fragile and feminine. *Reyla.*

Her cry sprang me into action, Shadoe following along side me. Having regained my equilibrium, I sprang over small objects in my way, not bothering to go around them. Shadoe followed suit when he needed to.

We arrived just in time to see Berwyn push a man off his knife, Eden behind him. The man crumpled to the ground, his shoulder gushing blood. I had never seen Berwyn look so tall or bulky in my life. He looked like his namesake as he towered above the man and I expected to hear him growl a warning to the others to stay away from his wife.

"Berwyn!" I shouted, announcing our approach to ensure he didn't mistake us for the enemy in his rage.

Eden wheeled around to face one of Wallace's men, rage burning in her eyes. Her hair flew behind her as she lashed out, kicking the man. She quietly reeled back in pain. Berwyn turned, landing a hard punch to her attacker, knocking him out.

I smiled at the scene, happy Berwyn and Eden were together again, but the moment only lasted until I heard another shout.

"Where is Reyla?" I shrieked, racing toward Dov's family.

Eden's eyes darted around wildly, searching for the girl.

"Where is she?" she echoed as Berwyn joined the search.

"There." He pointed.

In the darkness, Silas struggled forward, painfully taking each step. A body sagged in his arms.

Berwyn rushed forward. I followed quickly behind. The leader of the Baers took Reyla's broken body from Silas' careful grip and he nearly stumbled forward as the weight was transferred from his arms. I caught him, slipping under his arm to keep him steady.

Blood covered him, but I couldn't tell where it was

from as it dripped off of him. Silas attempted to rush after Berwyn. Eden caught his other arm, ducking under it to stabilize him. He kept his weight on me, ensuring he didn't hurt Eden further. Shadoe waited where we had left him, not bothering to help.

"We need to go," Berwyn said, carefully positioning Reyla in his arms. He shouted to the team that it was time to leave. "Fall back!"

Eden and I hurried Silas after Berwyn, Shadoe taking a position behind us to watch for Wallace's people behind us. Raselin appeared, moving alongside Berwyn in case he needed assistance.

Wallace's men backed up, unwilling to face us in light of Marty's accusatory screams as he charged his companions to take Shadoe out in revenge. Berwyn's men had already taken out the high ranking men watching the cells, leaving only the underlings to fight us off. They didn't risk it.

Berwyn led the way away from Wallace's camp. Fitch took Reyla from his arms when he joined us in the dense trees as we retreated, relieving Berwyn. I could tell he was still struggling to bounce back from the effects of the claw Shadoe had used to shred his arm in the cave before we were split up.

"You're hurt." Silas said quietly, eyeing me as he stumbled forward.

"Look who's talking…"

"Nah, this is all surface-level." He tried to grin, wincing. "What happened?"

"Made it to the wall before they cornered us. Shadoe showed up and Dov pushed me up to him. He gave himself up to make sure we made it over."

"Sounds like Dov." He shook his head. "And Canton has him?"

I nodded, reliving Devin's report once again.

"Reyla?" he asked, nodding ahead of us.

"I don't know."

"Silas, what happened?" Eden asked, joining the conversation.

"They attacked us. It all happened so fast." He struggled to catch his breath at the pace we were forcing him to move at. "She fought hard. She looked like you, Auluria. If her hair were more like yours, I might have thought it *was* you for a second. You would have been proud."

I *was* proud—of both of them.

"And you thought carrying her while you were this beat up was wise?" Eden chastised.

"We had to move, Eden." He said, not joking back. Whatever had happened, the gravity of the situation weighed on Silas. I had never seen him unable to find levity in a situation afterward.

Eden cast me a worried look as she moved a bit closer to Silas' side.

"I'm fine, Eden." He insisted as he attempted to walk more on his own. He failed.

Ahead, Reyla started to move in Fitch's arms.

"Reyla." I said when I noticed, lurching forward before I remembered I was holding up Silas.

"Go," he said, obviously worried about her.

Reyla's head lolled back as she fell unconscious again.

"She's out, don't bother," Fitch called over his shoulder.

"I didn't realize we were so loud," I mumbled, looking at the distance between us.

"I have good ears." Fitch replied, hearing even my quiet muttering.

Eden's face fell.

"Who is that?" She resorted to whispering.

"Fitch. He's one of my guys from over the wall." I replied. "He's been a real asset to us. You'll like his wife, Lydia, too."

"Less talking," Shadoe demanded, reminding me he was behind us.

We continued our harsh pace, trying to put as much distance between us and Wallace as possible.

The quiet should have been my first indication that

something was wrong. It was hard to hear it over the soft crunching of leaves and branches under our feet, but it was there, screaming at us to take notice.

I failed to listen.

The attack was brutal as the Society soldiers divided us. We were far enough ahead that we weren't touched. The back of our team, however didn't fare as well.

We moved our injured men as far away as we could, sheltering them from the soldiers as we heard the fighting in the distance. Our secondary team heard the commotion from where they waited for us a mile away.

They ran to aid us. Berwyn sent them back to help as we pressed forward toward the storehouse. We had to hide our men before we were caught.

When our men made it back, they brought a story of horror with them. The soldiers had cut them off from the group. The secondary team was able to fight them back, causing a retreat.

"They have them, Berwyn," Henry said. "We couldn't get to them. We only managed to get a few of the men on your team back."

"The soldiers captured at least a dozen of our men," Gregory confirmed, glancing at Silas where he leaned against me in the circle.

Silas insisted on being there, even though he needed medical attention. He swayed against me.

"Okay, that's enough. You're getting looked at now," I

insisted. Glancing at Shadoe, I decided to ask for help. "Justin, help me."

Justin moved to Silas's side and together we forced him to a small room in the storehouse where Eden was recovering. Reyla had been given a separate, tiny room because her injuries were far more severe.

"Do not let him move," I directed the woman watching over them. I turned to place him under a stricter charge. "Eden."

Pointing my finger at her was probably a bad idea, but she didn't snap at me. Instead, she watched Silas closely as the women helped lower him to a cot.

"What happened?" Eden asked softly.

"They captured our men. We're planning a rescue," I answered.

Justin hovered outside the room.

"Auluria, we should get back."

"How many?" Eden asked.

"A dozen." Silas winced, and he moved back on the cot. "We'll get them. They got us out, this won't be too much harder."

"I'm going to go back and help with the plan." I cut Eden off when she opened her mouth to speak. "I'll come back with details. I'll probably even beat Berwyn."

It was surprising that Berwyn wasn't sitting next to Eden to conduct the meeting from the tiny room. He always put his loyalty to the group first and this was no exception it seemed.

"Hang on," I said to Justin once we left the room.

I detoured to the next room where Reyla was lying on a mattress. Her body was hidden under a blanket, but I saw her chest rising and falling in a steady pattern.

"Reyla," I whispered into the quiet room.

Her eyes fluttered open, and she inhaled deeply.

"Can I get you anything?" I asked, kneeling by her cot.

I brushed her hair back and waited for her to think about the question. Her lip was broken open under a swollen cheek. A small cut by the side of her eye was already starting to scab over.

"Are you okay?" she asked. "Did he hurt you?"

"I'm fine. Marty didn't get very far."

"Don't worry, Shadoe lent him a hand." Justin said dryly.

"What happened?" Reyla's eyes grew as round as mine.

"Marty pulled a knife on me." I paused. "Shadoe didn't take that well."

"What did he do?" the brunette prompted when I didn't continue.

"He might have, um, cut off his hand." I looked down, guilt flooding me, tightening in my chest.

Reyla looked horrified.

"He…?"

"He cut off his hand," I confirmed.

"The poor thing." Her hand flinched under the sheet.

"The important thing is that Auluria is safe." Justin chimed in, refocusing us.

"Did everyone get out?" She clenched the sheet in her hand nervously.

"We got Silas and Eden out," I replied. "But the Society found us. I'm assuming Wallace had something to do with that. I wouldn't be surprised if he had a few men in his pocket like Lowell did. They got a dozen of our men. We're staging a rescue now. We want to strike before they're ready for us."

"You should go," Reyla insisted. "I'll be fine."

It only took a minute of arguing before she kicked us out.

"Hey, Rey?" I paused at the door. "You did really good. Silas even said you looked like me while you were off fighting the bad guys."

I grinned from the door. She smiled, her tiny attempt at a giggle radiating pain that made her body seize up.

"Yes, I made the bad guys run for their lives." She gave me a sad look. "Go get our men back. I expect flowers when you return, Auluria."

She managed to yell the last part loud enough for me to hear it as I walked away. Necesta nodded to me as she slipped into Reyla's room, a satchel in her hands. I knew my friend was in good hands.

"A girl with priorities," Justin mused.

"She certainly has those." I smirked. "Are you going on the mission?"

"Have I missed one yet?"

"No, you haven't. Is Devin coming?"

"Probably. They let him help with the backup group today, and I imagine Berwyn and Raselin are going to want as many hands as possible."

Berwyn nodded to us as we approached, finishing what he was saying to the group.

"Auluria, you and Shadoe are in charge of a team. Arin and Raselin will be leading a team. Fitch and I will be leading the first team," he said, mixing up the team to ensure he had one of his trusted people with each group.

"Are you sure it's such a good idea you lead the initial strike, Berwyn? You're still recovering," I say softly, hoping only Berwyn could hear.

He turned sharply to glare at me.

"I'm just saying, maybe Shadoe and I should go in first. You can follow with the second wave." I held my hands up as if I was trying to calm an angry animal. "*One of us needs to make it back, Berwyn.*"

"We'll go," Arin said, stepping into the conversation. "She's right… All of you have been through a lot recently, but my team hasn't sustained as much damage. Let us go in first, and you act as our back up."

He rolled his eyes when we agreed that I had a point.

It was amazing how the man still didn't trust me. He leered at Shadoe for a moment. Maybe I wasn't the only one he didn't trust.

All eyes were on Berwyn when he reluctantly agreed to Arin's plan. But even with a solid plan, I knew nothing ever worked the way the Baers planned it to, and I wondered how many more we would lose in an attempt to save lives.

Chapter 9

THE SOLDIERS WERE WAITING FOR US WHEN WE ARRIVED. We never made it into the town. They lined the streets facing the woods. It didn't matter where they were—they knew we would find them.

Our captured men were lined up, each the length of two men apart, spreading the group out over a great distance. The soldiers had them on their knees, resting in the dirt uncomfortably. Rocks dug into one man's knees as I watched from a distance.

When our lookout delivered the news of the stand off, the team leaders raced ahead to assess the situation. Their men were watching for us, alerting the soldier in charge when they saw us at the tree line.

"This is what happens when you work against the Society. Magistrate Canton has found these men are guilty of treason." The soldier quickly listed the charges against our people. "The sentence is death."

Before any of us could move, the soldiers pulled knives from their belts and ran them across the throats of twelve of our men. They fell at their feet, blood pooling around their bodies. Shadoe clamped his hand around my mouth to keep me from screaming, his strong arms holding me back as I tried to push forward to help the lost cause.

Berwyn's eyes were glassy as his fists tightened so hard I thought they might break. Raselin wore a shocked expression, realizing, perhaps, that taking down the Society would not be as easy as he thought, despite our numbers.

"Tell your leaders," the soldier shouted, "that if they give this battle up and work under Magistrate Canton's command, they can prevent this from happening again."

He waved his hand at the bodies as he stepped forward to kick the corpse of a man around Justin and Devin's age. The body moved slightly with the impact, jostling his hair out of place, making me nauseous.

"Run along, little spies. Or you'll join them."

They thought we were spies. They didn't realize we had come with a team. Surprisingly, they had missed our actual spy. We would have to remember to let him take the lead on spy missions from then on.

"Go." Berwyn whispered harshly.

We retreated quickly, running back to the waiting teams. Before we reached them, we gave them the signal to retreat. After a few miles, we stopped to tell them what had happened. Everyone was devastated.

"They expect us to retreat," Berwyn said. "They want us to disappear. The Society wants us to submit to their will and fight their wars. But today we will do what they do not expect. Today we will bring the war to them."

His voice rose in power as he spoke until he was shouting. He grew taller, rising up on his feet, taking up as much space as he could. Berwyn leading not by emotion, but by some master plan he had conjured up in the few miles we had traveled.

"We're going back," he said, a wild smile slipping onto his face. "They took our people, now we will take theirs."

"Berwyn!" I was horrified.

He looked to me, but never faltered.

"We're going into the Society to find their men. We will take their leaders and question them. We can't get Canton, but we can get the men who work for him. They'll never suspect we're coming for them. We've never dared to abduct their men before."

I was catching on to his plan.

"We will take Canton's men and find out what his

plans are. Once we have information, we'll release them and Canton will never know."

"You want to release them?" Justin said incredulously. "They'll run straight to Canton."

"No they won't," Arin said, a darkness encapsulating his voice.

No one questioned him further.

Berwyn divided the team, sending many of them back to the storehouse. I didn't question him when he directed me to return.

Shadoe watched long enough to concern me before he turned and left with Arin. I started to shake once they were out of sight.

"I know you're upset," Berwyn said, slipping his injured arm under mine, "but you have to keep it together."

I tried to nod, but my body rebelled.

"I know Lowell and Shadoe trained you to withstand interrogation, but did they ever teach you how to extract information from a person?"

"In a way." My voice quivered.

"In the time I've known you, I've watched you coerce your way into our group, manipulate your cousin, withstand Canton's torture, and rally an entire division of men and women to follow you over the wall.

"I think you've seen enough in your lifetime to handle

getting information from one of the Society's men, don't you?"

I glanced up at him as we walked back to the storehouse.

"You have the motive, Auluria. You're using the men we capture now to find Dov."

The spark caught. My head whipped up to look at the tall man who was guiding my steps, fire racing through me.

This was how I would get Dov back.

"And that's all you needed to know." He smiled at me as I stopped shaking, dropping his arm from mine. He wandered away, leaving me to consider my moves the rest of the way back.

I didn't speak to anyone when I returned, brushing off Sharone when she raced up to me.

"Later," I promised, not knowing if I could keep my word.

I paced in one of the rooms that was hidden off of the main area; formerly a storage area, transformed into a multipurpose room that was used for medical needs, private meetings, or as a place to hide from the crowd.

I debated going to Silas. I even considered teaming up

with Shadoe, but I knew his tactics would not sit well with me. No, this was something I had to do on my own.

I played with my thoughts, running through every possible tactic I could think of, but nothing felt right. Lowell had trained me to be smart. Shadoe had trained me to be fierce. But in the end, Brittella's manipulation training won out. I knew what I had to do. I would need to be patient.

Eventually the men returned, four of Magistrate Canton's underlings in their possession. I watched quietly as they brought the men, bound and blindfolded, into the storehouse through the main entrance.

Everyone was silent as we guided the men down a separate set of tunnels, keeping them far away from the main storehouse. We gave no indication of how many of us were walking alongside them.

Each man was given a room far enough away that they couldn't communicate with each other, but close enough should we need them to overhear the screams of their friends.

Shadoe, Arin, Berwyn, and another of Berwyn's men followed into the rooms. Berwyn had agreed to work with my plan, substituting his extra man in for the fourth captive. I waited, listening to the grumblings that came from behind the closed doors as the men interrogated Canton's people.

Knowing I didn't want to oversee Shadoe's work, I

asked Raselin to monitor him. Fitch stood between Berwyn and the fourth man's cells, while I wandered over to Arin's, looking in the window.

He stalked around the man much as he had done the day he questioned me. His knife glinted in his hand as Arin walked quietly around the terrified man. He looked like he never spent a day outside of his fancy home in his entire life.

When the interrogator walked back into his line of sight, he leapt forward, throwing his hand against the table, creating a noise that must have made the man in Shadoe's room jump as well. Arin yelled at him, demanding information. The tiny man shook, tears forming in the corners of his eyes. Arin had a system for his interrogations and he did not deviate.

"Are you okay?" Raselin asked from a few feet away. He leaned back against the wall, arms folded across his chest.

"I've been on the receiving end of one of Arin's interrogations. Shadoe trained me well enough to play along, but Arin certainly has this guy worked up."

Berwyn stepped out of his room, motioning us to follow. We left our posts and walked out into the hallway. A moment later, Arin and the other man joined us.

"We managed to get some low level intelligence out of them, but we're not done yet." Berwyn said after each man had told the group what they had learned.

They debated whether it would be wise to continue to work with the same captive or to switch out the interrogators, eventually deciding to attempt to work with different Society men. Berwyn went to inform Shadoe.

"Auluria," Berwyn called to me before opening the door. There was an edge to his voice that I couldn't convince myself wasn't there.

I reached the window just as Shadoe stepped out.

"What did you do?" I said, horrified.

Berwyn held me back, blocking my path with his arm. He grunted as my stomach collided with his mostly healed cuts.

"Not yet," he cautioned. "You have a good plan, you just have to get the timing right."

Shadoe eyed me, knowing what I planned to do.

"He will be ready for you," he said, wiping his blade.

He must have removed the gag the man was wearing while he used the knife on him. We wouldn't have missed what must have been pained screams otherwise. I cringed thinking of the pain my former handler had inflicted, my thoughts floating back to Canton's presence.

"It's nothing he wouldn't have done to you," Shadoe said. Dropping his voice, he added, "And far less than Canton *did* to you."

Was this retribution?

"Give it a few minutes and then go in," Berwyn instructed.

I took the time to gather a few rags and bandages. My hand floated to the necklace Necesta had demanded I hide below my clothing. This man would not be receiving that kind of help today.

Stepping inside, I adopted a demure demeanor, walking over to the man gently. Bending down, I dropped to my knees and dipped a rag in a small bin of water I brought with me. He hissed when it touched his open wound.

I continued to say nothing as I worked, waiting for him to speak first. As I started bandaging his arm, he broke his silence.

"Who are you?" he demanded as I continued to work, wrapping gauze around his forearm. "Where are we?"

His body grew tenser the longer I went without speaking.

"Look at me, girl," he demanded, flexing his fingers in an attempt to grab me. His attempts were in vain as his wrists were tied to the arms of the chair.

Berwyn burst into the room, stomping over to where I knelt on the floor.

"You're not done yet?" he bellowed, grabbing my hair and throwing me to the floor. "We don't have time for you to waste."

He stormed out of the room, leaving me to pick myself up.

"Are you being held here against your will?" the man hissed, hoping to convince me to help him.

"I can't help you," I said quietly.

"We can help each other," he said, gaining strength, as he leaned forward to formulate a plan.

I finished wrapping his cuts as he spit out idea after idea.

"Even if I could get you out, where would we go?" I finally hissed at him.

He smiled.

By the time I reached the fourth cell, playing the game with each one, I had answers. I wiped the blood off my finger where I pinched down on Shadoe's victim's injuries. I let it sit through all of my interrogations as a terror tactic, and it sickened me.

Each man wanted the same thing: escape. Each captive reacted differently as I played the part of a helpless woman they thought they could manipulate. It was too late by the time their other interrogator walked in: I had enough information to use against them.

When I switched from innocent, naïve girl, to strategic interrogator in front of their eyes, they were terrified, desperately trying to convince me they had lied. They had no grace as they flailed about, trying not to pay for their ignorance. By the time I left their cells, they were more afraid of me than they were of the men in the room.

They gave up everything they could about the Society's plans. We knew more about where they were keeping Dov than we had been able to find out since they took him. The men gave up information about the war over the wall, the camps, and the soldiers than we had ever had access to in the years we had been working against them.

Berwyn was elated. Shadoe looked proud of me for the first time ever as he took up his place at my side.

"Looks like Lowell was right about you. You are a leader. I think we owe Brittella a debut of gratitude too. This was her doing, wasn't it?"

"I thought you hated Brittella." I walked along side him back to the main storehouse.

"I hate what she teaches, though I see its importance. Just don't ever use that stuff on me."

I refused to test what I had learned from the woman out on Shadoe when she had first educated me, and I refused to do it now.

"We have a problem, though," Berwyn said loudly once we rounded the corner. "We can't send them back. Not after the damage Shadoe did to Justice Kenton."

"There will be retribution," Fitch said. "Are we ready for that?"

"We'll have to be." Berwyn glowered at Shadoe.

Shadoe glared back, refusing to justify his actions to anyone. I wanted to slap him again. It was a stupid move; one that would likely cost us. We had lost too many lives already.

"Can we use them to negotiate Dov's release?" Fitch asked.

"I don't know," Berwyn replied, "Right now the Society doesn't know what their men have told us. We have the upper hand. But if we trade, they'll interrogate their men too, probably kill them afterward, and they'll know exactly what we know and can change their plan."

"They didn't have enough information for us to bring down the Society, Berwyn, just to mess up Canton's plans," I commented, unsure of how I felt about releasing the men as a trade.

"We're not done talking to them yet." Raselin turned to us as we walked. "Let's give it a few days to see how desperate the Society is to get their men back."

Unfortunately, giving the Society time was a mistake.

Chapter 10

THE CROWD WAS CHARGED WITH TENSION AS WE SNUCK into the masses, weaving our way through hordes of people. The air seemed to crackle with each step I took. I moved my hand to brush my hair back, but I had tied it down earlier in an effort to keep it hidden. I was too well known in the city after my escape.

Four days after capturing Canton's men, he had retaliated. Our men found word of a public spectacle, but we knew he wouldn't kill Dov. He wanted a trade. We also knew he would never trade Dov, but rather use it as a ploy to get us to come out of hiding and release his men. We quietly snuck into the city, waiting for what would happen next.

I crept forward, making my way to the same stage I had once stood on, noose around my neck. The noise of voices hummed around me as spectators guessed the extent the Society would go to this time.

My breath caught as they dragged him out. He stumbled up the steps, tripping as he walked out onto the stage between two guards. His hair was matted with dried blood, the color drained from his face. Bruises covered his body as they threw him to his knees.

A fixture had been placed toward the front of the stage. They pulled Dov's hands from behind him and fastened them to the device he knelt in front of. He leaned forward, placing his weight on his arms.

Magistrate Canton walked on stage, his robe flowing behind him as he walked. Taking his place slightly in front of Dov, he stared at the audience.

"Where are they?" Canton asked.

"I don't know," Dov croaked, sounding as though he hadn't had water all day.

"Where is your brother?" he inquired.

Dov grunted in response, trying to adjust his hands into a more comfortable position.

"One more time. Where are your people?" Canton queried.

"I don't know," Dov said, looking up at him.

The lash came down on his back, making a horrific sound. The entire gallery gasped.

"Dov Baer, you have been charged with crimes against the Society, as have your brother, sister-in-law, and entire group. Tell us where to find them and we won't kill any more than we have to. We'll give them the chance to confess and surrender."

"I do not know where they are." Dov glared at him.

The soldier with the lash reached out and kicked Dov in the stomach. He wasn't prepared to be hit from that angle, assuming he would be lashed again, and he crumpled in on himself. His shirt dangled in front of him, a hole torn by the man's boot exposing his flesh.

"Where is your brother?" Canton turned to look at him.

"You won't win, Canton." Dov said as fiercely as he could in his state.

The guard kicked his hip, tossing Dov to the ground. I could almost feel his shoulders pop as his body moved away from where his hands were tied. He struggled to right himself quickly to avoid another blow that might actually dislocate his shoulder.

Once he had positioned himself on his knees, he stared out into the crowd.

"Where is the girl?"

"What girl?" Dov challenged, his eyes taking a sad turn.

"The one that works for Lowell. Where is she?"

"She's gone. You'll never get your hands on her." Dov smiled just enough to infuriate Canton.

"We'll find her, Baer," Canton tormented him. "When we do, we'll do a lot worse than the last time we had her."

"Good luck with that," Dov offered. "You'll never hurt her again."

Canton fumed. He rushed around behind Dov, to the man with the whip. Ripping it from his hand, he towered over Dov.

Dov's entire body stilled as he found me in the crowd. My hair was back, I had covered as much of myself as possible, but he held my gaze, questioning me. I nodded just enough that he could confirm it was me, and his entire body went tense.

"Where is she?" Canton demanded, hand raised in the air.

Dov watched me. He never moved from where he held my gaze. The lash came down again, ripping into him. The second hit forced him to fight against squeezing his eyes shut so he wouldn't lose sight of me.

I stood, frozen, knowing I couldn't move or I would give him away. My jaw clenched with every strike, but I didn't look away.

Canton kicked him, knocking Dov off balance. He fell to the ground again, angling his head to see me.

We're coming, I mouthed, hoping he had seen.

"Where are they?" Canton yelled as he stepped back for the soldier to take over.

Dov remained on the ground. When the guard neared him, he kicked, pushing the man over. The crowd hummed.

Canton nodded to another soldier. He and his partner stepped forward quickly. The second man reached out, untying Dov from the fixture he was bound to. The first man pulled Dov up by his chin, wrapping a hand in front of him to force him up, while his dominant hand held a knife to Dov's throat.

I was about to rush forward when Canton roared.

"This is the last chance you will have. You have one week to give yourselves over, or I will kill him."

The soldiers dragged Dov away. His face was tipped up so high he couldn't have seen me if he tried. The man holding him practically carried him off the stage.

Canton turned back to the crowd.

"Anyone found helping the Baers from this point on will be executed on the spot. If you have contact with them, get word to them today that this is their last chance. They know what we want in addition to their surrender.

"The Society has always worked to protect its people, both from forces outside the wall and threats in our own country like the Baers. We will not stand for any more loss of life because of these people!" Canton roared to the masses.

"If they come after any more of our people, I will see to it that their leaders are sentenced to death for this. There will be no mercy for them. If their people give themselves up now, we will rehabilitate them and welcome them back into our community."

He gave his speech pledging benevolence we knew would never come. If he got his hands on our people, they would be sent to the camps, if they weren't exterminated.

"If anyone attempts to harm my men again, I will send Dov Baer back in pieces!" he threatened, anger radiating off of him matching his red flowing robes.

"Now go!" the magistrate demanded, charging the crowd to find and turn over the Baers.

"We have to go." Devin tugged on my arm.

When I didn't move, he tried again.

"Auluria, please. We have to go." He pulled harder. "*Lur!*"

I snapped out of it and allowed him to drape an arm over me as if I belonged to him—sister, lover, wife—I didn't know. He guided me away from the crowd.

"He's worried for his own safety. He doesn't care about his men. He thinks we're going to come for him," Berwyn said when we reached him where he waited out of sight at Raselin's suggestion.

"If we're going to survive this, we need more people," Raselin insisted as we evaluated our options. "We have your group and ours, but Canton has an army bigger than I thought. We don't have any other choice."

The two men looked at each other, silently communicating. Their eyes argued, back and forth, over a conversation the rest of us were not privy to.

"We have to, Berwyn."

Our leader looked reluctantly at Raselin. He turned to face us.

"We need your men," he said to Shadoe. "Go get Lowell's men and bring them here."

My heart dropped.

"We will send a few men with you," Raselin said, reminding us that Shadoe would be watched. "You were second in command to Lowell, which means these are your people now."

"No one has heard much from them since Lowell died. They have no leadership that we can tell." Berwyn added painfully, "You are their leader now, Shadoe."

I knew once Shadoe returned to his men, he would not be helping the Baers. He was only there for me.

"We need to take the Society out, once and for all. This is the only way we will ever be free of them." Raselin played into Shadoe's vanity. "After we bring them down, you will be responsible for your people and their wellbeing. But until then, we need to work together to stop

Canton and bring down the entire government structure."

Shadoe stood in silence for a moment. He looked to me, considering my role in this.

"She comes with me," he announced boldly.

I was about to refuse, demanding to stay with the Baers, when they stopped me.

"You will go with him, Auluria," Raselin informed me. "Lowell wanted you both in charge, and now you are. Go do your duty and bring your men here."

I started to argue until Berwyn pulled me aside.

"Listen," he demanded. "We have to get Dov out now. Canton isn't going to draw this out much more. We need Lowell's men, and right now that means we need Shadoe to lead them. If we give him free reign, he'll probably resort back to Lowell's tactics, but *you* can control him.

"Pull yourself together and go get them."

"They won't accept me, Berwyn, I betrayed them." I insisted.

"They will do anything Shadoe says. They know Lowell trained him to take over. If he brings you back to them, they will have to accept you.

"The faster you find them, the faster we can save Dov and take down the Society. I don't care what you have to do, just do it, and get those people back here and ready to fight. I don't care if they kill every Society man along the way if they have to at this point. We are saving Dov and getting control of Canton."

"Auluria," he softened. "I know this won't be easy for you. I understand that we're asking you to walk into a bad situation, but you won't be alone."

"Auluria." Silas puts his hand on my shoulder as he approaches from behind me. "I'm not going to leave you alone with them. You'll be safe."

He looked to be almost back to his normal self. Necesta's brightly colored little jars had worked miracles. He stood at my shoulder, waiting for an answer.

"No one will force you to do this, Auluria," he said softly, "but from where I stand, this is the only way I can see for all of us to survive this. I promise, I won't leave you. We'll save Dov together, and if that means we use Lowell's people to do it, so be it."

"What good can come from following Lowell's plan?" I asked.

"But we're *not*. You'll be in leadership, just like he wanted, but that's all. You'll never run his group the way he wanted you to.

"Besides," he added, "that's not the wedding we're planning here."

Berwyn's jaw dropped as far as mine did. I turned so quickly I nearly collided with Silas.

"We were all thinking it." He shrugged, grinning.

Berwyn sputtered.

"Time to go." Silas wheeled me around. "We'll be back with reinforcements, Berwyn."

"No," Shadoe said when we arrived at the tree he had retreated to to wait by.

"She's not going alone," Silas insisted.

"You're not coming," Shadoe forbade him.

"You don't get a choice," I interjected. "Silas is coming with us. It's one of my conditions."

"You don't get to *have* conditions," Shadoe challenged me.

"Oh, yes I do, Shadoe. Lowell put us *both* in charge. You and me; together. If you showed up by yourself, maybe they'd follow you. But what happens when I show up too?

"Let's just say for a moment that I walk into the camp with an elaborate story about how Lowell instructed me to continue on with the ruse even to the point of us hanging. I mean, how else would anyone be able to explain the fact that you cut me down or that you climbed the wall with me?

"I'll tell them all about what Lowell had planned and how you didn't follow his strategy."

"I have followed—"

"Followed *what,* Shadoe? Are you and I married? Are you and I together? Here's a hint: *we're not!*"

I dropped my voice the way Brittella had taught me to do, sounding sad and meek.

"I couldn't help it that you didn't want to follow through with Lowell's plan." I pouted, "But it turns out *Silas* could be bought."

For a moment, Silas looked like I had slapped him. He grinned, leaning an elbow on my shoulder and pretended to examine his hands.

"Yeah. You heard the lady… Money talks." Silas looked up to catch Shadoe's eye before pointing at me. "And I'd bet money that this little lady can spin a better tale than you can, Shadoe. So I suggest you be practical if you want to keep control of your group."

"Not sure what's happening here," Talley said as she joined us, "but I'll side with Auluria. Seems she has a way of beating the odds around here."

"Not you, too," Shadoe complained.

"Yes, *me*. Devin, Fitch and Lydia, and Nian, too," she responded. "And before you go protesting, we're here in case you have trouble taking back command from whoever is overseeing your people at the moment."

I turned back to Shadoe and nodded. Surrounding myself with friends was a wise choice, especially if I was about to step into unfriendly territory.

"Fine," Shadoe grunted. "Let's move."

A day and a half later, we walked into the temporary camp Lowell's men were using. Their transient lifestyle made them hard to find, but Shadoe and I watched for the markers they left that only people from Lowell's fold would be able to decipher.

The men overseeing the group quickly turned over power to Shadoe... after he broke a few bones in the scuffle. Their new leader explained that we had been following Lowell's plan, escaping over the wall and rallying more fighters. Shadoe told the plan of working with the Baers to bring down the Society as if it had been his own idea. He didn't mention the part about saving Dov.

My former colleagues had torn down the camp and were ready to move within hours. They begrudgingly accepted me back into the fold, having no choice but to listen to Shadoe as he forced them into submission.

Several of the men I had known from my time training with Shadoe watched curiously as I stayed between Silas and their new leader. Shadoe did nothing to claim me and Silas refused to leave my side, leaving the group unsure of my standing.

The group followed behind Shadoe toward the place we would meet the Baers. It took several hours before we reached the location. We moved the group into the burned out storehouse the Baers used before Shadoe had torched the place to prove a point. Dov's pond was within walking distance, but I couldn't risk the excursion.

Berwyn and Eden were waiting when we arrived, surrounded by their best fighters. They walked out to meet us, allowing Shadoe's people to file into the storehouse while the leaders talked outside.

"We're leaving tonight." Berwyn said, Raselin and Eden taking equal positions on either side of him, their arms crossed. "We're almost out of time."

"We're not ready to take on the Society yet," Shadoe countered.

"We need to get Dov out."

"If you want to go after your kid brother, fine, but my men are not getting involved.," Shadoe pressed.

I knew he would pull something like that.

"Our job is to bring down Canton and destroy the Society. Not to rescue your family."

"He saved you, Shadoe," I protested.

"No, he saved *you*." Shadoe turned on me. "I was already on the wall. He stayed behind for *you. I* owe him nothing."

"He saved your *fianceé*." I reminded him.

"*Are* you?" he leered at me. "Are you my fianceé, Lur? Because I'm pretty sure fiancés aren't allowed to kiss other men."

His lecture might have hurt if I had cared.

"*They* don't know that," I said, pointing to the storehouse entrance. "So in their eyes, you *do* owe him. Don't forget, I still hold some power here. You *will* help us rescue him."

"I insist," Berwyn said. "Or else I can easily block your men in the storehouse right now and turn them over to Canton as a peace offering. Don't you think he'd be willing to trade my brother for *all* of those people in there? And then where would you be? You can't take down the government without an army."

"He's right, Shadoe," Raselin said. "We're all in this, and we will win or lose by what we choose now."

I wrenched myself closer to him and whispered in his ear, "You help us now, and we'll help you later. You're going to need something later on, and this will be your bargaining chip."

He pushed me away. I stumbled back into Silas, catching myself on his arm.

"Fine. But we do this my way." Shadoe took authority over the situation. "My men will be the distraction. They will not be taking the risks for one of you."

"Fine," Berwyn said.

"We'll rescue him while you draw the soldiers away," I confirmed.

"No." He stopped me. "*They'll* rescue him while *we* draw the guards away."

I furrowed my brows, ready to correct him.

"I'm helping save Dov." I tried to keep my voice even.

"Yes, by being a distraction with your team," he corrected me. "That was part of this deal. I'd go back to lead Lowell's men and you would be alongside me, and together, you and I would lend our people to *him* to defeat the Society."

He jutted his chin out at Berwyn.

"Baer wanted our group back together so we could help him. You are the price he paid for that. You're back with your people. If you want to help your precious Dov, you do it with *us*. Otherwise, we conveniently slip away during this little distraction mission and the soldiers return right in the middle of your jailbreak and ruin any chance you have of getting him out."

Eden looked like she was ready to pummel Shadoe. I wished she would have. I wish *I* could have.

Silas stepped up behind me, taking my wrist gently between his fingers. His arm brushed against me, every muscle in his body pulled tightly in anger, but his fingers held loosely onto me without hurting me.

"I'm staying with your team, in that case," he said, voice low and dangerous.

"You can't," I whispered. "They need you. Dov needs you."

"You are not going to do this alone," he insisted quietly. "Dov wouldn't let you and neither will I."

"Dov is not going to pay the price for this," I hissed back, instantly regretting my tone. "Dov gave himself up to save me; now it's my turn. I'll be fine. When this is all over, we'll handle it. But right now, Berwyn and Eden need your help. Between the three of you, you'll get him back."

"Auluria," Silas insisted.

"Silas. This is how it's going to be." I stepped away from him.

Shadoe practically beamed, grinning over his victory at Berwyn as I approached him and turned to face the Baers. He cast Silas a withering look that would make a lesser man back down.

Three leaders watched one another. Three groups faced off in a circle of wills. Shadoe's team would be a distraction, entering the city first and drawing the guards away. Berwyn's men would breach the city and retrieve Dov. Raselin's team would assist, acting as the hidden second wave that would stop any soldiers that chased Berwyn's men.

The three men watched each other, Eden and Silas with Berwyn, Fitch with Raselin, and myself standing by Shadoe. The leaders of three very distinct groups, with very clear lines drawn, stood on opposite sides of the circle, all willing to work toward one goal, despite the conditions and the mistrust. The very thing Lowell had lost everything over was happening: the Society was going to burn at the hands of enemies.

Chapter 11

"Now," I whispered to myself, begging Shadoe to be thinking the same thing.

My hand gripped the wooden crate, a sliver of metal icily touching the tip of my little finger. I tensed my muscles, waiting to push. Rocking on my toes, I tried to see around the box, hoping Shadoe was ready.

This has to be now.

Movement caught my eye as Shadoe stepped back just enough that I could see his hand fall.

Now.

Without bothering to inhale, I pushed, toppling the crate. The metal latch broke open, toppling the contents out. Food spilled out, bouncing across the floor. I kicked a piece out of the way as I started to run.

I threw myself at the entrance, grabbing the door frame to swing myself out into the fresh air. It was a relief to be out of the stale stench of the makeshift building that housed the boxes we were destroying.

Shadoe had several of his men carrying boxes with unknown content. One didn't need to know what was inside when one was planning to drop it along the way.

Locust, a boy I met while training with Shadoe, held a crate with another man. It bounced between them, slamming into their legs as they ran out of sync.

"Pick up the pace, boys," one of the women shouted as she raced by.

"You try running with a crate and an idiot," Locust snapped.

"Move!" I shouted, not waiting to see if they would find their footing.

"Stop!" the soldiers shouted as they rounded the corner, hearing the commotion. Shadoe had timed it perfectly so that they could hear our escape, but were not close enough to do any real damage.

A moment later, I heard a crash as the crate Locust and the man were carrying fell to the ground. It splintered, wood cracking as it slammed at their feet. The boys kept running.

The group shouted to each other, making it seem as if

we had been accidentally discovered and the dropped crates were actual losses. The Society men kept running.

We wove through the city, spreading out through alleys, hiding in houses. Shadoe's men forced their way into hiding, quietly holding families hostage for minutes at a time until it was safe to run again. Shadoe ran ahead as I darted into a quiet alley, hiding in the shadows.

I breathed heavily as the soldiers ran past the entrance, casting long, dark shadows down the walkway, cutting off the glimpses of gold the setting sun threw into my walkway. Pressing against the wall, I waited. I glanced down, noticing my hair had fallen from where I had tied it back.

A loud thud at the mouth of the alley screamed for my attention. A soldier slammed a boy into the wall. The guard was surprised when I appeared at his side, kicking him into the road. He sprawled in the dirt while I leapt over him, the boy's hand in mine as I dragged him away.

I threw him ahead of me, turning to face the soldier. I found him still in the dirt.

"Go!" I commanded, letting Shadoe's man run ahead.

When I felt it was secure, I ran, focusing on the path ahead of me in a desperate attempt not to worry about Dov. Each pounding step urged me to focus more. The woods loomed ahead of me, our meeting point once we had lost the guards. I sprinted for the trees, prepared to dive into the tall grass that separated the tree line from the roads of the city. I skirted around the city onto the gravel road that outlined the space.

Before I could reach where Shadoe stood just behind a tree, watching, I was forced to a stop. My team struggled against an unexpected attack by the Society. A small group of men appeared from the neighboring town line, striking our men.

They struggled, drawing blood as knives were brandished. I raced forward to help, knowing if we could use our numbers, we could survive. A hand clamped around my arm stopped me, swinging me back into the arms of a young man with red hair.

"You have to go," he hissed, checking to see where our team was. "He's not watching, you need to go."

"What are you talking about?" I struggled to pull away.

"Shadoe is fighting. Go save your boyfriend," the man hissed.

The minute his eyes connected with mine, I remembered a scared, redheaded boy held in the cells of the Society as I broke out members of the Baers' team before Silas and I were temporarily captured.

"Just go!" he hissed, repaying the debt he never owed me in the first place.

Without thinking through the implications of betraying Shadoe, I ran. My breaths felt heavy as I forced my way through the streets, back the way I had come. I raced to the center of the city, hiding from the soldiers I nearly met along the way.

"Please let me make it in time," I whispered. "Please let us get him out."

The sun glinted fiercely off of roads and buildings alike. I could barely see as I charged into a haze of yellow, arms pumping furiously by my body.

"What are you doing here?" Arin yelled, seeing me approach.

"Where are they?" I shouted back.

"I don't know. Eden was separated from us. Berwyn is looking for her. That way." He pointed to where I was running as he took the opposite direction, rushing after soldiers we could hear around the corner.

I wanted to burn the buildings to the ground to create a path for myself. Instead, I leapt over carts and darted around buildings as I sped forward. At the break in the buildings, I paused, determining which way to go out in the open space.

Chaos was everywhere and Berwyn's men fought to keep control as their leaders fought their way into the prison where they held Dov.

"Eden?" Berwyn shouted in the distance, not close enough to where Dov was being held.

I saw the stage I had once graced and turned, angling for the entrance. I saw something out of the corner of my eye as I ran. My feet were pulled out from under me, nearly flipping me over the arms of a soldier who grabbed me. Smoke burned my eyes as he tried to subdue me.

"Eden!" Berwyn shouted again, closer to where I was being held captive.

"Berwyn!" I tried to scream. The man muffled my cry.

I bit down, forcing *him* to scream instead.

A second man pushed in between us, revealing the first. I struggled against him in vain as another man joined him to restrain me.

All I could hear was yelling. Soldiers, rescuers, and people inside the prison all shouted out in an orchestrated attempt to survive and win. The men behind me stilled.

Looking away from where they held onto me I saw what had stopped them. I watched in horror.

A single figure ran out of the prison, taking on three men. The soldiers were cut down, one at a time. They flew into the air or dropped dead to the ground. Eden systematically took them out, beating them with her fists and cutting them with her weapon. She lifted one and threw him farther than I imagined even Berwyn was capable of throwing a man.

Turning, the blond woman, having cleared a path, ran back into the prison, returning instantly with a battered and limping Dov Baer.

Fighting, I slammed my head into the men behind me, trying to knock them off balance. The man I bit was running toward where Eden was, far across the yard. She turned and threw her knife, sinking it in the man's chest.

Dragging Dov with her, she retrieved it and hurriedly guided him away. Eden blocked a soldier who ran at them, slamming her knife at him. He backed up, barely avoiding her strike. He readied himself to strike, but Eden moved quicker, breaking something in his hand loud enough for me to hear it all the way across the yard.

She scooped Dov up off the ground, slinging his arm around her shoulder. They moved further away, my heart cheering them to run, while, at the same time, breaking as Dov was moving further away from me.

A sharp hand on my shoulder reminded me I was being held. The men came to their senses, realizing they had me in their possession, and forced me toward the cells. Digging my feet into the ground, I tried to counteract their movements. The two men worked together to push me ahead of them, digging up the ground in the process.

I heard a grunt before I was propelled into the ground. My arms, now free, jerked in front of me to protect my face. I hit the ground, hair flying out in front of me in a massive wave of gold, covering my arms and tangling in my outstretched fingers.

"Move!" Berwyn shouted, pulling hard on my arm under my shoulder.

"Berwyn?" I gasped as his fingers dug into the soft flesh under my arm. I tried to point. "Eden…"

"I saw." He looked shocked that his wife had just defeated multiple Society soldiers and managed to carry his brother away from the prison. "We have to go."

He shook his head to refocus himself. Dropping his shoulders, he ran toward his wife. I limped after him, having twisted my ankle when I fell. Halfway across the yard, I figured out how to move without causing too much pain and picked up my pace.

"Berwyn!" I screamed, seeing the oncoming soldiers that ran into the yard after he had passed.

He turned, looking at the men. Berwyn reached them before I did, engaging in battle. A fist struck him, causing him to rear back. He lashed out, looking like Shadoe the day he had cut Berwyn with his clawed contraption. His eyes were deadly, holding no remorse.

Ignoring my ankle, I attacked. The man turned to me, weapon in hand. Reaching down, I grabbed my extra knife from my boot. I cut deep into his arm as he attempted to drag his knife through me. He was tall, tall enough that my knife easily found its way into the flesh on his chest.

Blood trickled out of his wound as his hand clutched it. A moment later he toppled to his left, a hand appearing where he once stood.

"I heard things went sideways." Justin appeared next to me. "A couple of us left the backup group to come help.

"Time to move, *Goldilocks*," he said, pushing me until I was running with him.

"Spending time with Necesta again?" I asked.

"Simple rule, Auluria: never turn down time with Necesta. You'd be amazed what you will learn."

"The fact that she was taking care of a couple of pretty ladies the last few days didn't hurt either, I'm guessing."

"What can I say? I'm a sucker for unavailable women."

At least I wouldn't have to remind him that Eden was married and Reyla was in mourning. I added Justin to the list of men I had to find girlfriends for, right after Silas.

"I have some good news though," he said, ducking as we ran under a tree branch as we reached the tree line. "Eden brought Dov out. At least, I'm assuming it was him. We were running pretty fast and she was having a hard time keeping him upright, so I basically just saw a guy having trouble running."

"We saw." Berwyn said as he caught up to us. "We need to get to them."

His voice caught, making him cut off his words. We raced around trees, deeper into the woods. Raselin's men were waiting as the soldiers followed us. Berwyn and I didn't stop as Justin turned back to help his team.

"You saw him, right?" Berwyn asked when we were alone.

"He looked terrible, Berwyn." I cringed. "Do you think he will be okay?"

"I don't know." The seriousness in his voice made my blood run cold. I sprinted faster.

"At least Eden got him out," I responded. "How did she even do that?"

"Serious motivation?" Berwyn suggested. His voice turned dark again. "She's wanted to get back at the Society for a long time, Auluria. I think that, mixed with her fear over losing Dov, resulted in what we saw. I don't think she could have physically done that otherwise."

"Berwyn, I don't think *you* could have done what your wife did today."

He smiled softly for a moment before it iced over.

"He didn't look right, did he? Something was really wrong…"

"Something was wrong," I whispered, tearing up.

"I can't lose him too." Berwyn mumbled as we ran.

"We won't." I said my wish as a promise, hoping it would be true.

"Sit down." Eden pushed me back, forcing me against the wall. "You will wait your turn."

For suffering at the hands of Wallace's men not too long ago, Eden had gained incredible strength, much of which I assumed must be credited to Necesta.

"You *will* sit down or so help me—"

"How will you stop me?" I threatened, trying to stand up as she pinned me against the wall, forcing me to bend my knees in an effort not to fall to the ground.

Indignation rolled across her face, darker than any storm cloud I had ever seen. She looked ready to slap me. We were in public so I knew she wouldn't, but I wanted to dare her too, just to have reason to escape.

Instead, she held me there, with the same strength she used to rescue Dov hours earlier.

"You will allow his brother to do whatever he needs to do. He will not leave his side until he is ready and you will *not* interfere." She struggled against me as people watched our argument.

Justin looked sympathetically at me, Devin hovering close by. I was one of them; Eden was not, but even though they wanted to help me, they knew whose house we were in. What the Baers said was law.

Silas stood by the door of the room Berwyn had entered, guarding his friend as Necesta scurried in and out. Maylin quietly fetched items for her. They were a good fit.

I wouldn't see anything through the door when it briefly opened for an entrance or exit. No bed, not glimpses of even his feet or a hand hanging out of the cot. I couldn't even tell where Berwyn was situated in the room.

"*You* got to see him," I protested, near tears.

Silas looked pained as he watched me grapple against Eden's wishes. I cast him a pleading look, begging him to speak to Eden. He would be the only one other than Berwyn she would listen to.

He shook his head slightly, telling me there was nothing he could do. I turned back to Eden, not above begging.

"I got to see him because I dragged him back. You'll see him when Berwyn is done talking to him."

"At least tell me *something*, Eden, please," I implored. "*Please.*"

"I don't know anything, Auluria, or I'd tell you just to get you to shut up. Sit down!" She shoved me hard on the ground. "He was messed up, that's all I know. That woman kicked me out as soon as we arrived. No one has been in there since, except for Berwyn."

I pushed against her.

"I *will* hit you to get you to calm down." She leaned in to hiss at me. "Now settle down. You're causing undue stress out *here,* which certainly isn't helping in *there.*"

I calmed, knowing I had used up the last of her grace.

I had taken too many hits recently; I knew I couldn't survive whatever blow the back of Eden's hand would deliver should I speak again.

Sharone and the girls inched closer to me, trying to make eye contact in an attempt to support me. I continually looked away, knowing it would be my undoing.

Shadoe's gaze made me wither. He judged me as he had judged the weak, young girl he had met the day Lowell brought me into his fold. Vulnerability was a blemish on one's record, a stain on life meant to be rubbed out and replaced with strength and cold valor. Trembling on the ground, I was everything Shadoe despised. His perfect creation, the girl built to destroy, sat wrecked on the ground, leaving his reputation as a trainer in her wake.

He couldn't stand to look at me, pulling his eyes from me whenever I looked at him. I didn't blame him. Lowell would have been ashamed.

Each time the door opened, I flinched so hard Eden looked like she was prepared to pummel me to the ground just to keep me from moving. I didn't try to stand, but every fiber of my being was being drawn to that room.

When Berwyn finally stepped out, Eden held me in place until he approached.

"What did she say?" Eden asked through her teeth and she tightened her grip on me.

"He's been drugged. That's why he couldn't walk or stay upright. Necesta is working to remove the toxins now. She's bandaging his wounds."

"Berwyn, can I see him?" I pleaded, interrupting the account of what had happened.

"He's not really with us right now. I'm not sure…"

"Berwyn, *please!*" My tears burst from my eyes like an angry waterfall, misting as they hit my legs and chest as I hunched over myself. I rocked forward, hands gripping my calves so tightly I thought I'd do more damage than the Society people had. I choked. *"Please!"*

He looked away. "Go."

I scrambled to my feet, falling along the way. My hand touched the floor halfway to Silas, who was no longer at his post. I pushed myself upright, refusing to fall all the way.

Silas heard me coming, crashing as I raced to Dov's door. He stepped outside just as I entered. I heard him pull the door closed as I fell on the floor inside the threshold.

He was sitting up in the bed, propped against the wall, his breathing labored. I crawled over to him, quickly and slowly all at once. I didn't want to spook him; I knew I had to be careful. He watched my every move, tracking me with his eyes as I approached him.

He looked so tired, dark circles forming deeply beneath his eyes. His hair was wild, like the day he ran out of the storehouse fire…the day he first kissed me. His eyes held a certain weariness in them and I could see the pain written across his face from the torture he had endured.

Moving closer to him, my only intent was to make sure he was all right, but I longed to touch him. My fingers itched to reach out and trace his face, his lips. I couldn't help myself; I moved closer.

My hand found its way to his shoulder, resting gently near the side of his handsome face. His gaze held mine, finding recognition, then traveling to my lips for only a moment. I could see the hesitation in his eyes as I inched closer and closer still.

So much time has passed. I didn't know this new Dov; the broken man before me. He didn't know me, this leader who was willing to compromise everything and work with the enemy to get him back. We were strangers; so familiar with each other's touch and yet, so fragile that the slightest rebuff might break us.

I knew he needed time. I knew *I* needed time. But time was something I wanted to bind up and cast aside, banishing it for the remainder of our lives, so that this moment would only be me and the man I cared for and once knew so well.

I leaned in as he stared, motionless. He felt so warm beneath my touch. Everything in me sparked to life under his gaze. He called to me without a word.

"Tell me to stop," I whisper, closing the space between us until I rested over him, lips just out of reach, waiting for him to lean into me.

His throat made dry clicking sounds as he breathed out in response, eyes still fixed on me.

"Dov, tell me to stop," I whispered. His eyes dilated as he registered how much I desperately needed him in that moment, to know that he was still in there behind the drugs that made him hazy.

I waited as he swallowed hard, the moment causing his eyelids to close slightly in pain. We breathed together, heavy and deep, waiting. His hand found its way to my hip, his touch so weak, but his grip firm.

"Tell me to stop," I whispered so quietly I doubted he could hear me.

Dov pulled me to his chest, leaning against the wall for support. I supported myself, propping my knees along side of his hip, leaning against him only enough to let him feel my presence against him. My movements were careful and protective.

His touch was so weak, yet full of more power than I'd ever seen from him. Such strength existed in his broken and damaged hands.

Everything I loved about Dov that I thought must have been stripped away during his beatings still existed, just beneath the surface, hovering under his bruised skin.

His scars reminded me that every one of them had been for me.

I kissed him, driving our lips together again and again. He let me explore him as he rested against the wall, my mouth tracing his jaw, his neck, his shoulders. His hands traced up my back sending a shudder racing through me.

"Auluria," Dov whispered as my mouth found its way to his jaw again.

I couldn't think.

"Come here." He groaned, pulling me against him so that I was no longer supporting myself, my dress tangling around me.

The effort it took for him to reach up and tangle his hands in my hair nearly broke me. I hated seeing Dov in pain. I willed my kisses to heal his defeated body, removing all of the scars I had left there in my wake.

Instead, his lips cleansed me, purifying my transgressions against him. Forgiveness so sweet I could cry coursed through his lips, pressing into my very soul.

I loved this man.

I loved him, I loved him, I loved him.

Reaching my hands up to his hair, I wrapped my fingers around him, cradling his head between the wall and me. He fought to keep me close, forcing me to abandon any ideas of pulling back to keep him from hurting. His hands tugged at my hips and my back, bringing me as near as possible.

"Auluria," he breathed again, forcing me to lean back just enough that he could see me. I lingered with my eyes closed, not wanting to be present for fear the communion might end.

"I thought... " he started, his words lost. "I thought... how... how do I have you here, with me, now? How is this possible?"

His anxious eyes betrayed him, screaming to me how Dov had thought he had lost me for good.

"I will never leave you, Dov, never," I replied softly... forcefully, as I clutched at his face with my hands. I stroked the sides of his face, brushing his hair down, as he stared at my lips.

"I never want you to," he sighed, and everything in me broke. I wasn't sure he'd want me back, not after everything, but he had admitted it... *committed* to it. I was his and always would be. Nothing could break us.

"Shadoe!" Silas called from outside a moment before the door swung open.

"Let's go." Shadoe grumbled, crossing the small room as he reached for my arm.

His nostrils flared as he saw me perched on the cot by Dov's side. Dov started as Shadoe burst into the room, lurching forward in surprise. My hands, resting on his shoulders, gently pushed him back against the wall as Shadoe latched on to me.

"Out!" Silas commanded, following Shadoe into the room.

"We are leaving. We have a mission," Shadoe growled.

Silas clamped onto Shadoe's shirt, dragging him to the door. Turning, he pushed hard, sending him into the doorframe. I knew Silas would pay for that later.

Dov was wild-eyed when I turned back to him, hands still resting on his arms.

"Why was he here? We have to get you away." He tried to get up.

"Dov." My voice silenced him. "He's working with us now. Shadoe and Berwyn made a deal. We needed Lowell's men to help rescue you, and we're planning to take down the Society."

"We can't trust him," Dov insisted.

"We're not," I promised him. "But, Dov, we have an agreement with him."

I cringed.

"I'm so sorry, Dov. I have to go with him right now."

"No." Worry filled his blue eyes.

"Dov, listen." My hand found its way to his cheek. I stroked it gently, trying to sooth him. "Shadoe wouldn't reclaim Lowell's group unless I was there too. And, honestly, I had to go to make sure he actually did what he promised. Lowell's men listen to me…kind of."

"Auluria, no." Dov shook his head sadly.

"It's okay." I sounded like I was talking to tiny Jasleen. "We just have to defeat the Society. Once we do, I can come back. I don't have to help Shadoe anymore."

"I saw his body." Dov said.

"What?"

"Lowell." He looked away. "They brought his body by my cell to show me what would happen to you if they caught you without me turning you over. They threatened Berwyn and Eden, too."

"But you didn't, Dov. You stayed strong." I moved closer to him.

"Every day they told me they had found you. Every night they questioned me about where you were." His voice was heartbreakingly sad.

A bang on the door told me I had to move quickly.

I leaned in, kissing Dov again.

"I have to go," I whispered. "I'll be back as soon as I can. I'll be okay. Shadoe will keep me safe. He's trying to prove a point.

"As soon as we can bring down Canton, we can be together again."

He nodded, understanding.

"Don't go," Dov whispered.

"I have to." I smiled at him softly, hoping he would let me go.

Instead, he pulled me in, kissing me. He nodded when I pulled back, saying goodbye.

The door flew open just as I reached for it.

"Let's go." I pushed past Shadoe.

Chapter 12

THE DENSE AIR SEEMED TO WEIGH ME DOWN AS I WALKED through the light fog bank. Moisture rolled over the ground, pale and thin at my feet. The area was illuminated with it in the early morning hours as light in the atmosphere reflected off the bank of clouds. It grew thicker the further I looked out, blocking things from sight.

The fallen leaves on the ground were a dull color, muted by the opaque fog. They crunched quietly with each step as we crept forward.

Shadoe had sent most of his men back to the burned out storehouse Berwyn had provided as shelter. His elite team and backup group stayed by his side, moving strategically toward the city. Shadoe's mission was to gain intelligence on Magistrate Canton in the hours after the escape when the Society soldiers would assume everyone had fled.

"Martin," Shadoe whispered, flicking a wrist to the left, instructing the man to go around the outskirts of the city to enter. Hopefully he would hold his temper if he ran into any of the Society men.

Locust crept to the right, careful to avoid me. He clicked his tongue to get Shadoe's attention as he nodded to the right. Our leader dipped his chin down once, giving the man permission to split off.

I followed along beside him, fighting to keep focused on the task at hand and not the tiny room on the right side of the storehouse that held my heart. I dug my nails into the side of my legs every time I found my thoughts straying, using the temporary pain to bring me back.

Slowly the group disbanded, taking different routes into the city. Shadoe stayed by my side as we walked.

"Ready to put your training to good use?" he asked unexpectedly.

"Sure," I said lifelessly.

"You're going to have to do better than that," he chastised me, scowling.

I turned to him sharply, working a smile onto my face.

"There. Happy." I said, sarcastically playing the happy girl who was out walking with her fiancé.

I threw my shoulders down, elongating my neck, and leaned over to him, wrapping my arm through his. Shadoe had never been one for physical contact with a person unless it was in combat, so I didn't mind making him uncomfortable as we moved through the city.

It took a while to see the dark smoke rising up in the air after we heard the deafening collision of rock meeting rock as a building was being ripped apart several streets over. An explosion rocked the ground, making it tremble beneath my feet. Shadoe's arm unexpectedly steadied me.

He looked to me and for the first time I saw fear. It reminded me of the day I made him believe he had drowned me during my training, though this time, I was the only one he knew *was* safe.

We ran, darting to the scene of the explosion. My ankle caught again, pain jabbing into me where I had twisted it not a day before. Limping was not an option, so I kept up with Shadoe, despite the pull I felt.

Smoke poured from the rubble, casting a black trail into the sky, outlined by the white fog in a slow motion version of life. It drifted in front of us, commanding our movements.

"No," Shadoe whispered harshly under his breath. "He didn't."

"Who?" I looked at him, furious that he knew what was going on.

"Martin," he said. "He's been talking about this for ages. Lowell always said no."

"He wanted to blow something up?" I asked.

"He wanted revenge for his sister. They took her when he was too young to stop them." He looked at me. "You're aware that he has anger issues."

Eden had anger issues. *Berwyn* had anger issues. *Martin* beat people for the fun of it.

My fingers glided to my stomach, remembering my encounter with him during one of my tests in training.

"So he did *this*?"

"And destroyed any hope we had of capturing Canton."

"Wait," I paused. "We were *capturing* Canton?"

"Not *technically*." He rolled his eyes, pulling me away. "But had the opportunity presented itself…"

The opportunity would have presented itself. Shadoe would have seen to that.

A second explosion cut through the air, another building in Martin's wake. Pieces of wood and debris flew all around us as we retreated. The heat was over-whelming as I fell to the ground.

Lifting myself up, shards of wood tumbled out of my hair. Miraculously it remained tied back. It was just like my hair to stay in place the *one time* I would have granted it an excuse to fall out of place.

Shadoe was on his feet, engaged in battle with two soldiers. His silver claw lashed out at the men, striping their arms with bloody streaks. I wondered if he had had time to dose his prize before the attack. As the men began to react as Berwyn had when he had been struck, I knew he must have laced the metal contraption.

My lungs burned as smoke filled the air. A sharp pain shot through my right shoulder that, I assume, had taken the brunt of the fall. I rolled to the left, hoping to prop myself up with my good arm. My eyes rolled back in my head with the pain of the effort.

"Stay down," Shadoe yelled, trying to keep me from being noticed by the soldiers that were running to join the onslaught against him.

I waited for the men to pass me before I stood up. Finding a wood board ripped loose in the blast, I staggered to my feet. My balance was off.

Taking aim, I slammed the board into one of the soldier's heads. He fell unconscious at my feet. His partner turned to me, seeing his friend fall, and attacked. I swung hard, striking his arm with a loud crack. His knife toppled to the ground.

He looked at me, daring me to go for the weapon. I

lurched forward as if I were going to stoop to retrieve it. When he bent to catch it, I slammed the board into the back of his skull. Taking his knife was easy while he lay sprawled out on the ground.

Standing back up was not so easy.

Nausea crashed over me. My head felt like it was floating.

"Come on," Locust said, appearing out of nowhere.

He grabbed my arm and guided me to Shadoe. Together, they killed the soldiers that had been fighting our leader, returning to me. They braced me between them, running from the city.

"Did you see anything?" Shadoe yelled as we ran.

"No, the explosion hit before we could get close enough." He yelled over the roar of noise. "What happened?"

"Martin happened," Shadoe said, righting me as I stumbled.

Despite my efforts to watch the ground as it raced by under my feet, I could see the boys share a look over my head. Either Locust had risen in the ranks since I had left, or Martin had become a big enough problem that most of Lowell's men had heard about while I was gone.

"We don't have a choice, Shadoe," Locust said, pulling me faster. "We have to call it off… for now."

I knew Shadoe well enough to know he wanted to argue, but he knew I was in no position to fight.

"I know." He admitted coarsely. "We have to get out of here."

The soldiers burst out of a walkway in front of us, forcing us to stop in our tracks. My feet kept moving, nearly flipping me forward as my chaperones slammed to a halt.

"Back," Shadoe commanded as he stepped in reverse, quickly wheeling us around to run in the opposite direction, just as I had started to regain my balance.

They ran with me, half carrying me as we moved, taking a street that brought us to a new part of the city.

"Go," Shadoe instructed, shoving me toward Locust.

He caught me as I pitched forward, increasing our speed as I gained my strength back. Shadoe turned, knives in hand, and took out our attackers. I heard at least one of his men join him, executing the other soldiers that followed us.

Locust slowed us, hearing it as well. He leaned me against a wall, holding my shoulder to brace me, as if I would fall, as he leaned out to check the status of his friends. He looked back at me, nodding twice as he sighed in relief. For all of Locust's faults, he wasn't *entirely* bad.

Then he grinned at me and I lost my faith in him yet again.

"Let's move," Shadoe commanded, Sherman and Ella trailing behind him.

I pushed Locust off, considering stealing one of his knives in the process. I knew I would feel miserable if he ended up needing it and I had stolen it, so I left it in place. I considered running alongside Ella, one of the women just a few years older than me, but she was still angry with me over my work with Lowell, so instead, I lagged behind Shadoe, watching everything that surrounded me in the city.

Sherman, one of Shadoe's elites, broke off from us a mile later, taking care of a Society man. The sound was sickening as he beat the man's head into a wall. Shadoe grumbled under his breath, distracting me momentarily.

Eventually we made it to the meeting point in the woods. Most of Shadoe's team was there, waiting for our arrival.

"Was anyone followed?" Shadoe looked at the group.

"None that made it this far." One of the men answered, a hint of achievement in his voice. Lowell's careless appreciation of life had infiltrated the majority of his flock.

Once he was sure we weren't being followed, Shadoe led us back toward the storehouse. We climbed the side of the hill, ducking under low tree branches and crawling over enormous roots that grew into tangled nests above the ground. The wind felt good on my face, bringing me back to life after what had happened in the heart of the city.

Shadoe glowered the entire trip, fuming at losing his shot at capturing Canton from the Society. I assumed his plan was to use the man against the government; something Lowell's training would have encouraged *me* to do also had I been calling the shots. I wondered if Shadoe had discussed this with Berwyn.

The group quieted as we reached the top of the mound, cresting at the line of trees that formed a sad attempt at a wall. Shadoe glanced to the edge as the rest of the group followed behind us, using the exposed roots as ropes to scale the steep incline.

We walked, high above the world, for a mile. Forming several lines, we walked behind each other in groups of no more than three. Shadoe let several of the others take the lead, falling further back with me where I had planted myself toward the far end of the middle of the team, decidedly far from Locust and Ella.

The birds sang overhead, reminding me that soon I would be back with Dov. I would survive until then. The scream made me rethink that.

Shadoe launched himself out of the line, toward the precipice, carrying Martin with him. The boy struggled, Shadoe's hand around his throat as he propelled him backward.

"Shadoe!" I screamed, pushing a woman out of my way.

He pushed Martin further toward the drop off and I prayed he was only trying to scare him.

"Lowell never would have tolerated this," Shadoe bellowed loud enough for the entire group to fear him. "You will never disrespect me or my decisions again."

He pushed the boy again and he stumbled on the edge, teetering several inches out before flinging his body back at Shadoe. I had hoped Shadoe had been talking to Martin; he had been speaking to the group, warning them that their actions had consequences. He glanced back at them to make sure they were listening as I pushed past another team member, knocking them to the ground.

"Shadoe, don't!"

He focused his speech on Martin again.

"You jeopardized our plan. You risked our lives. *For what?* Revenge?" Shadoe taunted him, tightening his grip on his throat. "Never again."

Shadoe pushed him just as I reached them. Grabbing onto Martin however I could, I fought to pull him back. His hands flailed, digging into my flesh like a cat might, clawing to get to safety.

I threw myself back, hoping to counteract the fall. His foot slipped, jerking him backward as I pulled to save him. Martin's foot caught, finding a steady step. He pulled himself up on my arm quickly, finding his footing so fast that it threw me off balance. He stepped forward, throwing me past Shadoe, over the edge.

I saw panic on Shadoe's face as I pitched over the edge and plummeted. I wasn't sure if I screamed, but my hands flew out, desperate to grab anything that could sustain me. I registered the pain of sliding down the face of the cliff, but didn't have time to think. I saw brown, likely dirt, as I slid.

Shadoe had attempted to catch me, scratching at me in the air. His hand hit mine at some point, pulling me back enough that I skidded down the face of the cliff instead of free falling several feet away.

Suddenly, I jerked to a stop, crashing into something. I paused for a moment, before feeling the wind rush around me again. Another hesitation in my fall, an interruption in my descent, and I found myself cascading again, clawing at the earth and air.

A final body-shaking stop ended it.

Chapter 13

"T HERE NOW," A SOFT VOICE SAID, "G OOD GIRL. T AKE IT easy."

A hand, much less soft than the voice, touched my face. I held still, not opening my eyes until I figured out what was happening.

"Now, now, dearie. Don't be like that. I know you're there."

I inhaled the much needed air, letting my lungs expand. My eyes shot open when I realized if I was with Necesta, I must also be with Dov.

"Where is he?" I demanded, pain shooting through my body.

"Sit back." Necesta growled at me, the first time I had

ever seen her annoyed with me. "If you're talking about your young man, he's fine. If you're talking about the young man you saved, he's fine too. If you're talking about Silas, he's outside."

"Where is Dov?" My voice sounded gravelly and harsh.

"He's at the storehouse," she responded, picking up a bottle of something.

My eyes clicked from her, to my lap, to the wall, to the door. She handed me something, but I didn't move to take it.

"Where are *we*, then?"

She studied me for a moment, then paused to force-feed me the liquid in the bottle she held.

"You thought we were in the storehouse?" she asked. "Well, we are. Just not *your* storehouse. They brought you back after your fall. The Baers were so intent on figuring out what to do next and taking care of your young man, that they didn't hear about the incident right away. When they did, they sent Silas and a few men to check on you all.

"Shadoe's physicians looked at you, but they're nothing compared to this old girl. Silas was smart enough to come get me and bring me here.

"You took a nasty fall. You've been in and out for days. You've spoken to me a few times. Do you remember that?"

I shook my head.

"I didn't think so." She smiled at me. "You'll be fine, though. You're body just had a great deal of trauma. Sleep helps the body heal, Goldilocks. You'll be fine soon. You just need to rest."

"Is she awake?" Silas asked, sticking his head in the door. He grinned when he saw me, relief washing over his face.

"Nice to see you, Sleeping Beauty."

"Wow, you *have* been hanging around Eden too much." I tried to laugh and ended up coughing.

"Easy," he said, slipping quietly into the room.

Necesta nodded to him and walked toward the door. Silas took a seat in the chair near the bed.

"So you thought going back and forth to the store-houses was a good idea, but you didn't think to just take *me* to *them*…?" I goaded him.

"Dov may be in the business of carrying women around after injuries, but I, madam, am not."

"Reyla might think differently." I raised an eyebrow to him, challenging him to disagree.

He smirked.

"You were in no condition to be traveling." Necesta added.

"Oh, *Auluria*…" He sighed. "You just had to go and be noble, didn't you? What were you thinking? You nearly died."

I stared at him.

"Oh, don't give me that look. You know he'd say the same thing."

"How is he?"

"You threw yourself off a cliff, Auluria, how do you think he is?"

I could feel the color draining from my face.

"*He knows*? Why would you tell him that?"

"Because you almost died, Auluria." He dragged his hand down the side of his face. "But to be honest, we didn't at first. We knew he would try to get to you and he was still in no condition to be traveling so far.

"I brought Necesta here first, and once she determined that she could help, we told him what had happened. You have no idea how hard it was to convince him to stay." He paused. "Necesta might have had to knock him out."

My face fell.

"Just until I could get out of there." He held up his hands against whatever verbal attack I might launch at him. "No one bothered to tell him where you were. If he couldn't track us, he couldn't find you."

It was sound logic.

"Go tell him I'm okay," I said, attempting to lean up.

"No." He laughed at me.

"Excuse me?"

I attempted a second time to sit.

"I'm up. Go tell him I'm fine."

"You are not fine, Auluria, you can't even sit up." He reached out a hand for me to pull myself up on, his other slipping behind my shoulder to assist me. "I'm not leaving you alone with him."

"Necesta's here," I insisted, my hair catching as Silas lifted me up.

He gave me a doubtful look.

"Yes, and how will she protect you?" He questioned. "By throwing bottles of medicine at him?"

"She knocked Dov out," I pointed out.

"Dov was only partially conscious to begin with." He patronized me. "Shadoe is *fully* awake and very much aware that the Baers are furious with him. I doubt he's slept at all for fear of retribution for throwing you off a cliff."

"He didn't throw me off a cliff… He tried to throw *Martin* off a cliff." I made a vague attempt at rolling my eyes. "And Shadoe isn't scared of anyone."

"You're defending him?" He looked shocked. "In all this time, haven't you figured this out yet, Auluria? Shadoe is not the good guy here."

"I'm aware of that. You don't think I know that?" I was annoyed. "But he didn't intentionally try to hurt me. In fact, he tried to catch me. He almost did and, frankly, he's the only reason I survived. He pulled me into the cliff enough that I was able to partially break my fall."

"I'm still not leaving you alone with him." Silas said stubbornly.

"And how did you manage that with all the running back and forth between the storehouses, Silas?"

The storm in his eyes cleared, flashing a brilliant green, as his smile returned.

"Please," he said smugly. "You don't think I'm here alone, do you?"

I gave him a quizzical look.

"Talley is here. And Devin and Justin. They haven't left your door this entire time. Shadoe may still be in charge around here, but they haven't let him anywhere near you without one of them outside the door and the door left open."

I sat still for a moment, deciding whether to be annoyed that I had babysitters or grateful that they cared enough to watch over me.

"You can go," I said. He looked at me until I continued. "If they are here, that means you can go to Dov."

An inner war played out across his face as he debated whether or not to listen to me. I waited, as I had been taught, until he had had enough time for my words to sink in.

"It's me or him, Silas. You know I'm going to be okay. But he doesn't know that, and you're the only one that can tell him. Don't you think he will focus more on getting better if he's not stressed out over me?" I said calmly, focusing him on my goal.

"I won't talk to Shadoe, if that makes you feel better." I grinned, knowing I was winning him over.

"Don't look at me like that." He grinned back. I knew I had him.

"Seriously, I'll be fine. Go take care of Dov. It can be a race to see which of us heals first." I hesitated. "Silas, how is he?"

"Worried about you." His smile didn't slip. "He's getting better. I don't know what Necesta learned on her side of the wall, but she's better than anyone I've seen over here."

"When I first met her, I watched her work. She was magnificent," I agreed.

"You're going to have to fill me in on your time over the wall sometime."

"I'll fill you *both* in. But, Silas, you've got to get one of us to the other."

"I'm working on it, Goldilocks." He laughed. "I'm working on it.

I tipped my head, unimpressed that he picked up Necesta's nickname for me.

"Don't."

"Don't?" he smirked. "Don't get you and Dov back together? Doesn't it seem like that's all I ever do these days?"

He squinted his eyes at me, daring me to play along.

"Don't call me that." I didn't rise to the bait. "That's Necesta's name."

"I'm going to tell Dov. We'll see how you like it after that." He winked, making me giggle.

"Time to let me work, young man." Necesta entered, carrying a bowl.

"I'll come back soon," Silas promised. He stood to go.

"No you won't," Necesta said, setting the bowl down on the small table beside the bed. "You have work to do over there."

She turned to me and dipped her head as if she was about to say something important and needed me to listen.

"You and I need to have a little talk, Goldilocks. He's not going to be back for awhile, so say your goodbyes." She leaned back and waited patiently in her chair.

Silas shrugged.

"Don't sass me, young man," Necesta said without looking back. Silas' eyes grew wide.

"I…"

"Yes, you did." She grinned conspiratorially at me. "Now go. Berwyn and Raselin need your help. Take the bag I left outside the door for Dov. That should help. Twice a day, Silas. Don't forget."

"Yes, ma'am." Silas said, stepping toward the door.

"Auluria, if you need *anything,* send one of guys to come get me. Berwyn will send an army if you need us."

"I know." And I *did* know.

"He's a fine young man," Necesta said. "All of the Baers' group is, so it seems."

"How is Reyla?" I asked.

"She's fine, dearie. She was nearly back to normal when I came to you. Silas, as you saw, has recovered nicely."

"And quickly," I pointed out.

"She followed my instructions well—like you did." She grinned. "But we'll get back to that. Reyla is a strong girl. She'll be fine.

"Poor thing… She told me about that young man of hers. How terrible. You're a good friend to her.

"Your friends are quite lovely, really," she crooned, rocking forward in her chair. "I especially like that young man of yours.

"I think you'll be impressed to know that his family took very good care of him. He and I had a little chat after you left and before I came here. He had some old scars that were of particular interest to me."

She reached forward to the table, something scraping along the wood. She handed the beads to me, waiting for me to take them.

"Before I forget," she commented, "just like I said. You're a good listener."

I gave her a questioning look, but she waved me off.

"His family, like I said, took very good care of him. Eden and Berwyn stayed by his side the entire time. They were about as adamant as your other friends were about staying by Reyla's side. Maylin, Katarina, Gregory… Silas refused to leave her side unless he was allowed to go in to see Dov for a few minutes. Prying those Baers away from him was harder than climbing that wall. They all took wonderful care of both Reyla and Dov. You'd be very proud of how they handled themselves."

"So it would seem." I didn't need Necesta to tell me how helpful they had been, but I was glad she had.

"Now, we need to talk, dearie." She grew more serious. "There are two things we need to discuss. The first is what happened out there. What do you remember?"

"Martin caused an explosion," I started, leaning my head back against the wall. "He destroyed Shadoe's plan and nearly got us killed. I got hurt in the second blast."

"How so?"

"I was very dizzy. Shadoe and Locust had to help me back. I'm sure I had a concussion…it certainly wasn't my first.

"When we finally escaped the city, we went to the rendezvous point. We had to walk for a while. When we reached the cliff, Shadoe decided to make a point.

"Martin nearly got us all killed *and* he possibly cost us an opportunity to defeat the Society."

I paused, shocked I hadn't realized it yet.

"Necesta," I said urgently, "Where is Martin?"

"He's fine, Goldilocks. He's locked up with the Baers. Berwyn didn't trust Shadoe enough to leave him in his care. Shadoe couldn't argue at that point because they could have accused him of throwing you off that cliff. He didn't, did he?"

"No." I attempted to shake my head only to be met with searing pain.

"Don't do that, Goldilocks," she chastised as I flinched.

"It's probably wise that Berwyn is in control of the situation. Arin is probably busy terrifying him as we speak."

"Something like that," she murmured. "Goldilocks, do you know what happened after you fell?"

I tried to think back, but only my hands grasping at dirt came to mind. I blinked at her blankly, refusing to shake my head again.

She eyed the necklace around my neck. I absentmindedly reached up to brush it with my fingers.

"Somewhere along the line, you told Shadoe how to use it. It probably saved you," she said, admiring her handiwork. "They brought you back here and eventually Silas and a convoy came to see what had happened. When he saw you, he left all of his men to guard you and came immediately for me."

She explained what she knew, most of which I had

already learned from Silas. I waited patiently, not telling her Silas had already explained it to me, but she kept it brief.

"Now, Goldilocks, we need to talk about something else," she said gently. I waited for her to continue. "Your scars, dearie."

Suddenly self-conscious, my fingers inched their way to the burn marks on my thighs, remembering the marks Canton's interrogator had inflicted on me in front of Dov. The twisted feeling in my stomach returned, sharp and metallic, reminding me of every painful thing I had ever endured.

"Canton's men did that. They wanted information, but really, they just wanted to torture us. They made us listen to each other being hurt; Eden, Silas, Dov, and me.

"Lowell got involved, and the Society realized Dov and I were more than just members of the same group. They made us watch each other being tortured."

"Ahh, so that's where some of those came from. He didn't give much detail," Necesta said knowingly, tapping her arm where the men had sliced Dov. "Unfortunately, there's not much I can do for scars. We can help them to fade a bit, if that's any consolation."

"Get back!" Justin's voice rang out on the other side of the door.

"I imagine that would be your intended," Necesta frowned.

I groaned. I didn't want to see Shadoe after he had nearly murdered Martin to make a point. Necesta stood, walking to the door.

I could hear Talley arguing as Necesta reached for the door.

"Now or later, dearie? You'll have to get it over with at some point."

I sighed, knowing she was right.

"Now."

She opened the door, stepping outside to talk to my keepers. I could feel the tense pause where they all considered Necesta's request to let Shadoe inside.

"It's fine," I attempted to call out.

After a moment Shadoe stepped in. He attempted to close the door, but forceful hands held it open, reminding Shadoe once again that in the struggle for power, he did not have the upper hand.

He stood by the cot, until I motioned for him to sit. He refused until I flicked my eyes at the chair again, daring him to provoke me as I lay wounded in a bed due to his choices. He sat.

"Are you okay?" he asked, the moment eerily similar to the time he had checked on me after I was beaten at the hands of his men as part of Lowell's initiation.

"Do I look okay?" I challenged, refusing to break eye contact.

"Necesta says you're healing."

"I am." Hostility took over, tensing every muscle in my body. "What do you want?"

"To check on you. They haven't let me near you."

"You think that's a bad thing? You think it's unwarranted?"

"Lur." His voice grew icy.

"No, Shadoe," I interrupted. "You tried to kill Martin. What were you thinking?"

"He nearly got us killed," Shadoe protested. "He's never going to listen. He will always try to do things his own way, and it would always cost us."

"Shadoe, do you even hear yourself? How can you be so judgmental when that is *exactly* what Lowell did to the Baers?" I asked. "Or didn't you know that? When Lowell wanted to do things his own way, what happened? He split off from Griz, got people killed, and started his own group. All of this was because of that, and you sold your life to it.

"You've done the same things Martin has done. Even when we went on your mission to find Canton… Was that something Berwyn was okay with, or did you do that on your own?" I demanded. "Considering I knew nothing about that part of the mission, I'm willing to bet the Baers knew nothing about it."

I waited for him to deny it.

"We have an obligation to Lowell's—"

"No," I interrupted him forcefully. "We don't."

He glared at me, returning my own furious gaze.

"We owe Lowell *nothing*. Lowell didn't care about any of us. Even when I was locked up in that prison with him, his own flesh and blood, he had his inside men work to punish me. He didn't attempt to help me. He didn't attempt to save the little cousin he helped to raise. He didn't do one thing to honor his mother's last wishes about protecting me.

"Shadoe, he never cared. Not about me, not about you, not about anything other than his revenge mission!

"He was sick and twisted, and he is dead, Shadoe. He's gone. We don't have to listen to him anymore. You're in charge now. Be a man and make decisions for yourself.

"You *have to* know that this isn't right. The *only thing* Lowell ever got right was that we needed to bring the Society down. Lowell wanted to do it so he could be in charge, but you... You know we need to bring them down to save this country. You know these people need help. *Our* people need help Shadoe. The only way we can do that is if we stop thinking about ourselves and actually work together to stop the Society. Canton is only the start, but if we can use him to destroy the government, we have to be smart about it."

Shadoe fumed, the muscles in his face clenching so tightly, I thought his lower jaw might burst through the top of his head, sending teeth shattering everywhere. He leaned forward viciously.

"You of all people should remain loyal to Lowell. He kept you alive. I know those Baers have you sucked into their world, and I don't know how Dov managed to seduce you into his illogical little plan, but you're smarter than this. You know being nice isn't going to win this war.

"Martin is a threat to our standing in this war. Any smart leader would have cut it off at the head. Don't you blame me for putting our entire group of men and women ahead of one misguided life, Auluria."

"Lowell thought I was a misguided life," I provoked, letting a small laugh escape my lips. "And you went against him and saved me. He died while you saved *me*, remember? You chose *my life* over *his* and his mission."

"Maybe I shouldn't have," he said quietly, ensuring no one but me heard. "Maybe I would do it differently now."

"But you didn't. You're turning into Lowell. His ideals cost him his life. Is that a price you're willing to pay?"

"I've always been willing to pay that." He sat back in the chair, deflating, looking at his folded hands.

"You are not Lowell," I said quietly. "You can still be redeemed."

His head shot up to look at me, anger rippling through him.

"You have no idea what you're talking about, Auluria. You are a confused and foolish girl. We never should have let you go to the Baers. We should have trusted Anetta to go. She, at least, was loyal.

"You have been nothing but a disappointment."

He stood to leave, but I wasn't finished.

"I'm not the one who let Lowell die."

"You're the entire reason he is dead," Shadoe whipped back to me, roaring loudly enough to propel Justin, Devin, and Talley into the room, hands on their knives. "We will work with the Baers, because you're right, we need to take the Society down, but mark my words, Lur, you will *never* be going back to them. This is the price you will all pay for this."

Shadoe stalked out of the room. I knew he was right. We had all agreed this was the price, and Shadoe would never let me leave. He had too much of a point to prove now. He was a man who was true to his word: he would work with the Baers and I would never again leave the fold.

Devin, Talley, and Justin stared blankly.

"That is incredible." Justin laughed, dropping a card on the pile at the edge of my cot. "I can't believe they actually pulled that off."

"What did you expect?" I laughed, tossing my own card on top.

"I really need to spend more time with those two when we get back." Justin wiped at a tear in his eye as Talley placed a card on the pile.

"They seem nice." Talley smiled, brushing back her blonde hair. "You really found yourself a good crowd of people to run with, Auluria."

"I don't know how, but I really did."

Dov had sent the cards over a few days ago when he sent Silas to check on me, flowers carefully tucked away in the small package. They sat on the table next to my cot. Justin had pushed away the chair, giving himself and his sister room to sit on the floor for our game.

"It's really not fair that I don't get to play." Devin leaned over from where he was sitting on the floor outside the room, hovering over the threshold.

"No one said you couldn't come in, Devin." I motioned for him to enter.

"I'm on duty," he complained, grinning.

"This is silly," I said, loud enough for him to hear me. "No one is going to try to come in with the three of you here. Just come inside."

"Nope," Devin said, turning back around to face outside.

"You might trust them, Auluria, but we don't," Talley said, putting another card down when it was her turn.

"What do you think they're going to do, lock us in here?"

"Yes," the siblings said at the same time.

"And just what will that achieve?" I asked.

"World domination?" Justin asked.

"Hostages," Talley murmured.

"Test subjects for whatever mind control project your cousin passed on to him," Devin leaned in and shouted into the room, careful to make sure Shadoe's men weren't listening.

We had been very careful to keep a buffer around the room. Shadoe's men kept their distance. He hadn't returned after I had yelled at him. No one bothered us. I guessed it had something to do with Shadoe keeping them away from me—I still had cards to play that wouldn't be found in his favor.

I laughed at Devin's suggestion.

"Manipulation and persuasive power of speech do not equate to mind control." I rolled my eyes. "Lowell just found the right people at the right time and knew how to talk to them. Once he had a handful of people, it was easy to convince other people he was right."

Getting people to believe in something was always easier when there were people to back it up. An idea on it's own was simply that: an idea. But an idea with force to stabilize it and give it roots was practically unstoppable.

Lowell showed the world people believed in his way of doing things. One follower lead to another follower, and eventually he amassed a following so large it rivaled the one he had left.

When people feel they have permission to think and act in a certain way because it is perceived as accepted by others, there is no stopping the wildfire that started from one tiny spark.

It is how evil and goodness continue to exist in our world. One man or woman convinces a second and third person that what they are doing is right, and the entire world is transformed because of it.

Lowell did it when he convinced his people to go after the Baers. Raselin and Necesta did it when they persuaded their people to band together to fight back against their government and ours. I did it when I convinced Dov to trust me. Dov did it when he showed the world his goodness and they too gave selflessly like he did for them.

Even Shadoe was doing it now, as he made his choices for his new command. Every action, every step, every choice gave the people he interacted with permission to do things, one way or the other.

"Auluria?" Justin sang, breaking my thoughts. "You with us, Goldilocks?"

"Seriously, you have *got* to stop calling me that," I said, shaking my head, for the first time without much pain. "What did I miss?"

"Where were you?" Talley prompted softly, moving her legs so one was in the air under her elbow and the other was wrapped around it, reaching her opposite hip.

"I was thinking about Lowell."

"Your cousin?" Talley asked, settling in for a conversation.

"He manipulated people. He manipulated me," I confessed what they already knew. "But I did that too. Lowell trained me to manipulate. Shadoe trained me to manipulate. They even sent me off to a woman specifically for manipulation training. She did a bang up job too." I glanced down, thinking of all the people I had exploited in the last few months.

"You weren't trying to hurt people, Auluria."

"Wasn't I? I mean, I didn't *want* to hurt people, but I wanted to help my cousin. I did what he told me to do and that involved hurting Dov and Berwyn. I willfully did that."

"That doesn't make you the same," Justin said earnestly, sitting forward. "You were protecting your family. Any of us would do the same thing."

"Doesn't that make us all just as bad?" I could see him questioning himself.

"None of us are guiltless in this, Auluria." Talley leaned her chin on her hands as they rested on her knee in front of her. "You and I, we both have flaws. We've both made bad choices. But we've also both made choices to protect our families.

"What Lowell did was wrong, and he paid for that. Somewhere along the line, doing what he thought was right crossed the line to hurting people. I'm sure that wasn't his intention starting out, though, do you think? Just like it was never your intention to hurt people when you started out. The difference is that you realized it and did something about it."

"We all mess up, Auluria." Justin said. "You're thinking about Shadoe right now, I can tell. He's at that place where he has some very big choices to make. We can't make them for him. It's up to him to decide what side of this he will fall on."

"But you *can* influence him." Talley picked up. "He's watching you. He's *been* watching you, and I'll wager he's been watching you since the day you met him. He's seen your choices during all this.

"You've saved the Baers. You were willing to give your life for them. You fought when you didn't have to. You honored your word to Shadoe and Lowell about caring for this group." She motioned to the door. "You came back to help, even when you were safe over the wall. And here you are, sitting in a bed, recovering from falling off a cliff, because you would rather die than let someone who nearly got you killed die. I promise you, Shadoe sees all of that."

"Just keep making the right choices," Justin chimed in, "or fixing them when you make the wrong ones. Your actions affect everyone else... you can either influence them for the better or for the worse."

"That was deep," I joked, making him crack up.

"He gets that way when delivering the truth. Even as a kid, he'd have these deep conversations with the others and send them crying to their mothers." Talley laughed.

"And then Talley would have to console him because all his friends ran away." Devin leaned back into the room, laughing.

"I had more friends than you did," Justin retorted.

"Necesta doesn't count." Devin tried to keep a straight face.

"You're just jealous because she thought I was more adorable than you." Justin smirked at his older brother, turning back to wink at me.

"Because you were a child." He emphasized the last word.

"Necesta was good to us all," Talley interrupted, quelling the fake fight. She turned back to me. "She watched out for us when we lost our mother right after we climbed over the wall. It wasn't easy being so young and in charge of these two monsters."

Justin acted offended, clutching his hand to his heart.

"That is harsh, sister."

"That is *Hersh*, brother." Talley played off of their last name. "And *you* try raising two little hooligans *and* make enough money to survive. Thank goodness Necesta let you two hang around while I was working at the market."

She turned back to me to finish her story.

"Necesta would set up next to me and the boys would run between us. When I had to go to the far side of the city, she would watch them closer to home for me, especially when I had to go to the rougher areas."

"Hey! *I* was helpful." Devin glanced back to the main room before spinning to partially face us. He leaned forward on his crossed legs, looking like he was Jasleen's age.

"If you say so, baby brother."

"Ten years is not that much younger," he quipped.

"I can't really talk here; she's fifteen years older than me." Justin shrugged.

"Necesta was very kind to us." Talley tucked a strand of hair behind her ear.

"When will she be back?" I asked.

"A few days, assuming everything is fine at the other storehouse," Devin said from the doorway.

I had sent one of the flowers Dov had sent me back with Necesta that morning as she traveled back to the Baers' storehouse. It had started to die, withering away, when Necesta helped me to dry it. She carried it back with a message of well wishes from me as she checked on his progress.

"Okay, enough of this." Devin stood up, hand on the back of his neck. "My neck is killing me. Justin, out. It's your turn to keep watch."

Justin reluctantly stood up, winking at me. "We've got your back."

His hand shook the cot as he used it to balance himself. Devin took his seat as Justin settled on the ground outside, back against the doorframe.

"Just don't leave me out this time," he called in to us as we giggled over lowering our voices the day before so even when he strained he couldn't be a part of the conversation.

"Okay," I called, before dropping my voice to a whisper. "Let the games begin."

Shadoe sulked in the main area, skulking past my line of sight every so often. He scowled whenever he saw me talking to one of the Hersh siblings.

The days dragged on, each one bringing more strength back to my body. Necesta's bottles worked wonders, though I might have felt better than I actually was.

"I just want to talk to her," a voice outside said.

Talley glanced inside, waiting for approval. I nodded and she stepped back to let Anetta inside. She walked in, tall and graceful, standing several feet from the cot. I swung my feet over the edge, keeping the blanket draped over me.

"Hello," I said cautiously.

"Hello, Auluria," she said tentatively.

I watched as she hovered, rocking onto her heels.

"What is it, Anetta?" I encouraged her to speak.

Her eyes dragged the length of me, reminding me of how Lowell used to examine me before a test. Perhaps she had learned this technique from him during her time with him.

"Was any of it true?" she finally questioned. "Did you ever care?"

"What do you mean?" I was confused.

"Did you ever actually try to help Lowell?" she said, accusation in her voice.

"Of course I did. I did everything he asked, Anetta."

"Then why is he dead?" she whined.

"Lowell made some bad choices, Anetta. His goal of taking down the Society was admirable, but he let his revenge get in the way of actually helping people. How many people did we lose during his campaign of retribution against Griz Baer? You lost friends, I remember it happening."

"But Lowell didn't have to die," she persisted.

"No, but Lowell made his choice. His revenge was worth more to him than surviving."

"You could have helped him." She sounded like she was pleading.

"How?" I waited for her to answer. Tears started to drip down her face.

"Why did this happen?" she asked as she sunk to the floor, a puddle of tears forming in her lap.

I remembered once thinking it would be nice if any of Lowell's friends had taken an interest in me. Now one finally had and it was *still* all about my cousin.

"Your aunt would be so ashamed," Anetta sobbed. I wondered if she had ever met my aunt. I didn't think Lowell had ever introduced any of the girls to my aunt.

"Yes, she would, but not of me," I addressed her. "She never would have been okay with what Lowell was doing had she known."

"She was okay with the food and money Lowell brought you." She looked up at me defiantly. She wiped her eyes. "She never questioned that."

"She couldn't question that. Lowell was her son. She had to trust him or she had nothing. I heard her questioning it to herself once. She knew something was strange, but he was her son and he was taking care of her. She didn't want to push him away; he needed her. And she needed to take care of me."

"She would be horrified that you turned your back on your family."

"I didn't turn my back on Lowell; I tried to get him to stop the disaster he was creating. Lowell turned his back on me though. Do you have any idea what happened once we were caught, Anetta?"

She stared at me, daring me to go on.

"When Magistrate Canton had us in our cells, we were taken out for interrogation. Lowell had at least one of the soldiers in his pocket. Instead of bribing them to get him out, he traded for an empty room alone with me.

"He used his time to threaten me. He made me choose who would be hurt worse—Dov Baer or me. Anetta, he had so much power that Magistrate Canton actually listened to him when it came to our torture. You think a man like that couldn't have found a way out of all of this?

"He used his opportunity on revenge. That was his choice."

She looked furious, realizing that Lowell had done this to himself without a thought for his people...or her.

"His mother would have been heartbroken to see what he had become. He was always cold, but he changed once he left the Baers. My aunt never would have been okay with what he did to me or how he betrayed me. When I didn't do what he wanted, he threw me away.

"Lowell didn't care about anyone other than himself.

I'm not even sure he truly cared about my aunt. Everything he did for her was a show of power."

"He loved her," she said. "He talked about her all the time. That's why he took you in. He had promised her he would look after you."

So Lowell wasn't completely heartless.

"Did he *ever* care about me, Anetta?" I asked quietly. "I mean, more than for what I could do for his mission?"

"I don't know." She breathed deeply, another tear falling off her check into the ocean that sat in her lap. She dragged a hand through her blonde hair. "I honestly don't think I know anything anymore."

"Did you love him?" I asked.

"Yes," she replied. "But, then, we all did. He didn't love me; I know that. But I think he was fond of me."

"I think he was too." I smiled. "I think I saw more of you than any of the other girls."

"Except Marjorie." She smiled ruefully.

"You two always did spend a lot of time with him."

"He was obsessed with you while you were gone, if that's any help," she suggested, hoping that would mean something to me. It didn't.

"Thank you, Anetta."

"He talked about your aunt all the time. He really felt that she would be proud of him."

"She would have been, even though she wouldn't have agreed with him. She loved him, even if they didn't see eye to eye. She would have loved him unconditionally, even in the face of all this."

"She must have been very special."

"She was." I paused. "I still love Lowell, Anetta. He was my cousin, and even though I didn't agree with him, I still love him because he is my family."

She glanced up quickly at me.

"I couldn't support the choices he made, but that didn't make him less of a person to me, or less of a relative. We get to make our own choices, Anetta, but we can still love and respect people as humans even though we don't see things the same way."

After a moment, she nodded. Anetta crawled over to the cot, putting her head on the mattress by my knee. I stroked her hair as she cried.

"I'm sorry he left you, Anetta. But you're strong." I smiled at her as she looked up at me. "I've seen you fight. You'll be okay."

"Maybe," she mumbled.

"You will," I insisted.

"I'm sorry you lost your cousin," she whispered.

Tears sprung to my eyes.

I had lost a cousin. I had lost my only remaining family.

We cried together as I forgave him.

Chapter 14

"Necesta is here." Talley grinned as she reached around the doorframe.

I pushed myself up, arranging my skirt in front of me as I stood to show Necesta my progress in the week and a half that she had been gone. The dark fabric fell in front of me, cascading around my feet. She took an exceptionally long time reaching the door and I assumed she had stopped to talk to someone.

Talley walked away from the door in my line of sight, Devin and Justin going with her. My protection detail left me. Fear washed over me. They hadn't left my side since they arrived. Something was wrong.

Coldness crept over me and I looked for something to defend myself with. Footsteps approached the door. Twenty feet away, a figure stepped into my line of sight. The man approached quickly, coming straight for the door.

I nearly fell when I recognized the face. I shouldn't have been seeing him, but he was there.

My breath caught as he reached the door. It was real. *He* was real.

Blue eyes, so deep and true, moved slowly toward me. His smile hitched up on one side, showing his dimples as his hands tangled in my hair.

Dov's lips touched mine, as soft as I remembered them. He panted slightly in pain as I reached up his back and embraced him, accidentally touching his injuries. I pulled back, breathing in as I released him. Dov held me in place.

"It's okay," he whispered, finding my lips again.

His hands found my hips as he smiled against my mouth.

"Auluria," he sighed.

I reached a hand to his face, cradling it as he kissed me.

"Are you okay?" he asked between kisses.

"Mmm," I murmured against his lips.

I ran my hand up his arm, making him shiver. I

jumped when he touched my shoulder and neck with his mouth. His warm breath rippled through my body as I quivered.

I stepped toward him, forcing him back. He moved with me, letting me guide his steps.

The door had closed at some point, giving us a modicum of privacy. He found the wall beside the door, leaning against it. I rested my hands on his shoulders, wanting to work out the knots, but terrified I would hurt him. He pulled at my back, moving me closer.

I pulled back, unable to breath, and watched him through half closed eyes. It was like a dream. He smiled at me, one hand in my hair, the other possessively on my hip.

"Took long enough," he finally said, making both of us burst into laughter.

"Sorry, the other side of the wall was a bit of an obstacle course." I giggled.

"From what I hear, it was *this* side that tripped you up." He smirked.

"Less tripping, more tangling," I corrected appreciatively, brushing his cheek with my fingertips.

"I think we need to work out a better plan next time—one that avoids cliffs. We seem to be making that a trend here." His moved his face to hover over mine again.

"And prisons. Let's avoid those too," I added.

"And that awful stage in the center of the city. That's the worst of it all."

"Agreed." I nodded, nearly bumping his nose. I thought twice and nudged his nose with mine.

He pulled me toward him, kissing me.

"How are you here? Shouldn't you be resting?" I asked when he pulled away.

"I have my ways." He shot me a flirtatious look. "But I've been holding out on them, so we can't wait too long to go back."

"What do you mean?" I pulled back and guided him to the chair.

He pulled it close to the cot as he sat, our knees touching.

"We have to come up with a plan. They aren't doing anything until you and I are back on our feet, but I intentionally stayed pretty quiet about what happened while I was gone, otherwise Berwyn never would have let me come." His smile faded into one a little sadder. "Silas knows, just in case we needed the information."

"Silas always plays a hand in everything, doesn't he?"

"I can't even imagine a life without Silas knowing everything before we do." Dov laughed.

A fist pounded against the door as we chuckled.

"Okay you two, that's about enough, we're coming in."

The door swung open to reveal Silas and Reyla. I

jumped up so fast, Dov nearly toppled backward off the chair. He grinned as I raced past him into Reyla's arms.

"How are you here?" Tears pricked my eyes, more from the surprise of seeing her than the pain that pierced through my back.

"I was better off than Dov was, and he's here." She frowned. "They couldn't have kept me away if they tried. I tried to come the last time Silas was here too, but he wouldn't let me."

"You weren't ready yet. You needed to heal," he told her quietly. "But she's here now."

"I'm doing much better, and apparently, you are too." Reyla nodded to the cot before guiding us there.

I moved the pillow against the wall to give us more room. Reyla sat at the foot of the bed, leaving me to sit near Dov's chair at the head of the cot. Silas sat on the floor near Dov. As we sat there, I realized just how much each of us had endured.

Talley and her brothers resumed their posts outside of the door as we settled in to catch up. She closed the door over again, giving us space to openly talk.

"Auluria, what happened?" Reyla said urgently as soon as the door was closed.

I glanced to Silas to see what he had told them. He raised his hands in the air.

"I told them everything you said," he offered.

"I know what Silas said, but what *really* happened with Shadoe?" she persisted.

"Nothing. He was trying to teach someone a lesson and I interfered. He had nothing to do with it ending badly. Martin pulled himself up and landed poorly enough that it swung me out over the cliff. Shadoe tried to reach me." I noticed Dov grimace as I spoke. "But at least he pulled me closer to the face of the cliff so I could slow my fall. I just couldn't catch myself."

Reyla looked horrified.

"I don't like him," she pushed.

"I know," I said at the same time the boys said they didn't either.

"He hasn't come near me since I woke up, if that helps."

"Because you told him off," Silas added, his smug look suggesting I should consider him helpful.

Dov pursed his lips, a grin tugging the corners up. I wanted to kiss it off. I got lost staring at him, making him grin for real.

"Should we leave you two alone?" Silas smirked.

"Yes," we both said, refusing to break eye contact. Silas gaped at us until we laughed.

"So what is our plan here?" I finally asked when we calmed down.

"For what?" Silas asked, indicating there was a lot we should probably be discussing.

"For handling Canton. For reigning in Shadoe. For all if it."

"Well… I'm pretty sure *you're* the only one who can handle Shadoe at this point," Silas pointed out as Dov scowled.

"I don't like this," Dov said.

"Well, of course not," Reyla jumped in. "That's a terrible idea. She shouldn't be anywhere near Shadoe without some of us there."

"I agree. I don't want you alone with him," Dov said, reaching for my hand.

"I've been alone with him this whole time. I'll be fine," I said softly, trying not to upset him. I knew Shadoe was a sore spot for Dov. I brushed my thumb over the top of his hand.

"But he's angry now."

"Isn't he always angry?" Reyla asked.

"I think that's called 'personality.'" Silas answered.

"What about Canton?" I redirected, glaring at Silas's joke.

"Well, we've been talking about that," Dov said, glancing at Silas. "We think Shadoe is right. We need Canton. If we can get our hands on him, we can use him against the Society to bring them down."

"Dov knows his way around inside Canton's mansion," Silas supplied, looking between Reyla and me. "He can create maps for us."

"They dragged me around enough while I was there," he said sheepishly, not wanting to discuss what had happened to him in Canton's possession. I'd have to ask him about it later. "There are ways we can get our people in."

"The trick is getting close enough to get in," Silas said.

"So what do we need to do?" Reyla asked, hand running through her hair. She leaned over and started brushing her fingers through mine, beginning to work it into an intricate design, needing something to occupy her.

"We're not sure yet. We really need to discuss most of this with Berwyn and Raselin." Dov hedged.

"But you have *something*?" I prompted.

"We have our people already planted in the city," he started. "And we're pretty sure Lowell has people planted as well…"

"He does, but not as many as you. At least, not that I know of. More like people he paid off and worked with. Shadoe probably knows more about that though."

"We're thinking maybe we could slip in. We could hide with our people and slowly start to, umm, replace the soldiers." He coughed, glancing down.

"Define 'replace,'" Reyla said.

"We would isolate a soldier or two and have our people inside the city hold them. We'd take their uniforms and pose as them for awhile," Silas informed us, looking as unsure as Dov.

"And then what?" I nudged Dov's foot with mine.

"Once we're all in place, we make our way to the mansion. We slip inside, try to avoid anyone who might figure out that we aren't really soldiers, and take over the soldier's duties inside the mansion," Dov finished.

"How do we get *inside* if we're the *outside* soldiers?" I asked.

"Turns out they rotate them every two weeks. If we're involved with the soldiers outside, we'll get rotated into the mansion. Once we're inside, we can get a hold of Canton and use him to control the soldiers.

"Once we rotate again, we can imprison the soldiers that we switched with. They won't think anything of being sent to the cells on their way back in. We'll lock them up and then pose as them again, with the end goal of using Canton in his position of power to bring down the Society." Dov grinned.

"And because no one will even realize the soldiers have been replaced by *our* people, no one will be the wiser." Silas looked between us, waiting for approval.

"So we quietly invade his precious mansion as his own men, and then coerce Canton into doing whatever we say, because no one will be there to stop us. Guys, this is brilliant."

"Can it really work?" Reyla hesitated.

"I think so," Dov replied. "I saw a lot while I was there. Canton dragged me all over that place. I might have acted a little more out of it than I really was."

Dov locked eyes with me.

"You were spying the entire time." I laughed. "I knew there was a reason I liked you."

"You like me for my charming personality." He smirked.

"And maybe a few other things too," I hinted.

"Reyla?" Silas interrupted.

"They already had their time together." Reyla shook her head jokingly. "Besides, I'm not done with her hair yet."

I hadn't even realized she was still braiding little pieces of my hair back, I was so absorbed in Dov's plan.

"We need to learn the layout of the mansion. Once our men are inside, we have to make it look like they know what they are doing. How much of it do you know, Dov?"

"Not everything, but enough to make it look good. Canton had me locked in different rooms. He was pretty paranoid that you all were coming for me."

"We were," Silas and Reyla said together. They glanced at me.

"I was dealing with a wall," I said in mock exasperation. "I got there eventually."

"Speaking of which, that *was* you that day, wasn't it? In the courtyard by the stage? I wasn't making that up, right?"

"No, that was me."

"I was pretty proud of you not running up to take another beating."

I always noticed how long Dov's lashes were when he was having meaningful discussions with me. They made me jealous. Everything about his eyes made me jealous.

"Yeah, well, they wouldn't let me. I tried," I teased back. "Devin had a pretty good grip on me at that point. I would have ended Canton had I made my way up there."

"Well, then I like this Devin guy."

"Have you met them yet?" I asked, glancing back at the door. "Devin and Justin and their sister, Talley?"

"Not really."

"I like them!" Silas says. "You'll like them too. I trust them."

"Oh I trust them. You left them to watch Auluria. I won't ever question them if you trusted them that much."

"I really did." Silas nodded. "But a lot of that came from Auluria's trust of them. She had a lot of faith in Raselin and his men."

"They've worked as hard as any of the teams I've worked with. Shadoe trusts them too, or at least as much as Shadoe trusts anyone," I added.

"How are we going to get Shadoe to go along with this?" Reyla picked up on his name.

"He wants to take down the Society. This is a good way to do it. He just has to understand that he can't try to go solo again. We all have to work together." Dov reached up to brush his hair out of his face, wincing when he reached high enough to tug on one of his injuries.

I started to lean forward to reach out to him, but that wasn't the place. He looked disappointed when I pulled back. I lowered my eyelids slowly, opening them back up to lock on him as I flirted from a distance. Brittella had taught me how to use my eyes to communicate when I was still in Lowell's care. Her lessons were paying off. His breath caught quietly as Silas smirked at his best friend.

"When are we going to tell *him* that?" Reyla brought up another good point.

"Soon," Dov said. "He's going to have to come back with us."

"We're going back?" I asked excitedly. I didn't know when I'd get to see any of my friends again with Shadoe's new rule. "When?"

"When Necesta says you can," Reyla cautioned. "And not before."

"Where is she?" I suddenly realized I hadn't seen her. "Talley said she was here and then you all showed up."

"Relax there, babe. She's outside with the others," Dov

said soothingly. He tried to keep from smiling, but his lips quirked up, making me fight my own smile.

"She said she would give us a few minutes once Devin told us you were doing better," Silas added. "We should probably let her in though."

Silas stood, offering his hand to Reyla to help her up. I reached out and took Dov's hand. He stayed in the chair.

"Fine." Silas laughed. "We'll get Necesta."

They walked to the door, opening it enough to slip out. Necesta walked in, beaming.

"I've been waiting awhile for this scene," she said, motioning me to lie down. "Now, dearie, what do we have here?"

"I'm feeling a lot better." I tried to look confident enough for her to release me from the room.

"I'm sure." She hushed me. "But that doesn't mean anything. Your man is back… You're on top of the moon right now."

She glanced at Dov. He smiled back. He would have no problem convincing her that he was fine. Probably.

"Have you been taking this?" She motioned to the bottle sitting on the table next to me.

"Yes, ma'am." My hair bunched next to my face as I tried to nod against the pillow.

"And you're standing and walking now?"

"I am," I confirmed.

"You two are a matching set," she said, looking from

Dov's arms to my legs, both hiding the scars with cloth-ing. "Now get out, I have to check over Goldilocks here."

Dov smirked, standing. I wanted to say he could stay and just turn around while she checked over my injuries, but I knew I shouldn't. He leaned down, carefully hiding his pain as he bent over, and kissed my hand that he was still holding.

"Soon," he whispered, meaning so many different things.

As soon as the door was closed, Necesta nodded for me to move the fabric of my skirt. She examined me, running her fingers over my damaged skin. I wound myself up so tightly to avoid reacting to her touch that she lectured me.

She made me stand and walk around the room. I did better than I thought I would. By the end of her overview, she gave me permission to walk around the storehouse. If I could handle functioning normally over the next few days, we could go back to the main storehouse and put our plan into action.

Dov's laughter was deep and careless as he leaned into me. I doubled over, folding into his shoulder as tears filled my eyes. The last time he had been this care free, we were dancing in his house, long before he ever found out Lowell had sent me to him.

Justin righted himself, wiping a tear. Devin slapped him on the shoulder, nearly choking as he laughed.

"You can't blame me for that, Necesta," Justin claimed. "I was seven, how was I supposed to know?"

"Oh, dearie, I can," the older woman said knowingly.

"Can we please talk about Devin?" Justin grumbled, feigning embarrassment.

"I'm not as amusing as you, baby brother," Devin rumbled, smirking.

Justin shot him a look, winking at him, hidden meaning in his actions. Devin looked affronted.

"I'm going to let that go because we are in the presence of ladies." Devin gestured to where Reyla and I sat. "Anyway, here comes Talley."

Talley sat down next to us, asking what we had been laughing about. Necesta briefly filled her in on the stories she had been telling us from their childhood.

"It's time," she said when we settled down. "We need to get back. This needs to happen."

We collectively sighed. Shadoe had avoided us the last two days as we created our own camp around the room that used to be my cage. Dov, Reyla, and Silas didn't leave my side as we worked on the maps of the mansion and strategized how to get in.

I glanced at Dov, trying to decide how he would take my next statement.

"I'll go talk to him."

Dov's hand on my wrist stopped me from standing up.

"*We* will talk to him." He said.

"You know he won't respond well to you. He's been waiting for you to confront him since you got here."

"Auluria, the only way I'll be talking to him is if you are present. Otherwise, I'll kill him." He said. He meant it.

"Auluria, he's going to have to deal with us one way or the other, and if it's not with the rest of you around, Dov and I can't promise he will come back in one piece." Silas shifted, as if getting ready to jump up and catch me if I tried to make an escape.

"He needs to see that we're a united front, Auluria." Dov added. "He's going to have to work with all of us to get through this, and when he does, it's you and me, together."

"But it's not, Dov. It's you and your family, and me and him. That was the deal. Like it or not, he and I have to work together on this. For now at least, these people are my people." I swung my arms around, motioning to the group. "I'm responsible for them. Shadoe and I are leading them together."

"Shadoe doesn't need you. We do." Dov nodded as if it would help me understand.

"No, Dov. You don't. Your people have you. They have your brother and Eden. They have Silas. They have so many good people watching out for them and leading them. You keep them safe.

"But these people… They don't have anyone. Shadoe is as blind as Lowell was in his ambition. He only sees the mission; he doesn't see the people.

"He's still thinking like Lowell. He stepped off Lowell's path to help me, but now that we're back on this side of the wall, he's right back on it–minus the revenge part, of course. He's going after the Society to bring them to their knees and he's willing to play whatever part he needs to in order to accomplish that.

"Be honest. Do you really think Shadoe is going to make the best choices here?"

Everyone shook their head. I prepared myself.

"I have to stay with him," I said. Dov looked like I had slapped him. "I have to help him lead until we bring down the Society. He won't listen to anyone else while he's still listening to Lowell. My cousin put him in charge *with* me, so I'm the only one who can keep him in check."

Dov stood, taking my hand. He pulled me into the tiny room where I had been recuperating and closed the door.

"Auluria, please," he begged. "We cannot trust him and we certainly can't leave you with him."

"We don't have a choice," I argued.

"There is always a choice," he disagreed. "We can keep him in check while you're with us. Berwyn and Raselin will help. It's two major factions against one. He has to work with us or the entire operation will fail. You don't *have to* be with him."

"Dov, you don't understand."

"What don't I understand?" he challenged, eyes flashing.

I stared at him, unsure of what to say.

"Has something changed, Auluria?" He finally broke the silence. "Is something different? Because you've been spending a lot of time with him since we were separated."

"That wasn't by choice," I lectured. "You're the one that sent me over the wall with him, Dov. I didn't want to go."

"I wasn't about to leave you to be captured." He argued, raking a hand through his hair.

"You should have let me stay with you," I said quietly. "We could have fought."

"We did fight. You rallied more troops and I spied on Canton."

"And nearly died because of it."

"Better me than you." He tipped his chin at me as if proving a point.

"Haven't we been here before?" I asked, exasperated.

"Like we never left." He was short with me.

It was apparently the only thing that hadn't changed

in our time apart. He looked the same, as did I, but scars covered everything we once knew.

"What are we supposed to do from here?" he asked quietly.

"I don't know."

"I trust you, you know that, right?" he asked, stepping forward. He took my hands in his. "This isn't about you, Auluria. I trust you. But I can't trust him; not after everything.

"I didn't want to leave you with him, but you know I knew you could protect yourself against him and you'd never be able to fight off all those Society men. I didn't want to leave you, but I couldn't see another way."

"I know." I couldn't tell if his hands felt familiar or foreign in mine as I answered.

"Please don't do this," he begged softly.

"I can't see any other way," I whispered, looking at the ground.

"Auluria."

His voice tore at my heart as I was breaking his.

I stepped closer to him, reaching up to kiss him. We stood, holding hands, my lips on his, trying to convince him to let me go, at least for now. I released my right hand and it climbed up his chest to his neck, pulling him harder against my face.

It hurt so much knowing that I had to walk away.

His free arm reached up, cradling my head. He was

nervous, I could feel it in the hand he kept in mine. I was nervous too.

Pushing him back, we stepped deeper into the room. Slowly he moved, bringing me with him. I didn't want to stop kissing him as he worked to convince me to stay.

His shoulder rose in surprise as he inhaled once I had stepped away. I moved quickly, leaving him frozen in place.

"I'm sorry. I'll come back to you," I promised, slamming the door. I turned to Silas who was as shocked as Dov had been. "Do not let him out of here, it's for his own good."

Dov was at the door, attempting to open it. Justin leapt to his feet, locking it.

"Do what she says," he commanded Silas.

"You know I have to do this," I pleaded with him.

"Silas," Reyla said quietly, urging him to help me.

He nodded once and I ran.

"Dov, she has to do this," I heard him trying to explain as Dov shouted through the door. I hoped he wouldn't hurt himself trying to get out.

I heard him begging Silas to go with me as I rounded the corner created by the long supply table. I hurried faster.

"Where is he?" I asked Marjorie.

"Who?" she snapped at me.

"Shadoe, where is he?" I asked, not slowing.

"I don't know."

"He's outside, Auluria," Anetta intervened from far enough away that I hadn't seen her.

Marjorie glared as I nodded to thank her. I turned, making my way outside. Speeding through the tunnel, I nearly crashed into Shadoe as I exited into the light.

"Go," I commanded the people surrounding him, finding my voice as their leader.

They shifted uncomfortably, looking to Shadoe.

"Now." I left the dangerous tone in my voice. I was Lowell's blood and I would not let them forget it.

They retreated without another question, wandering back inside the storehouse.

"We need to talk."

Shadoe crossed his arms, narrowing his eyes at me.

"You wanted me to lead, well, now I'm leading." I crossed my arms. "We have a plan, Shadoe, and you *will* listen to me.

"We're breaking into the Society and taking control of Canton."

"I'm listening," he finally agreed.

"Sit down," I said, nodding to a fallen tree.

"Lowell had contacts inside the city, right?" I waited for him to nod. "Do you know them? We need to use them."

"Yes, I know who they are."

"You need to contact them. We're going to reach out to the people the Baers have planted in the city too."

"Why?"

"We're sneaking into the city. We're going in a few at a time and hiding with our people. The goal is to quietly switch places with the soldiers and make our way to the mansion.

"Dov knows the layout of the building. He knows how to get us in. Once we're inside, we can get control of Canton and use him to play the Society. Shadoe, this is going to work."

"How do you propose we do this?" He questioned, looking skeptical.

"We've been working on the plan, but you and I have to go back and talk to Berwyn and Raselin about it."

He looked impressed that I had aligned myself with him.

"But we have to go soon—today or tomorrow if we can. We have to time it right so that we can sneak into the mansion."

"And where do our people fall into all this?" he asked.

"We're all going in. We'll send a large initial group to pose as soldiers. Once we're inside and we handle the other soldiers, we can bring everyone else in. The Society won't have any idea that we replaced their men."

"Where do you and I fit into this?" He pushed, face stone cold.

"I'm honoring my word, Shadoe. I'm here to help you and our people."

The smug look on his face only lasted a moment as Dov burst into the forest, Silas and Reyla following behind him. Justin and Devin joined them as Dov stalked over to us.

Shadoe slammed into the ground, the cracking sound from where Dov's fist collided with his jaw reaching me just as my own jaw fell.

"Dov!" I shouted, turning to see where Shadoe had landed.

"You will not touch her," Dov threatened quietly, as terrifying as his brother.

He leaned over the fallen tree to where Shadoe was lying. Shadoe lunged, kicking out at the tree, shaking it so hard that I was propelled off of it. It slammed into Dov's legs, moving him backward. I caught his arm and steadied us both.

Shadoe jumped to his feet, ready for a fight. I didn't know if Dov could withstand Shadoe in this condition. He still hadn't fully healed.

I eyed the claw that sat on Shadoe's hip, an ever-present reminder that he was willing to do whatever it took to succeed. It swung, catching the light as he stood.

I attempted to stand between them, but Dov reached around me and moved me off to the side. I pulled at him, hoping he would let me go.

"You will not touch her. You will not upset her. You will never be alone with her." Dov grew louder, listing his demands. "One of us will be with her at all times."

"You still don't get it, Baer," Shadoe sneered. "She is still not someone you can control."

"I'm not controlling her, I'm keeping *you* from hurting her or *any* of my people."

"This is why Lowell always had the upper hand on your kind." Shadoe stepped closer.

"Dov," I hissed, hoping it would cause him to back down.

"You live by the rules, Baer, but out here, there are no rules. The Society doesn't play by rules. Rules will get you killed."

"Rules will get *you* killed if you don't play by them, Shadoe. Auluria almost died because of your recklessness. I will not allow that to happen again."

"How will you stop me?" Shadoe taunted smugly.

Dov stepped forward, prompting Shadoe to look to me. He waited.

I had to choose.

I wasn't about to let Shadoe win, but I knew I had to side with him. I stepped in front of Dov so quickly he didn't realize I was moving. I kissed him longer than I should have, making it uncomfortable for anyone watching, before I stepped back to align myself with Shadoe.

His hands trailed after me, latching on as they moved

from my back, to my hips, down my elbows and arms, to my hands. We held each other, separated by a chasm, clinging to each other with Shadoe by my side.

"We're going to see Berwyn and Raselin." I turned my face toward Shadoe without breaking eye contact with Dov. "Get the group ready."

Chapter 15

IT WAS STRANGE TO SEE DOV STALKING THROUGH THE forest, still livid as we neared the storehouse that housed his people. He glared at Shadoe every few feet, making sure he kept his distance.

Reyla stayed next to me, frequently wrapping her arm around mine to keep step with me. She and Silas kept Shadoe from me, forcing him to the far end of the chain. The Hersh siblings and Necesta walked behind us, mixed with Shadoe's men. The rest of his team would be joining us a day later after they had packed.

Shadoe refused to let Necesta look him over after Dov attacked him. I think his pride was hurt more than

254

anything. His chin was swollen where he had taken the punch.

"Auluria," a friendly voice greeted me. I looked up to find Henry walking out from behind a tree where he was keeping his sparkling green eyes on things. "Nice to see you back. The girls will be thrilled."

His eye flitted between Dov and Shadoe and his face grew reserved. Shifting, he turned his shoulders, aligning himself with Dov. He nodded to Shadoe briefly, letting everyone know where his alliance rested.

"Anything you need?" he asked Dov, giving him a forced smile.

"No, Henry, thank you. Please let the others know the rest of Shadoe's men will be on their way shortly."

Henry nodded. I had a feeling Gregory, Ben, and Carter would be joining us shortly. He glanced at Silas before we walked past him.

Dov and Silas walked slightly heavier as we moved toward the storehouse entrance. It took me a moment to realize they were trying to cover the sound of Henry moving quickly away to enter the storehouse before we arrived through a secret entrance. He was going to warn Berwyn. I walked harder.

Once inside, Berwyn was waiting for us, arms crossed.

"You're back."

Eden walked up behind him, eyes moving from Shadoe, to Dov, to Silas before coming to rest on me. Apparently I was the one she wanted to telepathically communicate with. I moved my eyes to the side, letting her know something was going on with Shadoe.

"We have a plan, Berwyn," Dov said, pulling the maps out of the supply bag he was carrying them in. "We need to talk. Now."

Berwyn nodded, eager to hear what his kid brother had worked out. We all started to follow when he stopped us.

"Just him. Then you."

Dov hesitated, hovering in place for only a moment before following his brother, leaving Silas, Justin, and Devin a warning glance.

We walked through the tunnel to the main area, Eden leading the way. Reyla stayed close by my side, ensuring Dov's wishes were followed.

"What is this idea?" Eden said once we reached the main area.

Shadoe's men broke off, eager to find food. Talley went to find Lydia while Necesta made her way to Raselin to fill him in on the situation. Devin and Justin took positions very close to Shadoe, allowing Reyla to be my bodyguard as Silas oversaw the production.

"You're back!" A tiny voice shouted as it collided with

my legs. "Mommy said she didn't know if you were coming back, but I knew you were."

"Well, hello, Jasleen." I bent down to see her, scooping her up in my arms. "Your hair is so pretty today. Did Katarina help you with that?"

She giggled, running her hand through my hair. The boys watched me curiously as I bounced the little girl around and talked to her.

"Where is Dov?" she asked sheepishly.

"He's in a meeting with Berwyn."

"Why aren't you there?"

"I wanted to come see you, of course."

She caught sight of Silas and ducked her head into my shoulder, suddenly shy.

"Do you want to say hi?"

She shook her head against me, tossing her hair in my face. Silas laughed.

"Hi, Jasleen," he called softly.

She swooned against me as I tried to suppress a laugh. Reyla leaned over, grinning viciously.

"But we know who you like better," she teased just loud enough for the three of us to hear. "*Dov.*"

Reyla stretched out his name, sending Jasleen into a fit of giggles as her tiny fists balled in my hair. She shook her head violently, begging Reyla to stop, grinning against my shoulder.

"Oh, I see. Somebody thought she could steal my man while I was gone, did she?" I asked quietly.

Even Shadoe looked amused as I looked up to catch the others smirking at what we had done to the little girl. She giggled as I set her down, letting her run off to her mother.

"What did you say to her?" Silas asked once she was gone.

"Nothing," Reyla and I replied in unison, as innocently as we could.

"Oh, please," Eden scoffed. "She's been pining over Dov since he got back."

They all looked at her in surprise.

"Since he *got back*?" Reyla yelped, making us turn back to her. "She's been obsessed with him since the day she decided she wanted to be Auluria when she grew up.

"No offense, Silas." She winked at him, taking away the sting of falling in second place. She looked to the other men standing with us. "Don't worry boys, I'm sure she'll find a place in her heart for you all too. Or maybe some of her friends will adopt you as their crushes. It's amazing how crushes race through the little ones."

Reyla and I giggled as male eyes grew wide. Eden laughed only long enough to change the subject.

"Speaking of which, I think it's time Auluria and I had a little talk."

She guided me away from the group, Reyla keeping a

watchful eye on Shadoe as she moved out to find our friends. Justin and Devin stayed by his side, leaving Silas to be a little less obvious about his surveillance.

"Speak," Eden instructed once we were alone.

"Hello to you too, Eden. Nice to see you again."

The look she gave me so deeply resembled her husband's that I knew she had been spending far too much time with him. Her hands found her hips as she jutted one out to emphasize her point of who was in charge.

I quickly recounted everything that had happened from the time I left her until we walked in the door, giving her as many details about Dov's place as I had. She listened intently, making comments as I talked, her blonde hair bobbing as she nodded.

"Once we have Canton, then what? What is our plan?" she asked. "Even with all three of our groups working together, are we really going to be able to control the entire Society?"

"If we do it strategically, I think we can, yes," I said carefully.

"But what if we can't?"

"Do we have a choice?" I shrugged. "This is the best we've got, Eden."

"So, we capture Canton, use him against the Society, somehow manage to control the soldiers in the entire country, and then live happily ever after?" Eden mocked.

"Those of us who make it, I suppose. I can't imagine we'll all live through this." My realistic side, well groomed by Shadoe, made an appearance.

"And those of us that *do* survive... What do they do?" she inquired.

"They run the government, I guess. No more dictatorships. They handle our enemies on the other side of the walls. We already know we have to free Raselin's people, so that will be the first thing.

"They'll need to train our people," I continued. "And free the camps. We'll have to have something in place to help the people trapped in the camps."

Eden's face grew dark, brows furrowing as one of her curls fell in her face. She blinked several times, processing something.

"What if we didn't free the camps after?" she asked, to my horror.

"What?"

Her head snapped up to me.

"What if we didn't free the camps after we defeat the Society?" She grinned wickedly. "What if we got them out before?"

I inhaled sharply. *What if we did?*

"Think about it...the boys are sent to camps to learn to fight and then sent off to war. They would be incredible assets to us. The girls could learn to fight or do things around the country to be assets to us. Auluria, this could be huge! You know how many camps there are."

Her eyes were animated as her hands flew through the air while she was speaking. Excitement overtook us as both a brilliant idea and one of her revenge plans fell into place. She had wanted to destroy the camps for a long time.

"We can't force them to fight for us." I shook my head. "We have to give them the option of how they help us. These kids and people they send to the camps haven't asked for any of this. We free them, but they have the option of helping us bring down the Society that did this to them or not. We have to let them choose or we're no different than Canton and the Society."

She dimmed a little, but understood my words.

"We're not them," she agreed. "But they'll want to help. If we can take down the Society, then we can take down our enemies, and then we'll all truly be free."

"We need to talk to the boys." I gave us direction.

"Right." She grabbed my hand and pulled me back toward where Berwyn was meeting with Dov.

Arin let us pass without question as we approached. Berwyn and Dov were deep in conversation, looking over the maps Dov had created of Magistrate Canton's mansion. Dov sat in a chair as Berwyn towered over the table where the maps sat.

"We need to free the camps," Eden said, not taking

the time to announce our entrance. She walked up to the table and slammed a pointed finger on one of the maps.

"We will, Eden," Berwyn assured her.

"No, we need to do it now."

"We'll free them as soon as we have the Society under control. We can't give away our plan this early. The Society can't know we're working together or how strong our numbers are."

"Do you really think we have enough men to control this entire country, even if we follow this plan, Berwyn? It's a good plan, but we have to have every advantage."

"If we free the camps," I added quietly, "don't you think most of those men and women will want to join us?"

"Eden, Auluria, the Society will know if we free the camps. There is no coming back from that. Right now we will be able to slip in and not draw too much suspicion. We have to do this now," Berwyn said gently, trying to convince his wife it was better to wait.

"What if," Dov said, drawing out his words, "we get into the mansion and gain control of Canton, get all of our people on the inside, and then handle the camps before we take on the rest of the Society?"

Everyone paused to think through the implications. In theory, it was a solid plan.

"That way we don't lose our ability to rule through

Canton, but we still have the numbers to back us up when it's time for the real battle." I concluded.

"That could work…" Berwyn turned back to the maps, moving them to uncover the Society maps below. He charted the locations as Dov stood to join us, hovering over the pages.

We spent an hour working out patterns, deciding what the most strategic order to free the camps would be before we sent for Raselin and Shadoe. They, and a select group of their top people, joined us in the small room.

Shadoe forced his way in after Raselin, making his way to my side. Eden and Dov stood across the table watching as I was pinned between Shadoe and Berwyn. Silas slipped in, taking his post by Dov and Eden.

Raselin, the Hersh siblings, Reed, Fitch and Lydia, and Nian rounded out the far end of the table as everyone leaned in to see. Berwyn pointed out locations and Dov took charge, explaining the plan to everyone. Shadoe and Raselin each took turns challenging pieces until they were satisfied, tweaks being made to what we had worked on without them.

Eventually, we all stepped away to consult with our teams in private. Raselin led his men out before Shadoe and I followed, his men behind us. We convened down the hall, dark shadows falling across our faces from the lights on the walls.

Shadoe made comments. I responded. Everyone else

complied. After a few moments, we decided to agree with the Baers' plan, as if it hadn't been a given.

"We have to get into the city unnoticed. Our men will hide with the people Lowell planted in the city. We can bribe the rest of his contacts, although they may be willing to join us to avoid having to work under the Society for much longer." Shadoe nodded to each of us. "We need to move immediately. It will take a week to sneak us all in."

"We should get started," Nikko said. Shadoe glanced at him.

"Should we establish the order we send our men in before we go back to the leadership?" Sherman asked.

"Yes," Shadoe acknowledged them. "We need everything in order before we go back."

I had a feeling I wasn't going to like where that ended.

The first wave of people had already left. The second wave would be following. A third group remained in the storehouse, prepared to join us inside the city once we had taken over Canton's stronghold. I dropped the curtain, moving away from the window before I was lectured. Dov would arrive soon enough.

Shadoe had insisted we go with the first group of

rebels, finding shelter in the house of a man Lowell once traded with. He left the residences of our trusted contacts for our lesser-skilled fighters. Should any of the contacts we bribed turn on us, Shadoe would deal with them swiftly.

Ella turned to me, ready for an argument.

"I know." I cut her off.

"Leave her be, Ella." Anetta snapped, walking in the door. "I brought us food."

She shed the gray jacket the Society soldiers wear, dropping it on the back of a chair. Shadoe followed behind her. He placed a Society weapon on the table accompanied by a knife with barbed edges, like the back of a fish with a prickly spine. Definitely not Society issued.

I joined them at the table, happy to see food. I picked up the bread, ripping a piece off. Anetta glanced at me before looking down. She seemed to be warming up to me after all this time. Marjorie still glowered from a corner.

"Tomorrow we're moving to the mansion. We have to make sure everything is ready," Shadoe explained, joining in eating. "Is everything in order here?"

"Yes," Ella responded, not giving details.

"Ella and I will go on patrol when we're done here," I said, taking another bite of the bread.

"I will not. I've already been on patrol today. We're

not supposed to go back out until tomorrow," she protested, looking to Shadoe for support.

"I'll go back out," Anetta volunteered. "It's better than sitting around here all night. I don't like being cooped up like this."

She waved her hand around the house. Lowell had trained his fold to be mobile, constantly moving from location to location. It's what made it so hard for the Society to catch us. Staying inside houses for prolonged periods of time was suffocating to some of these people.

"Anetta and I will go," I said before Shadoe could protest.

He grumbled but knew he couldn't argue with me in front of everyone. When we were finished with our food, we slipped back into the Society uniforms we had stolen and stepped outside.

I tugged the cold weather hood up over my hair, concealing my long mane. Anetta did the same, tucking her short hair back so it wouldn't be noticed.

"Which way do you want to go?" I asked, walking out onto a main street.

"Whichever way we need to go to meet him," she said casually.

"What?" I questioned, turning to her. "Meet who?"

"You don't think I know you're out here looking for your boyfriend?" She warned me not to question her. "I saw you watching out the window as we walked up. "It's been two days and you're pining."

I stared at her and she started to walk.

"Which way?" Anetta demanded.

I guided us left, hoping I was correct. I didn't know where Dov was, or even if I'd see him, but if he was coming through, it would be in this direction. She kept step with me.

"Does he care about you?" she finally asked.

"Yes."

"It's more than Lowell ever did for me, so I say don't let it go." Her voice was quiet, as if reluctant to admit it.

"I don't intend on letting him go." I smiled, making her smile back.

"I'm sorry I ignored you back then," she admitted. "I shouldn't have done that. I was wrapped up in your cousin and you were just another thing to take his attention away from me."

"I never understood why you competed for his attention," I divulged. "He really wasn't worth it."

"No, he wasn't. But what girl doesn't want to be seen that way by the most important man she knows?" She made her point. "Speaking of…"

She pulled me off to the side of the street, a precaution in case it wasn't our people joining us. Only a few Society men roamed the streets, the last of the second wave of our men would replace them soon. We walked together with intentionality, hoping we wouldn't be questioned.

A small group approached us, not wearing uniforms. They drew closer, detail starting to take form. It would have been easy for Shadoe to have stopped the oncoming group and question them, adding credibility to our deception. As women, we had to remain quiet to avoid suspicion.

The group kept their heads down, huddling on the far side of the road. One chanced a look, eyes raking across us for information so quickly I wasn't sure I had seen it.

"Justin," I said when my brain had processed what I had seen.

He stopped, recognizing my voice. The group halted, waiting for us to cross the street and join them. Reed grinned as we stepped in front of them.

"Do you know where you're going?" I asked quickly, knowing we couldn't stay long.

"Yes, we're near you… one street over. Berwyn has a family there that will take us in. Why are you out here?" Justin questioned.

"We're patrolling," I explained.

"He's not here," Justin said quietly when he noticed Anetta looking around. I wanted to smack her.

"Where is he?" she asked, not bothering to hide what she was doing.

"Dov is in the next group," Nian said, moving his hair.

I should have insisted he fix that before we started the mission.

A branch cracked. We turned, realizing someone was approaching. Justin's team darted into the trees. I grabbed Anetta's arm and propelled her forward. We walked down the road, faces tipped down. The team would be fine in the trees until the people had passed by. I was tempted to look back once the man walked by us, but resisted.

The road was quiet for the next ten minutes, each moment slowly dragging by. I counted leaves as they fell, turning the deep colors of the forest in fall. Each noise frightened us as we reigned ourselves in to keep from being noticed.

Two figures approached us, casually walking the road. Leave it to Dov and Silas to remain nonchalant in a time of crisis. They both nodded as they passed by, stopping only after they had walked by us, realizing it was me.

"You're safe," Dov said, breaking from his act.

"So far," I replied with a smile.

"Is everything going according to plan?" Dov asked, staying business-oriented even as his hand slipped around my wrist.

"Yes. We're just waiting for the last of you tonight, and in the morning, we'll breech the mansion. Shadoe acquired some extra weapons for us. He's been getting them to the men that are already here. He will give the rest out tomorrow."

"Nasty looking things," Anetta commented.

"But effective, I'm sure." Silas knew how Shadoe operated.

"Do you know where you're going?" I asked Dov.

"Yes, we've got another mile to go, but we'll catch up with you tomorrow at the mansion. You and Shadoe are going to meet us in the study once we get there, right?"

"We'll be there," I confirmed.

Dov looked over my shoulder. I stiffened before slowly turning. Society men were about to discover us. With no time to hide the boys, I pushed Dov around, facing away from the men. With his hand behind his back, I nudged the back of his knee, indicating he should fall.

Anetta saw what I was doing and reached for Silas. Slightly confused, she had to kick his knee out for him to understand.

"Be our voices." I hissed at them, knowing Society soldiers could not sound like women.

Dov and Silas slipped into commanding roles, shouting for themselves to get on the ground as if our roles were reversed. They were about to get their Society uniforms much quicker than expected.

"Get on the ground!" Dov yelled as he pretended to struggle against me.

"I said cooperate…and maybe we won't try you for treason!" Silas echoed back, effortlessly straining against Anetta.

Dov threw his elbow back, nearly catching me by surprise. I ducked just in time, missing the painful blow, but Dov made a gasping sound as if I had been hit. Silas wrenched around, making it look like an escape attempt.

We heard the men running over the noise of the fake brawl, attempting to assist us. I tossed a look over my shoulder in the dwindling light for good measure.

"You there, help us," Dov lured the Society men to our aid.

The men shouted, raising their weapons.

"Put those away and help us," Silas shouted.

As they approached, Anetta and I realeased our grip on the men and turned on the soldiers. I threw my elbow into one's face, crunching something. Kicking out, I connected with his stomach, doubling him over. From above, I brought my hand down on the back of his shoulder, making him fall to the ground.

Quickly, I dropped to my knees, touching the sensitive part of his neck that rendered him unconscious. When I turned, Dov stood, his face a mixture of shock and pride. I stepped over and helped Anetta knock the second soldier out.

"Well, gentlemen, I think we found your uniforms for this little event." I grinned.

"I think we have." Dov smiled back.

We helped lift the unconscious bodies to the side of the road, stepping back into view of anyone who was watching to block the scene as Dov and Silas swapped outfits with the men. Once the change was complete, we helped tie the men up to be taken to the house where Dov and Silas would be staying. If anyone saw, four Society soldiers were taking prisoners for questioning. We gagged the men to prevent them from talking.

I walked alongside Dov as he led one of the disguised soldiers down the street. Anetta walked beside Silas. If we were approached, we would let them speak.

We stayed silent as we moved, avoiding conversation to prevent the Society men from learning anything from us. When we arrived, they stopped on the street, allowing me to approach the house so we didn't scare the owner. Dov and Silas weren't meant to be dressed in Society uniforms yet, nor should they have prisoners.

I knocked on the door, waiting for the owner to greet me. I gave the signal, indicating we were on the same team, and waited for him to step back.

"Well, it's about time," Fitch said from the back of the house.

"Fitch," I said, smiling. "Is Lydia here too?"

"Back here." A hand waved from behind a counter as she climbed out of the cabinet she was hiding in.

I turned, waving the rest of my group in. They

hurried up the path and into the house, making sure no one was watching us. We explained what had happened.

"Well, at least you won't have to go back out tonight to find uniforms." Fitch smirked as his eyes made their way over to the soldiers tied up on the middle of the floor where Silas and Dov had dropped them. "I guess we should put these two away."

He stood, grabbing each man by an arm, and lifted them into the air. Lydia's eyes grew wide in appreciation of her husband. She winked at me, making me giggle.

Fitch locked the men in a cellar below the house, concealed in the floorboards so no one could easily find it. The family that Berwyn had planted here would watch them while we ran our mission to the mansion the next day.

"You were great today," Dov said when we found a moment alone in the corner. "You knew just what to do."

"Well, I tried." I giggled.

"You saved us…again, Auluria." He inched closer. "You never cease to amaze me."

"We need to find time to talk, Dov." I grew serious. "We can't keep going like this."

"I know," he whispered back. "Soon. Once we get into the mansion, we'll find time to talk and get all of this figured out."

He reached up and brushed a strand of my hair back.

"Besides, Goldilocks, we have a few other things to discuss too."

I batted his hand away at that name.

"Why haven't you forgotten about that yet?"

"Everyone has told me about that, Auluria. Did you really think it's not burned into my brain?" he teased as I rolled my eyes. "Besides, it suits you. *Goldilocks.*"

I gave up trying to suppress my smirk and stepped closer to touch his hair. He froze, waiting for me to move.

"Speaking of the whole 'golden girl' and 'golden boy' thing… Did you hear about Marty?"

"About Shadoe taking his hand off for touching you?" Ice crept into his words. "It's about the only thing I can think of to redeem him."

His hand wrapped around my wrist as I played with his hair.

"Are you okay after all that?" His eyes pierced into me, searching every inch of my soul for an answer.

"I'm okay. We need to talk about it though." I moved my finger around a wave of his hair, making his eyes flutter. "But for now I'm fine. I'm not hurt, so it can wait until after."

"Okay," he agreed, nodding his head. "I know this is going to be a battle, but I promise, we will find time to reconnect. I know we need to go through everything we've been through."

"I don't want any of this to come between us."

"We have enough working against us as it is, but we won't let all of this be one of those things. We'll get through this. Besides, if Silas and Reyla have it their way, we won't be apart for very long."

"Of course not. We really need to find Silas something else to do with his free time." I laughed.

Dov chuckled, his face lighting up.

"Reyla too."

"Reyla is still in mourning, we can forgive her on this one." I paused. *"For a bit."*

Dov laughed, as loud and free as we had in his house before he found out I was working with Lowell and Shadoe. I stepped into his arms, holding him. He felt good; he felt safe.

I inhaled, every feeling I had while we were apart came flooding back. He wrapped himself around me, protecting me. When he pulled back, he rested his forehead on mine.

"I'm not giving up on us," he promised. "Not after all this."

"Good," I murmured.

"And you're both making me sick." Anetta stomped across the room. "Time to go, Auluria."

She flipped her hood over her head and put her hand on the doorknob. I turned back to Dov.

"See you tomorrow?" I asked, running a finger down his jaw to his chin.

"See you tomorrow," he confirmed. "Will you be okay out there?"

He knew better than to ask to walk me. We couldn't afford to have him out there any more than necessary tonight. He also knew Anetta and I could take care of ourselves if need be.

Instead, he walked me to the door. I waved goodbye to everyone and stepped into the darkness.

Chapter 16

WE WAITED IN THE COURTYARD AS SOLDIERS PASSED US. Each one of their steps felt like a nail being pounded into a board next to us, inching closer. My soul wanted to jump with each slam of their feet, but I willed myself still. Even Shadoe's training had not prepared me for this anxiety.

The men emptied out of the mansion, walking past us to the streets to their patrols. Our lines slowly started filing into the gates, branching out in different directions. Our men made their way to their posts, attempting to make it look as though they were doing their jobs for Magistrate Canton. I was near the front, only a few dozen men in front of me.

Stepping inside was like being captured again. Every feeling I had had when I was brought before Canton the first time washed over me. Shadoe had no idea the terror that grasped me inside these walls. He made his way quietly over to me from his position a few lines away.

"This way," he mumbled softly.

We branched off, following the hallways Dov had marked for us on a map. Up a flight of stairs, we took a right, entering into one of the Great Rooms in the mansion. Red, like the robes he wore during our sentencing, filled the space. I almost wanted to stop and admire the tapestries and banners hanging from ceiling to floor, but I remembered why we were there.

The only men we saw along the way were our own as they hurried to find their stations. Dov had carefully chosen a route for us that would avoid the main areas that Canton might be occupying upon our arrival. Neither of us trusted Shadoe not to change the plan.

Footsteps echoed along the hallway as we drew closer to the study where we were meeting the other leaders. Raselin nodded to us as he slipped in the door down the hall. Shadoe and I approached cautiously, making sure no one was around to see us follow him inside.

Raselin stood in the room alone, weapon in hand. Shadoe and I swept the room, ensuring no one was there to hinder our success. Fitch tentatively stepped inside, only relaxing once Raselin nodded to him that everything was fine.

Eden's blonde curls gave her away as she entered. She took a position by me as we waited in silence. She tucked her hair back under her hood.

Silas and Berwyn arrived a few minutes later, having been toward the back of our lineup of men and women. They nodded to Raselin and Shadoe before coming to stand by Eden.

"Anything?" Berwyn asked quietly.

Most of us had been sent in different directions, an attempt at ascertaining where Canton was at that given moment. We all shook our heads.

"Hopefully Dov found something."

As if on cue, Dov bounded in the door, closing it behind him. He put a finger to his lips, warning us. He tipped his ear back toward the door, pressing it against the frame to listen. I watched his shoulders move as he breathed, waiting for him to tell us it was safe.

Berwyn started to lean forward, ready to move to the door for answers if Dov didn't release us soon. Raselin and Fitch traded nervous glances while Shadoe's fingers inched toward his knife. Realizing the Baers didn't have Shadoe's new toys yet, I held my hand out, collecting them from him while we waited.

Finally, Dov released us. Every shoulder in the room

lowered an inch in relief. Walking to Dov and Berwyn, I held out the new knives.

"Shadoe found them. Just go with it," I instructed, handing them the weapons.

"He's in the weapons room," Dov reported.

"Of course he is," Berwyn groaned.

"As if the day weren't hard enough," Raselin echoed his sentiments.

"He has a few men with him. We're going to have to neutralize them," Dov added.

"We'll hit hard and fast," Shadoe said, pushing his way into the conversation. "They won't see us coming. We'll need to get Canton isolated and then we can interrogate him."

"We can't hurt him, Shadoe," Berwyn instructed. "The people will have to see him. He can't be injured or they will know something is wrong."

"I'm aware, Baer," Shadoe sneered. "That doesn't change the fact that we need information."

"We'll get it." Raselin tried to calm everyone. "Let's just focus on getting him under our control. We can focus on getting information later."

"We need to focus on it now," Shadoe protested. "If we can't hurt him, we have to make him fear us. This is a man who is willing to sell out his own people to protect himself. If he thinks he can find help when we let him address people, or address the Society, than he will take whatever chance he gets."

"He's right." I take a deep breath. "We can never control Canton unless there is a reason for him to do what we say. If he thinks he can win, he will try anything. He has to know the only way he survives this is if he plays along."

"Auluria and I will take care of that," Shadoe announced.

I look to him, unsure what he meant. He refused to look at me.

"Leave it to us. Now," he continued before anyone could stop him, "we need to go. We know where he is. This is the time to strike."

Standing outside the weapons room door was like waiting for my aunt to die—painful and unending. She fought with every breath to stay alive and it seemed as though the door before us was prepared to fight to stand its ground too.

Silent breaths filled the air as we waited, listening for the proper moment to break in. From what we could tell, six men were with Canton. We assumed they were high-level soldiers.

We all came to life when Dov turned back to us, ready to signal our entrance. Fear prickled through me, rushing through my veins. Eden brushed against me as she leaned forward on her toes.

Dov motioned for us to prepare ourselves. Counting down, Fitch burst through the door, surprising everyone inside. Canton wheeled around, his red robe dusting the floor. Shock flashed over his face until he recognized Dov.

"Kill them," he instructed his men. "But not the girl."

His men looked to me, recognizing me as we attacked. Dov and Berwyn worked as a team, taking on the brunt of the attack. I heard an arm break, the soldier's scream filling the room, as I engaged with a man at Shadoe's side.

"Silas," Eden warned her partner over the noise of the fight.

I blocked the soldier who swung a knife at me, striking so fast he didn't have time to protect himself. He doubled over as Shadoe kicked him hard enough to knock him out.

We moved to help Fitch and Raselin as they battled two strong soldiers. The first was no match for Fitch as he slammed him into a wall, knocking the ax he had pulled from the wall display out of his hand. The second man reached for something along the weapons room displays, throwing it toward Raselin. A knife buried itself into his upper arm, causing him to cry out in pain.

"Look out!" Dov shouted, warning one of us. A spear flew past me, landing in a display of what I could only assume was something that was meant to restrain people during torture. It clattered into it, knocking the display down.

Metal crashed to the floor, bouncing in all directions as Fitch pushed the soldier back into the displays against the wall. I wheeled around to see who needed help as Shadoe helped Raselin.

"Don't move," Eden said, her words precise and calculated. She held her knife out at Canton, circling slowly like a wolf looking at its enemy.

He laughed nervously.

"Now, now, Mrs. Baer. Do you really think you hold any power here?" He held up his hands as if trying to appease an upset child.

"I do," she answered. Berwyn shifted to glance at her.

"There's..." He scanned the room quickly. "Oh, Mrs. Baer, there's only eight of you here. I don't know how you got in, but you certainly have no chance of making it out of here alive. Even if you do hold me hostage, my men far outnumber you."

"That's where you're wrong, Canton." Dov called from across the room. "You're men aren't here."

Another snap followed by a loud cry and a painful whimper signified the last of his soldiers losing control to us. Canton looked around nervously.

"You've won for the moment, but moments only last so long, young Baer."

Fitch moved to pick up the shackles that had been thrown to the floor during the struggle. We had brought rope to tie them with, but it seemed less effective now. We began binding the soldiers, chaining them to the heavy pieces of equipment in the corners. Raselin, Fitch and Shadoe moved everything around them, isolating each man in a separate place.

"Here." Canton held out his hands. "I surrender."

His self-preservation skills were on par with the skills of his torturer: unquestionable.

Eden, Silas, Dov, Berwyn, and I surrounded him, forming a half circle in front of him. He eyed us, waiting for us to strike. His face changed when he noticed Berwyn.

"The great Berwyn Baer. We meet at last." He chuckled, tormenting Berwyn. "As you know, I've met your *beautiful* wife and kid brother…"

Berwyn stepped forward, ready to hit him.

"No, Baer." Shadoe's voice cut through the room as viciously as his barbed knife had through one of the soldier's arms. "It's my turn."

Shadoe stepped toward us, daring Berwyn to fight him.

"Out. Auluria and I have work to do." He challenged Berwyn and Dov to argue. "Stand guard."

Raselin nodded, walking over to put a hand on Berwyn's arm.

"Let him," he whispered. "Let him do what we cannot."

Berwyn hated backing down, his temper radiating across his movements in stiff, angry motions. Silas turned Eden, convincing her to go. Berwyn followed her out.

"Don't hurt him," Dov warned Shadoe before leaving. He held my gaze, asking me to walk out with him.

When the room was empty of anything but Canton's men chained to walls, Shadoe stepped forward. Canton sat in the center of the room, fiddling with the shackles Fitch had placed on his wrists before he left. His legs tangled in his robe, making him sit awkwardly while he watched us.

I waited for Shadoe to give me an indication of what we would be doing since he couldn't torture Canton. After a long time—an intimidation tactic he used to throw Canton off—he nodded to one of the soldiers. He was the least injured of all the men, sitting directly to Shadoe's right.

My heart raced as Shadoe took careful steps toward the man, maintaining eye contact with the magistrate.

"Up." He instructed the man.

He scrambled to his feet, stooping because the chain holding him in place wasn't long enough to stand upright.

"Not a sound." Shadoe whispered in the man's ear, but I knew his words were for me as he held my gaze.

The man whimpered as Shadoe brought his knife up the side of his arm, quietly brushing the metal against his skin to terrify him. I waited for Shadoe to draw blood, slicing off a layer of his arm. I knew Canton had to be as mortified as I was, but the thin layer of skin never fell to the floor, because, instead, Shadoe suddenly raised the knife to the man's throat and slowly dragged it across.

Blood pooled out in a dripping line. Canton gasped but I couldn't look away. It felt like a year before Shadoe dropped the man to the ground, sliced so deeply that I couldn't save him.

I gaped, shoulders shaking in horror.

"Not a word," Shadoe instructed before striding over to Canton.

My eye stayed on the dead soldier until I realized how dangerously close Shadoe had moved next to Canton.

"Shadoe!" I prayed my voice would halt him. Instead, it spurred him on.

He walked within feet of the man. Canton cowered to the ground, holding a shaking hand out to protect himself as the other soldiers gasped in fear for their leader. Shadoe watched him closely. He stopped quickly, convincing both of us that Canton was about to suffer.

Whipping a hand out, he threw his knife at the man across the room. Canton paled even more as he realized the knife had been thrown over his shoulder at one of his men. He blanched as the guard toppled over, the others crying out, begging for leniency.

Before I could reach him, Shadoe lashed out again, knives flying so quickly I didn't have time to look back from the target before the next had struck. All six men bled from chests, abdomens or faces.

Canton nearly passed out, the only thing reviving him was Shadoe's hand as he struck him.

"Oh no, you don't get to leave yet," Shadoe said. He knelt down to whisper instructions in his ear.

A man stirred; a survivor.

I rushed to him. Knowing not to pull out the blade, I tore off my uniform jacket and wrapped it around, attempting to slow the bleeding. I grappled for the beads around my neck, praying it would save him, or at least give him the ability to last until Necesta could help.

I heard Shadoe in the background as I spoke to the man, telling him what I was doing. Canton whimpered, squirming at Shadoe's proximity as he told him what happened to Justice Kenton and his other men in our custody.

"Yes, yes, I understand!" he yelped, surprising me. I jumped, knocking into the man.

It was as if I was breathing again, oxygen filling my lungs as I realized the carnage I sat in. A man was dying in my hands. Five others lay as sacrifices to our mission in the mere minutes the rest of the team had been outside.

"Berwyn!" I screamed, still holding onto the bloody mess of a man at my feet.

The door slammed opened, Dov racing inside. The others entered behind him, pausing to see the horror that had befallen the room. Six sets of eyes blinked, processing the scene.

"How?" Berwyn asked slowly, not sure if he could trust his eyes.

"I need help." I pocketed the necklace until I could put it back on, Silas rushing to my side as Dov and Berwyn approached Shadoe with Raselin and Fitch backing them up.

"Eden," I begged, nodding for her to check the other men. She scrambled forward, nearly tripping over herself to rush to them.

"Help me," I said quietly to Silas as the men argued in the center of the room. "We have to stop the bleeding."

Silas pushed down as the man groaned.

"Where is Necesta?" I asked, hoping she was nearby.

The man started to gurgle, and Silas shook his head.

"Go," he whispered, not wanting me to see the end.

I refused, staying where I was. Eden checked the man behind Silas, obviously not finding anyone alive.

"Eden." Silas's voice carried just enough to get her attention.

When she arrived, he nodded to me. Eden glanced at the dying man, realizing what our friend wanted. She dragged me away with the same force she used rescuing Dov. I couldn't escape as she forced me to the back of the room.

I watched Canton's back as he trembled in front of the men. Dov eyed me but held his ground in front of Canton and Shadoe. A battle of wills played out, but in the end, we could not change the fates of the dead men in the room.

Silas joined us and overwhelming sadness hit me so hard I couldn't catch my breath. Silas and Eden took my hands in theirs, comforting me.

Berwyn nodded to Fitch, who stepped forward and lifted Canton to his feet, a sobbing mess. He nodded at every instruction, doing exactly what he was told to do. He flinched when Shadoe looked at him.

I didn't realize I had tears streaming down my face until they were gone, Berwyn, Raselin, and Shadoe following behind Fitch. Dov rushed over to us, dropping to his knees in front of me.

"Auluria." He wrapped me in his arms, pulling me to his chest as I cried.

I sensed Eden squirming, uncomfortable with emotions. Dov let me cry and I soon found myself mourning more than just the loss of the man who I couldn't save.

When I looked up, tears were in Dov's eyes too. I reached out to hold him again, wrapping my arms tightly around his neck. He murmured soft things in my ear as I looked between Eden and Silas, realizing it was the first time we had been together like this since the last time we were in Canton's dwelling.

I rose, Dov standing with me. Reaching out, I pulled Silas to my side. Eden wrinkled her nose, questioning my change in demeanor.

"We beat him," I said softly, eyes drifting from Silas, to Eden, to Dov.

When it clicked, Eden joined us, her body language changing completely. She put a hand on Dov's shoulder before both of the boys pulled her in.

"We did." Dov grinned. We had beaten Canton. We had all survived.

"But now the real work begins," Silas reminded us. "We survived him once, but now we have to survive the Society."

"And whatever torture we endured here before will be nothing compared to what we're about to go through," Eden added harshly.

"Are we ready for this?" I asked, refusing to relinquish my hold on Dov and Silas.

"We have to be," Eden said.

"We have Canton now," Dov reminded us. "Whatever Shadoe did, he is now in control. I'd say we have a pretty good chance of getting through at least the next part of this."

"We should go make sure they gave our men the signal to sweep the grounds," I commented, realizing we had left Berwyn, Raselin, Fitch, and Shadoe to handle everything.

"She makes a point." Silas nodded to Dov, smirking.

"Indeed, she does." He smiled at his friend before ducking his head back to me.

"Oh get over yourselves." Eden pushed Dov, releasing herself from the circle. He crashed into me, sending us stumbling back.

Silas was concerned for a second until we got our footing before he laughed at us.

"*She's* got a point *too*."

"You're just giving me more incentive to find you a girlfriend, Silas," I teased. "If you've been reduced to agreeing with Eden, then it's definitely time to find you new people to hang out with.

"Shut up." Eden shook her head at me and tried to glare, not quite convincingly enough. Eden was starting to lose her ability to stay icy toward me.

Dov wrapped his arm around my waist and we walked toward the door.

Canton slouched in the corner, wrapping his arms around his legs pressed tightly against his chest. Like a cornered rabbit, his eyes darted from one person to the next, assessing their threat level.

We ignored him as Talley reported back to us. Our people had made it inside, neutralizing the few soldiers that remained on the grounds. They patrolled the area, ensuring Canton had no friends to save him. We took turns peering over to make sure he wasn't trying anything, though the chains on his wrists and feet gave us a certain assurance.

"We'll keep him quiet for a few days. No one will think anything of it if they don't see him for three days," Berwyn said, formulating a plan.

"And after that?" Raselin asked, wondering what we would use the man for to convince people he was acting of his own free will.

"After that, he will have his own personal guard helping him." Berwyn nodded to Shadoe. "You can never be too careful these days, especially with all the rebels breaking out of prison."

"Berwyn?" I realized something. "Do you think they'll question that? I mean, Canton has lost *all* of us...more than once. The only one he actually managed to stop was Lowell. He lost Dov *twice.* Don't you think the Society is going to have something to say about that?"

"Probably. We'll handle that when it gets here. For

now, it just lends credibility to the fact that he wants a personal guard to follow him around." He turned, raising his voice to the man in the corner. "Doesn't it?"

Canton looked up and nodded. At least he was cooperating.

"I think it's time we find out a little more about what he knows." Raselin said. "Like if the Society has been questioning his abilities."

Arin stepped forward, walking menacingly toward Magistrate Canton.

<h1>Chapter 17</h1>

"Sir, there's something wrong outside." Reed ran into the room an hour later.

"What do you mean?" Dov asked, rising from the chair in the study where he was pouring over Canton's record books.

"I don't know. Something is happening in the court-yard. There are no soldiers."

"What?"

"There are no Society men outside. Everything is empty. It's never empty out there. Everything is closed up tight, and since it's Canton's men outside, we thought we should get you first." Reed tried to catch his breath.

"Have you found Berwyn yet?"

"No, you're the first one I found."

Dov nodded, motioning me to follow.

"Go find Berwyn, Raselin, and Shadoe and have them meet us by the entrance to the south courtyard."

Reed raced out the door ahead of us.

"Silas," Dov called once we were in the hallway.

"In here." A voice came from a few doors down.

Dov paused at the door where our friend was searching the room and explained what was happening. Silas set down the papers he was riffling through and followed.

"Dov, over here." Gregory waved us over to a window once we exited the stairs.

He stepped back, giving us space to see.

"Do you see anything?" I asked, squinting to make sure I didn't miss any sign of movement or life.

It was quiet. Far *too* quiet for the Society. Had they found out?

"Missing something?" a jovial voice asked. It was exactly how Lowell would have spoken had he been there.

"Wallace?" Dov asked as we turned.

He was surrounded by a group of his men. Jake found me in the crowd and grinned. Marty, likely still learning to cope after his loss, was nowhere to be found.

"Little Baer," he greeted Dov. "You really didn't think I wouldn't find out about this, did you?"

"Why are you here, Wallace?" Dov growled as he stepped forward.

Henry, Ben, and Carter filed behind Dov and Silas, ready to assist. I was getting a little tired of Marty and Jake's crew.

"Where are the soldiers?" Dov demanded, holding his ground even in the face of Wallace's intimidating weapons.

"Dead." Wallace shrugged. "They were in the way. You left all of your men inside, so it was easy to pick off the few that maintained the grounds. You didn't do your math right, tiny Baer."

He must have hidden the bodies out of view from the mansion windows. I wondered where that meant he had concealed them.

"Wallace." Berwyn rushed down the stairs, ready to face his enemy. "Why are you here?"

"Berwyn," he leered. "So nice of you to join us. I imagine by now you have Canton under your control. I want you to give him to me."

"No." Berwyn looked amused. Crossing his arms, he added, "Why on earth would I do that?"

Wallace beamed as two of his men stepped out from the back of the crowd. They held Anetta and Marjorie, arms behind their backs. The women struggled to free themselves as the men clamped dirt-covered hands over their mouths to keep them from talking.

Anetta struggled wildly, catching my gaze. Her eyes kept darting to Marjorie and then back to me, trying hopelessly to communicate. Knives were held to their throats by the men assisting their captors, making it impossible to struggle too much. Marjorie flinched as the man stepped closer, her red hair falling in her face like it used to when Shadoe had to save me from countless dinners with Lowell and his friends.

Shadoe burst into the room, assessing the scene. Anger washed over his face when he saw Wallace occupying the room, darkness trembling through his every step. When he noticed Wallace was holding our people captive, a flicker of fear crossed over his face, melting into deeper hatred for the man. He stopped where he stood, waiting.

"That's what I thought," Wallace proclaimed victoriously. "Now, I see that you're trying to take control of the Society, and I admit, none of us alone have the numbers for that. So, I understand your little plan here, but I don't like being left out."

His voice changed from jovial to cold and dangerous.

"Now, you're going to go get Canton and bring him here. You will work *with* me and support *my* plan for this, or we'll kill your people. Not just these two, but all of them. My men are hiding all over this mansion. They'll never see us coming."

"How did you get your men in here without anyone seeing?" Shadoe challenged.

"Wouldn't you like to know?" Wallace sneered. "Now where is he?"

"Not one of our people would ever let you near Canton," Berwyn refused.

"No? Then how did I get in, Berwyn?" Wallace waved his arms around. "If your security is so good that you believed the Society couldn't get in, how did I do it?"

We all realized at the same moment that we had a spy in our midst. *But who?*

Just then Anetta stomped on the foot of her captor, causing him to pitch forward with her. The man with the knife leapt back as they lurched forward, barely nicking Anetta's neck and shoulder, just enough to see little bubbles of blood prick through her skin. She threw her blond head backwards, a flash of white, as she slammed into her captor's face.

"Marjorie!" she yelped to her friend.

I started to rush forward to help them as Anetta toppled onto the ground. She kicked out at the man, trying to knock him over.

"No, Auluria!" she screamed at me, panic in her voice.

Before I could reach her, Marjorie was free. She rushed to her friend, bending low. She held a knife in her hand.

Anetta's eyes were wild as the redhead held the blade to her already bloody neck. I froze.

"What is this?" Locust asked from his place behind Shadoe as he surveyed the scene.

"Marjorie is a spy," I responded quietly, wondering how I had never seen it. I found my voice, demanding information. "When?"

"Always," she sneered, no longer the flirtatious ladder-climber I had always known her to be. "You don't honestly think I would have hung around Lowell all that time without a purpose, do you?"

"Flirting your way to power seemed like a pretty good goal."

"It *did* seem that way, didn't it?" She laughed like it was all a joke. "Wallace is pretty good about picking his spies."

"Lowell took care of you. So has Shadoe. And the Baers have never hurt you. Why turn on us?" I asked, hoping to find a way to break her and free Anetta.

"Oh, little girl. You're wrong there. Speaking of which, let's make a little trade." She pulled Anetta to her feet.

Anetta's face was pulled tight as she raged inside against the woman she once trusted. I willed her to stay calm.

"Dov Baer," she turned to address the youngest Baer leader. "Your life for hers."

"No," I yelped unintentionally.

"Fine," Dov said, stepping forward. It was remarkable how good he looked in the Society's uniform. It seemed perfectly streamlined for his body. "Let her go."

Anetta tried to get his attention with a small shake of her head but he ignored her. He stepped forward slowly, trying not to spook Wallace's men.

"Let her go."

"Why him?" I snapped. "Take me instead. You've never liked me. If you want to make a point, make it with me."

"I don't want you, Auluria, but make no mistake, I'll come for you later. Funny, I have a feeling that Lowell wouldn't mind one bit." She laughed, enjoying herself. "But right now, I want *him* to die."

Jake stepped forward ready to assist. Moving to Marjorie's side, he took control of Anetta, in a move I hoped would give her a better chance of escape.

"Thank you, lamb," she said to Jake, almost adoringly, before turning to Dov. "Do you know who I am?"

"No," Dov said, not pretending.

"Look closer," she instructed.

Wallace looked amused as he watched the scene.

"No, no, big brother," he sang when he saw Berwyn start to inch forward, forcing him to hold his ground.

Dov studied the girl, trying to puzzle out who she was. When it clicked, his face fell.

"Oh, and he figured it out!" Wallace shouted, as if it were a game. "Your turn, Berwyn. Have a go!"

"No," Eden said in disbelief, understanding before her husband.

"That's bad," Silas whispered.

I shot him a questioning look, pleading for an answer.

"Wallace sent *her* to *us* and sent *you* to Lowell. He was playing us both."

I felt like I had been kicked as I realized Dov was talking about the girl that had been sent to win him over before I came along. It was the same girl who was discovered and sent back to Wallace's men, where she died from her interrogation. She was the entire reason Marty and Jake came after us so mercilessly.

"And here we thought we were special," Berwyn growled.

"When your sister left us," Dov addressed her, hands up to prove he wasn't being aggressive, "she was fine. She was very much alive. Wallace is the one that hurt her."

"Oh, I know," Marjorie said. Taking a step back, she moved her hand sharply behind her, digging her knife into Wallace's stomach.

His eye grew wide as he realized what was happening. Falling to his knees, his men all rushed forward to help. Marjorie stepped forward, nodding to Jake who was willing to turn his back on his leader to get revenge for the girl he had cared about.

"But he's not the only one who will pay." She lunged forward at Dov, attempting to cut him.

Dov moved quickly, grasping her wrist before she could bring her knife down. She fought, pulling his hair to whip his head around. Using her head, she crashed into Dov's face, making him gasp. She clawed at the hand holding her wrist.

Berwyn reached them first, assisting his brother. Everyone else rushed forward, engaging with Wallace's men. Anetta grappled with Jake until I arrived. Having had enough with the man, I didn't hold back. He lay unconscious on the floor, badly injured by the time Berwyn and Dov had Marjorie under control.

"Are you okay?" Anetta asked, kicking Jake once for good measure.

"I'm fine. Are you—" My words faded as she ran at Marjorie who was kneeling on the ground in front of the Baers.

"How could you?" Anetta screamed, accosting her former friend. She ranted about how Lowell protected them, how they were friends, and how she had trusted her.

Everyone gave her a moment to handle her feelings. She got in a few good punches before Dov dragged her back.

"Enough," he said quietly, allowing the older girl to collapse against him as Marjorie screamed about her sister.

He made Eden take a sobbing Anetta from him,

making her uneasiness show as she patted the girl's back. Her eyes caught mine, begging for help. I continued to guard Jake, leaving her responsible for the crying woman.

Dov knelt down in front of Marjorie.

"I'm sorry," he apologized. "I know you don't believe this, but I was heartbroken when I found out what they had done to her.

"I tried to protect her and I couldn't. If I could have changed what happened, I would have. If I could have taken the punishment for her, I would have, but there was nothing I could have done."

Shadoe joined him, kneeling beside them. Fear raced through me, knowing what he was capable of.

"You betrayed Lowell," he started.

It was the worst sin she could commit.

"Shadoe…" Dov cautioned.

He stared at her as I counted his breaths. One, two, ten, fifteen. He waited long enough to scare her. She was no fool.

"Lock her up," Shadoe finally said, standing. "Take the others."

Devin had arrived, helping to stop any uprising Wallace's men had considered pushing after the death of their leader. Silas confirmed he was no longer a problem before instructing his friends to take the new prisoners to the cells. With all the extra bodies, we'd be out of space before long.

Anetta stumbled back to me as Carter and Ben picked Jake up off the floor. They carried him out of the room with the others.

"I should have known."

"You couldn't have. Even Lowell didn't know. You honestly think any of us could have guessed it if Lowell hadn't?"

"I've lost Lowell. I've lost my closest friend," she lamented.

"You still have all of us, Anetta. We'll be your friends. And we still have a mission to carry out, so don't give up yet," I reminded her.

"We have a problem," Eden's voice rang out, forcing all of us to look toward the door.

"Hoods!" Dov hissed as he saw what was approaching.

I peered out from behind the mantle, the fabric once again hiding my hair. I walked quickly to fall into line; the perfect soldier doing their daily tasks around the mansion.

"Where is Magistrate Canton?" a frantic soldier asked.

The foyer was filled with panicked men. They searched for someone to address.

"In his study." Raselin responded. "He is not to be disturbed. What is it?"

"Bodies." The scared soldier answered. "They're all dead."

"Who?" Berwyn inquired.

"The men outside. They're all dead. The courtyard is empty. We found the bodies while on patrol and brought the men back. Is everything okay inside?"

Wallace's disruption had cost us our plan. The soldiers were about to discover what we had done.

"Everything is fine." Raselin guided the conversation. "Nothing is out of place."

The door slammed open, revealing an army of Society men. They jostled in the door.

"Everything is fine." Raselin raised his hands. "We've already patrolled the mansion, there is nothing out of place."

Canton appeared at the top of the stairs, hiding behind the banister. He stood taller than I had seen him since we arrived. The man looked calm as he placed his hands on the railing.

"Everything is fine. Stand your ground outside. Look for the rebels who did this on the grounds," Canton ordered.

He shifted, revealing Justin standing behind him. I assumed he had him at knifepoint.

They waited until most of the soldiers had returned

outside. I saw Justin whispering to him, giving him direction. He had risked bringing Canton in front of his men, but it had paid off.

The soldier who addressed us began to argue, unwilling to let it go so easily. He grabbed a hold of Raselin, trying to force him to listen. Raselin tossed him off, sending him into the group of men that stayed with him. They pushed him back, angry at being overlooked in the situation.

The man swung at Raselin, one of his coworkers swinging toward Berwyn. The soldiers started to yell as Canton was backed off of the landing, presumably to go back to where we had him locked up.

A soldier stumbled forward, crashing into Anetta. She knocked into me, swiping my hood off. I rushed to cover myself, but it was too late.

"It's her," one of them gasped, as visions of our plan to release the camps, take on the Society, and free our enemy countries on the other side of the wall flashed through my mind as quickly as memories of Dov had when I was waiting to hang. Everything slipped away.

We had been discovered, and no matter what we did now, the Society had the upper hand.

They attacked.

ACKNOWLEDGMENTS

Two down, one to go. Sorry I hit you with a cliffhanger again, but did you really expect anything less from me at this point? You know I'm kind of mean to characters and readers!

In all honesty, there were some things I didn't see coming in this one, and I'm happily surprised by the appearance of a few new characters. *Oh, do I have plans* for them! I hope you enjoyed meeting them as much as I did.

The thing I love most about this book is that we really see Auluria grow into her new role. In Golden, Dov was this strong, selfless character that did whatever he had to do to save the people he cared about, and Auluria had a bit of trouble making some of her decisions in the first book. Dov's selflessness clearly brushed off on Auluria in Locked as she fights to save not only Dov, but an entire country from the Society. I love seeing Auluria really step into her own in this story.

Don't worry, we still have one more piece of this story to go and I have some major things planned for this ending. Get ready, this is going to be the wildest ride of them all. Here's to the finale!

Thank you to Alexis, my amazing interior artist. You never cease to amaze me with your talent, hard work, and creativity. I appreciate you more than words can say. Thanks, yet again, for being the first to read my new babies. I love when you gush over my characters and help make sure everything is just right!

Special thanks to Awnna Marie Evans, my stunning editor. Words cannot express how grateful I am to have you in my life, both as a friend and as a colleague. I appreciate you helping me to *level up*!

Thank you to Sissy and Jess for all of your help! This story wouldn't be what it is without you!

Major shout out to my beautiful Elite Street Team—you all make life so much better! I'm so grateful for your friendship and all your hard work! Yentl, Jess, Sissy, Alexis, you ladies are the best!

Thank you to my awesome Street Team–your help, encouragement, and involvement are so appreciated! You rock!

Of course, special thanks to you, dear reader, for sticking with me on this journey. Auluria and Dov's story has always been so important to me and I couldn't be more grateful that you're experiencing it with me. I can't wait to wrap this up with you in the third book. Edge is going to be interesting to say the least. Let's do this!

Keep reading for a bonus scene from Shadoe's perspective, the first chapter of the final book in the series, and to find out how to play interactive games to help Auluria get ready for her mission to see the Baers, get more bonus scenes, and even gain access to Golden filters for your photos and live broadcasts.

Stay inspired,

-K.M. Robinson

I LET THE OTHERS WALK AHEAD OF ME. I NEEDED THE TIME to think.

Martin had ruined our chances of capturing Canton. I needed to figure out what to do next and how to prevent this from happening again. Lowell never would have stood for an infraction like this. He would have murdered Martin on the spot.

Lur wandered somewhere behind me, mixed with the group. I wondered how she felt about Martin's actions. Surely she was as upset as I was. If my training had taught her anything, she already knew what a set back this was for us. But then, have I *ever* known what Lur was thinking?

Birds chirped around us, only adding to my rage. Each one was like a little voice in my head reminding me that I had failed Lowell. I owed Lowell and I let him die to save Lur, then I let his plan fail. Now, with Canton out of my reach, I'd never be able to recover this plan. The Society's fall was within reach and slipped away.

I'm making ridiculous choices. I let Lur get into my head. I believed we could lead together like Lowell had planned. But Lur isn't one of us anymore; she's one of the Baers, and the Baers don't know how to play well.

Martin walked beside me, scowling. He had one job, and instead of giving his allegiance to us, he threw it away for one insignificant moment.

I should understand where he was coming from—Lowell himself had a moment like that when he chose to stand against Griz Baer. We're smarter now, though. We have our war planned out. We've been meticulous.

Martin broke our trust today.

The others glanced at me as we walked, waiting for me to do something in response. Words filtered back through the ranks from somewhere ahead of us, questioning how I would handle it.

"Do you think he'll do anything?"

"Lowell wouldn't have stood for this."

"He's going soft. They both are."

Martin's face twitched when he heard the same things I did. He believed them. He didn't think the punishment would fit the crime. If Lur had any say in it, it wouldn't. But I wasn't Lur. I was a product of my father and Lowell's training, and I would not be swayed.

I ground my teeth together, locking my jaw. I couldn't lose control of Lowell's people too. If I had any hope of carrying out his plan, I needed to keep my leadership intact.

Martin shifted next to me, dragging himself along. He clearly knew he would pay; he just didn't know how. Being near me set him on edge, as it should.

I watched him as we walked, one slow step after the next. We stepped over a large stone in the path, careful not to catch our feet on it. I moved quickly, letting the person behind me know there was something to avoid. Martin waited until the last second, not caring about our people. He never would.

I knew what I had to do.

Lowell had trained me well. Strategy was the thing I was best at, aside from fighting. My mentor had taught me how to lead; how to protect our interests. It was in our best interest to remove the plague that Martin had become. I knew Lowell would approve.

I stepped out of line, surprising Martin. With his throat in my fist, I pushed him toward the cliff. He moved easily, not expecting me to react as quickly as I had.

"Shadoe!" Lur screamed, forcing her way through the

crowd of people. I didn't have time to wait for her emotions to get in the way.

I pushed Martin again, this time for Lowell.

"Lowell never would have tolerated this," I yelled, ready to make my point to the crowd. "You will never disrespect me or my decisions again."

Martin rocked on the edge of the cliff, trying to catch his balance. I took the opportunity to make sure everyone was watching.

Today, they would hear me. Today, they would see me. Today, they would respect me.

Lur barreled through people, knocking them to the ground as she struggled to get to me. She had to admit, this was kinder than what Lowell would have done to the boy.

"Shadoe, don't!" she pleaded with me.

I turned back to Martin, unwilling to give her a say.

"You jeopardized our plan. You risked our lives. *For what?* Revenge. Never again." I squeezed his throat harder, making my point. Once I let go, it would be out of my hands, but I wanted Martin to know he had not only betrayed me—the person who helped him become the fighter that he was—but he had betrayed the man who had taken him in and given him purpose. Lowell would be disgusted.

I sensed Lur's presence before I hear the slap of her feet on the ground. Time was up.

I pushed Martin over the edge.

Lur reached us faster than I had anticipated. She grabbed onto Martin as he clawed at her, ripping into her skin. Relying on what I had taught her, Lur tried to counteract the motions, flinging Martin back to safety.

I lashed out, hoping to catch her as she hurled over the edge, her face washed in panic. My fingers met her wrist but tightened only long enough to pull her toward me. I nearly caught her.

Every crash filled my ears with more panic and dread. The first two must have broken bones. The third *had* to have killed her.

The silence was what broke *me*.

She didn't stir. The trees stopped rustling.

"Lur?" I yelled, peering over the edge.

I couldn't see her.

When I raised my gaze, people surrounded the precipice. They waited for directions.

"Down," I commanded, instructing them to search for her.

"I've got him," Ella's voice sounded through the chaos of people climbing down the cliff. Over my shoulder, I saw her take control of Martin as he lay sprawled on the ground.

I dropped over the side of the cliff, hoping Lur had landed straight down and it would be easy to find her.

Broken branches and crushed limbs littered the path down.

"Here," Nikko shouted when I made it over the edge.

I dropped the last few feet, quickly moving toward my former fiancée. She was crumpled on the ground, clothing ripped. Twigs sat at strange angles in her hair.

Dov Baer was going to murder me for this, and so would his little friends.

"Is she okay?" I asked, hoping my voice was even.

Nikko was bent over her body as he checked for a pulse. I searched for signs of life in her.

Lowell would have killed me for this.

Or would he have?

"She's alive," Nikko confirmed, looking up.

"This is bad," I commented quietly, kneeling down.

"What do you want us to do?" Nikko asked.

I paused, trying to think it through. We needed to get to the storehouse and we needed to get her help or I would pay for it later.

Knowing I needed to prevent the situation from getting out of control, I decided to do the only logical thing—control the story.

"Go get Sherman and find a way out of here," I instructed him.

My hands found their way to Lur's side. I've examined her injuries so many times that this shouldn't be any different, but it is. Her breathing is shallow, but it's there.

I could see where the bruises would form around the cuts in her pale skin.

"On it," Nikko stood. He ran off quickly as I gently worked my hands under Lur.

Lifting her, I braced myself to avoid stumbling. I looked for a new way up the side of the cliff. I could climb it on my own, but not with Lur in my arms. She shifted, settling against my chest.

Her groan made me wary. It should have made me feel worse than it did, but I didn't have time for that.

"Shadoe?" Sherman ran to my side.

"We need to find a way up," I said, voice strained under the weight of carrying another person.

Sherman nodded.

"We did. This way," he darted forward.

The others gathered around me, ready to help carry Lur if I was ready to pass her off.

I would pay the price of my decisions by carrying her to the storehouse. I never meant to hurt her, but I also didn't regret my decision to handle Martin. I'd have to deal with him once we reached the storehouse.

"We can't let them find out, you know," Sherman grumbled quietly on the walk back.

"We'll handle it," I agreed. "We have physicians."

Lur shifted in my arms. A strangled noise escaped her lips. It's much worse than the beating she took during her training.

"Lur?" I asked, moving her in an effort to wake her up. "*Lur?*"

She groaned and turned her head away from me. I deserved that.

"Lur, I need you to wake up now," I insisted.

"I have a feeling this is going to be easier if you just leave her alone," Sherman commented, holding a branch up so I didn't have to duck. It snapped back behind me, nearly hitting Locust in the face. He cursed as he batted it out of the way.

"Nikko," I called. "Run ahead to the storehouse and get the physician ready to look at her when we get there. "It's going to be a long walk back."

Lowell would have said Lur brought his on herself. In truth, she did. All of her decisions lead to this point.

In the end, we all pay for our choices. Lowell paid for his. I was paying for mine. Lur was paying for hers. But unlike Lur's cousin, we were still here, and we still had a job to do.

I chose to ignore Martin when we reached the top and rejoined the group. Instead, I tried working out another way to find Canton and bring the Society to its knees. If that meant working with the Baers, so be it, but in the end, Lowell's vision would come to light…I'd see to it, no matter what the price was.

EDGE: BOOK THREE IN THE GOLDEN TRILOGY

GOLDILOCKS HAS A NEW ROLE TO PLAY. SHE AND DOV BAER will draw the final battle lines and win the war—or die trying.

Securing a stronghold inside the enemy's walls, Auluria and Dov must fight to keep their deception concealed, but Shadoe's hunger for power might undo all of their work as they race for the Camps to free the young men and women being held there who could become their new allies in the war.

In their greatest battle yet, Goldilocks and the three Baers will have to fight for the fate of their country, bring down a corrupt enemy, and topple the Wall—but they never saw this coming. No one will make it out unscathed—if they make it out at all.

Now available!
Learn more about Locked at
edgeinfo.kmrobinsonbooks.com

**FORGED: A GOLDEN TRILOGY PREQUEL
NOVELLA**

Goldilocks was innocent once, but her cousin's plan to turn her into a killer has changed that.

Before Lowell sent Auluria on a mission for his master plan of destruction, before Shadoe trained her to be a vicious and deceptive fighter, before she ever met Dov Baer and his family, Auluria was a young girl merely trying to survive.

When Auluria is brought into Lowell's fold after the death of her aunt, she's placed under the supervision of Shadoe, a cruel and careless mentor to teach her to be a weapon in her cousin's war. As her training continues, she finds herself in growingly dangerous situations, all leading to her greatest mission yet: to destroy Dov and Berwyn Baer and become the deceptive fighter that no one will survive.

Now available!

Learn more about Forged at

forgedinfo.kmrobinsonbooks.com

TEMPERED: A GOLDEN TRILOGY PREQUEL NOVELLA

Before Dov lead a rebellion, he was a son and younger brother working to protect his family.

When the Baers discover the Society has called for their father's execution, they won't stop until he's safe, but their former friend has other plans. Forced into the open, the Baers try to protect their people from destruction at the merciless hands of the Society, but even *they* don't have the power to stop what is coming.

After the unthinkable happens, the brothers are forced to choose sides and take on roles they never wanted, but a new arrival changes everything and throws their world into chaos.

Now available exclusively in the Golden Boxset/Omnibus!

Learn more about Tempered at

goldentrilogyinfo.kmrobinsonbooks.com

MY FINGERS FAILED ME, TANGLING IN MY HAIR. Everything was muffled as I struggled to hide myself. Voices echoed inside my head, but I couldn't make out what they were saying.

Suddenly, I was snapped forward, jolted back to reality. Fixing my hood no longer mattered. Anetta tried to support me as I crashed into her. I came alive, realizing that we were under attack.

The Society men lunged toward us in the foyer of the mansion. I was suddenly grateful Canton had been led away before the soldiers realized who I was. Justin had good timing.

The noise of the fight dulled over the loud tearing of fabric. A red tapestry boasted a long tear, threatening to topple from its place on the wall. The ripping cloth drew my attention when it shouldn't have, making me involuntarily turn. A rough hand on my shoulder forced me to reach for the knife resting on my hip, its jagged edges begging to be used.

I sliced the man's arm, silently hoping that it was the worst damage I would have to do. Blood bubbled up on his skin as his eyes grew narrow and fiery. The man's nails dug into me in what I assumed would end in yet another scar on my body which was already marred by so many tales.

Gregory took the man down just as I drew back to attack once more. He nodded at me solemnly; the first time I'd ever seen him anything less than flirtatious.

"Behind you," he nodded.

I spun on my heels to confront whatever waited for me, my hair splaying out with my movements. Instead of being confronted with an attack, I found Shadoe grappling with a soldier.

"Here," I announced just loudly enough for my former handler to hear me.

I stepped beside him, taking a defensive position.

Before I could help, Shadoe leaped forward and snapped the man's neck. Shock waved over me in the two seconds between the dead man hitting the floor and another soldier rolling over my shoulder as I ducked, tossing him effortlessly as he attacked.

Shadoe looked impressed as I stood back up, having felt the man's approach and flipped him over. I turned away from Shadoe to see where else I could help and was immediately confronted with Dov's eyes, ten feet away. They were wide and surprised, but that same brilliant shade of deep blue.

I smiled to let him know I wasn't hurt, but it immediately faded as a soldier approached him. I jerked my head to the side to give him warning before I raised my hands, using my left arm to steady myself, and released my knife at the soldier. It embedded itself in the man just before Dov attacked.

"Auluria!" Silas shouted a warning, looking beyond me. "*Anetta.*"

I followed his gaze to where Anetta was fighting off two soldiers and failing. One grabbed her around the waist, attempting to lift her off the ground. Eden launched herself at the second man, kicking him so hard in the hip that I thought I heard it crunch. He toppled into a man beside him, taking them both to the ground. Shadoe and Locust appeared out of nowhere, slicing the soldiers' throats.

I ran to Anetta as she kicked in the air. She bit down on the man's hand, making him shriek and swear. I pulled an extra knife from my boot, plunging it into her captor's arm. The blond fell to the floor, bouncing up as soon as she hit the stone. Pulling her own knife, she drove it into the soldier's leg. His boot helped to protect him from her attack. He grabbed Anetta's hair, ripping it out from under the hood that only partially covered her head.

Locust—having finished off the men Eden had kicked down—stood up and took three wide steps forward. His hand dug into the soldier's wrist as he held him in place. His grip forced the man to release Anetta. He pulled back, preparing to hit the man as I turned.

"Fancy seeing you here." The low voice sent tingles up my spine.

The knife glistened in his hand as it moved toward me. The blood had been wiped off, though only so much could be removed from the strange, jagged blade without a proper cleaning. My sight traveled up the length of his arm to his face.

"Your knife, my lady." Dov smiled before growing serious. "Are you okay, Auluria?"

I took the blade from him, heat exploding through my hand when our skin touched. Tucking my backup weapon away in my boot, I opted to keep the knife Shadoe had provided for us.

"So far," I replied. "You?"

"Yeah," he mumbled before another soldier moved toward us.

I moved behind him, taking a position to cover his back. Hearing Dov fighting without being able to see him made me slow as I focused on what *he* was doing. I forced myself to block him out of my thoughts in order to protect him.

I kicked a soldier causing a sharp pain to crawl up my ankle where I had injured it before the attack on the mansion. I sucked in a deep breath, trying to control the burn creeping through my leg.

The soldier came at me again, yelling something I blocked out. I lowered my stance just enough to get a secure footing, putting as much weight as I could on my uninjured leg without throwing myself off balance. When he moved, I elbowed him in the nose. Blood gushed down his face.

He stepped forward again, undeterred by my hit. I prepared to strike, but suddenly, he fell at my feet. Silas lowered his weapon, having used it to hit the man in the head, knocking him out.

"Miss me?" he asked as he turned our two-person team into a trio.

"Nice to see you haven't died," I could hear the grin in Dov's voice as he called over his shoulder.

"Reinforcements are here," Silas informed us.

I glanced around, noticing that most of our team was in the foyer. Berwyn had made his way to Eden and Anetta, who appeared to have formed a partnership during the fight. Ben and Carter must have finished securing Wallace's men if they were available to join the combat, leaving us one less thing to worry about during the battle.

"You all okay?" Raselin yelled from a few feet away as he fought with a soldier.

I stepped ahead, darting my good leg out to sweep the Society man's feet out from under him. He crashed forward, nearly taking Raselin down with him. A tooth bounced across the ground, looking like a horrifying white bug skittering across the forest floor. I heard every ding and scrape it made as it moved.

Raselin nodded and shrugged when the man didn't get up.

"Works for me," he added.

"Shadoe!" Dov warned loudly.

"Shadoe, no!" I echoed when I saw that my former fiancé was doing as much damage as he had when he threatened Canton in the weapons room. Bodies littered the floor. "We need them."

Nikko took out another Society soldier before looking to Shadoe for direction. I searched for Ella but didn't see her in the room. I tried not to think about what mission Shadoe had sent her on that would have prevented her from joining the fight.

Shadoe nodded, knowing he had to play by the rules in a room filled with people who would not tolerate his deadly behavior. Berwyn's people and Raselin's group would work together to outnumber Shadoe's team if anything were to happen.

"Give up now and you won't get hurt." Berwyn's voice filled the room, giving the remaining Society men an option.

Most of the soldiers relented and stopped fighting, knowing they were outnumbered. One man rushed forward, refusing to back down. He launched himself at Devin. I leaped forward, despite knowing I would not be able to reach him in enough time to help. Devin tossed the man over his shoulder, protecting his newly-healed arm. He kicked the man's arm, making him cringe into himself. Carter stooped down to bind the man's wrists behind him.

I found Silas and Dov giving me questioning looks when I turned back to them, having only made it a few feet forward to help Devin.

"You didn't actually think you were going to help that situation, did you?" Eden scoffed from behind me.

"I was going to try," I growled back at her, knowing she wasn't being malicious, but also not caring of her intentions.

"Get these men taken care of," Berwyn announced. "Quickly. We still have to handle the men outside."

"This isn't over yet," Raselin added.

We quickly scrambled to determine who was awake, unconscious, or dead. The men who gave themselves up were bound and taken to the cells. I walked a man down the dark corridors with Eden and her charge as Dov and Silas carried an unconscious man behind us.

The cells were as bad as I remembered. The chill seeped into my bones as the hollow silence filled every space in my body. The last time I was there, I was meant to die, and my cousin, Lowell, had been the one to sentence me. The walls held the memory of my last conversation with my cousin.

Eden tensed next to me, her gait becoming stiff. She pushed the soldier forward with sharp fingers to his back between his shoulder blades. I forbade my muscles from tightening around my captive's hands; he didn't need to know my terror.

Dov and Silas looked less concerned about being in the space. I assumed they had been down here since our arrival. Dov had spent so much time in the mansion during his captivity that it was practically his second home. It didn't seem to affect them to be back in the cells… or they hid it well.

"Right," Dov instructed as we neared the end of the hall.

We turned, finding another series of hallways.

"Take the first one," Silas said, his voice strained under the weight of the unconscious man he was helping to carry.

We steered our charges down the walkway and found ourselves in an entirely new wing of cells.

"I didn't realize this was down here," Eden mumbled.

The man in front of me started to say something. My nails dug into his wrists silencing him before he could start.

We locked the men up, keeping them bound to prevent them from helping each other inside the cells. Dov and Silas checked all the locks on the prison doors before we left.

"We didn't either until we explored once we got in," Silas explained, "once we were away from the Society men."

"*I* didn't even see all of this," Dov commented as I slipped an arm around his waist, tucking myself under his arm as we walked through the muted gray lights of the cell passageways.

Shadoe and Raselin walked toward us, carrying another unconscious man. I expected Shadoe to try to talk to me, but instead, he locked eyes with Dov. They held each other's gaze until we passed, continuing to the foyer to see if we needed to move more Society bodies.

Several of our people filed past us, moving the Society prisoners to their new living quarters deep below the magistrate's mansion. I watched for my friends as we moved.

"You okay?" Dov whispered quietly in my ear, his lips tangling in my hair.

I nodded, not trusting myself to answer out loud. His hand tightened against my hip, pulling me closer. I leaned toward him, resting my head on his shoulder for a moment before stepping into the foyer.

Berwyn noticed us as we stepped into the light, motioning us to join him. Eden hurried to take her spot by her husband. His fingers slipped around her hand quietly at their sides so that only our tight circle could see.

"We have control of the mansion again, but we're going to need to handle the soldiers outside," Berwyn guided the conversation, his angry tone ever-present. "We're going to have to use Canton to deal with the courtyard."

"Can we trust him?" Eden asked before I could open my mouth to speak.

"Where is he?" I followed up.

"Justin is still guarding him. Apparently, he got

Canton to a cell and kept him ready in case we needed to use him to end the fight down here." Berwyn grimaced at the thought of coming so far only to play our hand before we were ready. "He's still with him...I'm assuming because he's thinking what we're all thinking—Shadoe will do something reckless."

"No surprise there." Silas and Dov murmured at the same time.

"What's the plan?" I asked, knowing I probably wouldn't like it. I wasn't fond of not knowing the next step. It reminded me too much of my time with Lowell.

"We're going to have to take Canton out and have him calm the courtyard." Dov took my hand, mirroring Berwyn and Eden. "And, once we've done that, we have to get a stronghold in the towns."

Dov glanced at Berwyn.

"One of us is going to have to go out and tell the people what is going on. They'll side with us, but right now, they have no idea what's going on here. Once we do that, then we can start to use Canton against the Society."

"And who is going to go out into the towns to do that?" I asked.

Dov's eyes shifted to me.

"No," I forbade it. "You are not going out there. Someone else can go."

"It has to be one of us," Dov tried to persuade me.

"Berwyn can't go. He needs to stay here and lead everyone. If it can't be him, it has to be me."

"What if *I* go?" I insist, trying to find another way.

"No offense, Auluria," Silas interjected. "But even though people have heard about you, you still worked for Lowell, and Lowell is dead. They might not know which side you are on."

"Despite the fact that you did all this, babe, the famous Goldilocks is still not as well-known as the sons of Griz Baer." Dov grinned, teasing me.

"That's not fair."

"We can't all be famous, Auluria." Dov's eyes sparkled as much as they did the time we sat on the floor of his house, mending socks and fantasizing about taking on the Society soldiers.

"*Auluria* might not be famous, but Necesta has been awfully quick to start spreading tales of *Goldilocks*," Raselin said, sidling up to the group, running his fingers through his dark brown hair. "Don't underestimate her... she knows what she's doing."

"Which one?" Silas smirked.

"Both." Raselin leveled a glare at him, removing Silas's joking grin.

"The point is," Berwyn growled, "That we need to handle making Canton cooperate first."

"Are we considering letting Shadoe handle this?" Raselin asked with concern. "He seems to be the one the

Magistrate fears, but do we really want to let him oversee Canton?"

"Do we have a choice?" I asked. I trusted him more than the others did, but I still didn't like what Shadoe was turning into.

"Can Justin handle it? He did well before the fight." Silas suggested.

"He can handle it," Dov, Raselin, and I all said in unison.

"The better question is whether we can afford to have Justin be Canton's handler and lose him for everything else."

"Would it be better to let Shadoe oversee Canton and let Justin help with the missions we're running?" Eden added, tucking a lock of hair back over her shoulder. It caught on the hood of her uniform as it lay on her back, leaving the strand of hair at a strange angle.

The group took a collective breath, puzzling out the best choice for the good of the team. It was quickly interrupted as Talley walked up.

"Whatever we're planning on doing, we need to do it now. The Society men outside are not going to wait any longer," she announced. "What's the strategy?"

The tall woman glanced at me, then to Raselin, looking for an answer. When we didn't speak, she turned to Berwyn.

"Well?" she prompted.

"Do we have a plan yet?" Devin bounded up next to his sister, looking out of breath.

"Are you okay?" I asked as he leaned forward to calm his rapid breathing.

"Yeah, I just ran from Justin to find out what's going on."

"Is he okay up there with Canton?" Talley asked, concern filling her voice.

"He's fine. Canton is behaving. But Shadoe is up there, so we'd better get moving if you weren't the ones to send him."

Everyone turned, sprinting toward the flight of stairs. Deep red carpet covered the stair, so soft it felt like layers of moss piled on top of each other.

"Time to vote," Berwyn said. "Who do we leave in charge of Canton?"

"Justin." Eden cast her vote first.

"Justin," Talley added, assuming her vote counted as part of the leadership vote.

"Justin," Devin echoed a vote for his brother.

"Shadoe." I shocked the Hersh siblings into looking at me. "We need Justin elsewhere and this will give Shadoe something less destructive to do. Plus, Canton is already under his thumb. He's terrified of him."

"She makes a good point," Raselin nodded. "Shadoe."

"Shadoe." Silas grimaced.

Dov only sighed and nodded once.

"Shadoe," Berwyn finished the count.

"You're not moving him." Justin's voice rang out as we approached the room Canton was being held in.

"Get out of the way, Hersh. We don't have time for this." Shadoe threatened.

"You're not taking him until I have confirmation that he is really supposed to be moved," Justin argued.

"Are you really going to take me on?" Shadoe's strong voice filled the hallway.

"Enough," I shouted, still far enough away that I wouldn't be able to step between the men, even if I wanted to.

I rounded the corner to find Shadoe and Justin facing off, chest puffed out and standing at full height. Canton leaned against the corner as I peeked over Berwyn's tall shoulder. The magistrate looked defeated as he slumped against the wall, eyes bouncing back and forth between his captors. He perked up when he saw the top of my head peering at him from behind Berwyn.

"Stand down," Raselin said from alongside Berwyn. "Shadoe, we need you to handle the magistrate's announcement. Justin, you're working with these three."

He nodded to me, indicating Justin should follow us. My friend's eyes bounced from Raselin, to me, to his siblings, and back to me. I nodded, hoping he would cooperate.

Reluctantly, he stepped aside, moving toward the door. Shadoe turned toward Canton.

"Up," Shadoe commanded.

Canton scrambled to his feet, locking eyes with Shadoe, ready to obey.

"Excuse me," Justin said quietly, slipping through the door once Berwyn and Raselin had stepped inside to give Canton directions.

Devin and Justin traded a look. Talley looked unimpressed with her brother's decision to take on Shadoe.

"What's the plan?" Justin asked.

"You and Dov are leaving. Now," Eden said before anyone else could speak. "They're handling Canton and quelling the soldiers outside. You two are sneaking out while the men are distracted by the announcement and you're going to rally the townspeople. We need them on our side."

Justin nodded.

"And the rest of you?"

"We have things to do here. There really isn't time to explain. You need to go." Eden reached out and put a hand on his arm, pulling him into motion. Dov followed quickly behind.

It took everything inside of me to force myself not to argue. Dov needed to do this—it was the only rational way. I had to stay and keep Shadoe in check. I was the only one that could.

"We'll be back in a few hours," Dov whispered quietly. "I'm not that easy to get rid of."

He grinned before surprising me with a quick kiss.

"Don't let this get out of hand." He took my hand and placed it on his chest when we reached the door.

"I'll watch him," I assured him.

"Don't get caught," Talley said a few feet away. She patted her brother on the shoulder.

"Come on," Justin said, nodding to Dov. "Let's get moving before the announcement starts."

The two men slipped out the door into the bright light of day. The white light bounced off the mansion floor. The light colors reflected the white light harshly, temporarily adding a green haze to my vision as I watched the people I cared about disappear into the world.

"They'll be fine," Talley acted as the voice of reason. "They're both very good at this."

"Justin will watch out for Dov." I murmured, knowing that he would.

"He knows to watch for Dov's injuries. He's not quite back to himself yet. Besides, unlike the rest of you, Justin isn't well-known. He can blend in and watch, where Dov will likely be recognized. They'll make a good team."

"Auluria," Eden's voice echoed from the stairway. "Get up here!"

"Happy?" Shadoe asked sarcastically.

"Yes," I responded as he came to a stop in front of me. He squared his feet with his shoulders and glared at me from behind crossed arms.

He watched me as if hoping I could guess what he wanted me to say. I didn't care enough to try.

Shadoe had forced Canton onto a balcony overlooking his soldiers. He quietly stood just behind the magistrate's shoulder, off to the side, acting as his personal guard. Every word was precisely spoken to planned perfection as the man convinced his minions to do his bidding. In the aftermath of his announcement, he cowered in the next room over under Devin's watch.

"What?" I shouted, demanding my handler say something as I looked up from the map I was studying.

He continued to stare for a moment before storming off. I considered going after him, but after everything that had happened that day, I needed a few minutes to myself.

The paper crinkled under my fingers as I gazed at it. My eyes traced the town lines. I followed the length of the Wall surrounding the Society, marking each place I thought we should begin the teardown process once we had defeated the Society. Liberating Raselin's country to the northeast would be the next thing we needed to do.

"Learning anything important?" Silas's voice frightened me.

Two deep breaths and I banished my shock, returning my shoulders to their normal position after gasping. Anetta smirked as she took a seat across from me at the table.

"We need to free the camps." I redirected.

"I know," Silas agreed.

Anetta shifted her focus to the window on the side of the room. Her eyes bounced slightly as she focused on something. I turned to glance outside. In the dark, small green lights flickered on and off.

"Didn't you see enough of those with Lowell?" I teased.

"I like fireflies." She shrugged.

Silas moved his chair closer to mine, leaning into my space to look at the map.

"Here," he pointed. "This is the route Dov would have taken. He's starting here, then here, and here."

His fingers traced along the towns, showing me where my boyfriend would be completing his mission. My gaze moved outward to the other towns. We needed a plan to reach them.

"The first step," Silas said as if reading my mind, "is to

get control of the justices in these towns. If we can gain control there, we've got a shot."

"Once we handle that, we should be able to get at least two of the other magistrates," I added.

"And if we can get them, we've got them all. We know, we know." Anetta rolled her eyes, turning back from the scene outside the window. "But how do we get them?"

"Once we have the towns and the camps with us, it shouldn't be hard to do exactly what we did here." Silas looked up from the map briefly to address her.

"This one," I said, pointing at the piece of paper, making it crinkle again. "We need this one."

Silas inspected it.

"You're right," he said, making me grateful for Shadoe's training. "We need that one first. We have the best chance of getting in there unnoticed."

"But we also need the rest of them."

"Or at least most of them." Silas nodded. "We'll have to send out multiple teams."

"What are we going to do about Marjorie?" Anetta interrupted, demanding answers.

We both looked up, slightly surprised at her outburst.

"She'll stay locked up in the cells," I answered, "For now, anyway."

"But she *will* answer for this?" she pressed.

"She will. Just not today." I felt Silas's leg tense next to mine as he spoke. I bumped his foot with mine, assuring him he didn't need to prepare to stop Anetta from running down to the cells and taking her revenge on her former best friend.

"Just how do you plan on breaking into the camps?" She changed the topic.

"We have a few ideas," Silas said, glancing at me, telling me he and Dov already had a plan. "You probably won't like them."

THE COMPLETE GOLDEN TRILOGY

Did you know the complete Golden Trilogy is now available with all three books and two prequel novellas?

The ebook boxset and printed omnibus contains Golden,

Locked, and Edge, as well as the prequel novella, Forged, which tells the story of Auluria's training before Lowell sent her on that deadly mission to destroy the Baer family, *and* an exclusive bonus novella, Tempered, which tells the events in Dov's life before he met Auluria—including what happened to his father.

You can only access Tempered and an exclusive note from the author through the boxset/omnius.

For more information, please visit
goldentrilogy.kmrobinsonbooks.com

BONUS SCENES

Want to read bonus scenes from Golden? We're giving out exclusive bonus scenes over on the K.M. Robinson Facebook page where you can read scenes from Dov and Reyla's perspectives.

Get them by sending the page a direct message
at
www.facebook.com/kmrobinsonbooks

We're constantly giving out additional bonus scenes for preorder swag, giveaways, and more, so watch the social media pages carefully for the next scene giveaway.

K.M. Robinson also has bonus scenes and extras from all of her books on
newsletter.kmrobinsonbooks.com

Sign up now for weekly emails with special bonuses, extras, live broadcasts replays and upcoming dates, events, coloring pages, games, introductions to new authors+live broadcasts with them, and more.

WORLD PORTALS

Ready to learn exclusive facts about The Golden Trilogy and other K.M. Robinson Series?

World Portals are now available on www. kmrobinsonbooks.com

Learn behind the scenes facts, watch videos, play games, check out our book filters, find out where to get bonus scenes, view fan art, and get access to other secrets we've hidden away inside the World Portals on the website.

The World Portals are constantly changing and information is being taken away and added all the time, so check back frequently for new content!

GOLDEN MISSION INTERACTIVE GAME

Auluria is being sent on one last mission before Lowell and Shadoe send her to destroy Dov and Berwyn Baer and she needs your help. Are you ready to assist Goldilocks and locate the Baers?

This interactive, choose-your-own-adventure game is played through Facebook messenger so you never miss a mission. Played over the course of one-two days, you and Auluria will go on several missions to discover the location of her next target and then you can go back into the story and see how your actions lead up to everything in the book.

PLAY THE GAME

at

goldenmission.kmrobinsonbooks.com

Auluria will meet with you few times for different missions over the course of a few days, with gaps of time in between so you can "complete the missions" and report back. She will be in touch!

Have fun running missions to help Auluria find Dov and Berwyn and then go back in the story to see how your choices directly affect them in the story.

BONUS FACEBOOK FILTERS

WANT TO GET YOUR HANDS ON SOME INCREDIBLE Facebook filters for Golden? Now you have the ability to get filters for the story, characters, etc right inside your phone.

You can use these on your photos, profile pictures,

videos, and live broadcasts. All you have to do is like my author page and they will automatically show up in your filters!

I've even taken these clips and put them on Instagram Stories by saving them to my phone and uploading them to Instagram.

Visit www.facebook.com/kmrobinsonbooks to grab these filters for your photos, videos, and broadcasts! Bonus points for tagging me @kmrobinsonbooks so I can see how you're supporting The Golden Trilogy.

ABOUT THE AUTHOR

K.M. Robinson is a storyteller who creates new worlds both in her writing and in her fine arts conceptual photography. She is a marketing, branding and social media strategy educator who is recognized at first sight by her very long hair. She is a creative who focuses on photography, videography, couture dress making, and writing to express the stories she needs to tell. She almost always has a camera within reach.

Visit her at her website: www.kmrobinsonbooks.com

CONNECT ON SOCIAL MEDIA

facebook.com/kmrobinsonbooks

instagram.com/kmrobinsonbooks

twitter.com/kmrobinsonbooks

Get free excerpts and full novels from K.M. Robinson at excerpt.kmrobinsonbooks.com

ALSO BY K.M. ROBINSON

The Golden Trilogy

Book One: Golden

Forged: A Golden Novella

Book Two: Locked

Book Three: Edge

The Complete Series Boxset/Omnibus with Tempered: an exclusive bonus novella

The Jaded Duology

Book One: Jaded

Book Two: Risen

The Complete Series Boxset/Omnibus with exclusive epilogue

The Siren Wars Saga

Book One: The Siren Wars

Book Two: Darker Depths

Book Three: Beyond The Shores

Origins of the Siren Wars: Prequel Novella

Book Four: Forbidden Waters (coming soon)

The Legends Chronicles

Along Came A Spider: A Prequel Novelette

And They'll Come Home: A Prequel Novelette

The Archives of Jack Frost Series

The Revolution of Jack Frost

The Redemption of Jack Frost (coming soon)

Stealing Steam Series

Book One: Lions and Lamps

Book Two: Pistons and Prisoners

Book Three: Railcars and Rulers

Top Hats and Telegraphs: A Prequel Novella

The Complete Series Boxset/Omnibus with Vambraces and Victories: an exclusive bonus novella

Virtually Sleeping Beauty: A Novella Retelling

The Goose Girl and The Artificial: A Novella Retelling

The Sinking: A Little Mermaid Novella Retelling

Cindrill: A Cinderella Assassin Novella Retelling

Sugarcoated: A Hansel and Gretel's Witch Novella Retelling

Blood Is Silent: A Red Riding Hood Circus Retelling

JADED: BOOK ONE OF THE JADED DUOLOGY

Her father failed in his mission to take control from the Commander, a defeat that has cost Jade her life. She will die as punishment. Now she belongs to the Commander's son—as his wife. Knowing his intent is to quietly kill her in revenge, Jade's every move is calculated to survive—until she learns her death ensures the safety of her father and her entire town.

Roan doesn't want to kill Jade, but once his family isolates her from her father and community, his only choice is to go through with the plan. Jade doesn't make it easy as she tries to sway him into falling for her. Each misstep makes him question his cause. Each moment makes every decision harder, but the Commander won't allow him to fail.

One chooses life. One chooses death. In the midst of the chaos, only one will succeed.

Now available!
Learn more about The Jaded Duology at
jadedinfo.kmrobinsonbooks.com

THE SIREN WARS: BOOK ONE OF THE SIREN WARS SAGA

War has hovered around the kingdom of Scylla for generations ever since the original sirens left the mer collection generations ago after nearly drowning the human prince. Over the years, select mermaids from the royal bloodline have been trained as spies to work for the reigning kings and queens, keeping the collection safe from sirens and humans.

Celena and her partner, Merrick, work covertly for the royals—not even her twin brother knows. When they discover the sirens have broken through the barriers the mer set up to keep the sirens out, Celena and her friends must race to the old kingdom of Metten to stop them from starting a war within their borders.

When she's dragged to the surface, Celena realizes that the war above the waters is as deadly as the one below the waves—and sacrificing herself may be the only way to protect her family.

The Siren Wars have only just begun.

Available now!
Learn more about The Siren Wars Saga at sirenwarsinfo.kmrobinsonbooks.com

LIONS AND LAMPS: BOOK ONE OF THE STEALING STEAM SERIES

All wishes require sacrifice…are you willing to pay the price?

Cyra spent the last seven years being trained to steal an airship in a brutal competition that leaves the victor with millions. Last year, she won.

Aladdin spent the past year fighting to get enough money to take his mother away from Horallen after his father was murdered. Now, his evil uncle Kacper wants to force him into the competition and straight to his death inside the Collection Cave.

When Aladdin discovers a genie said to have been banished a century ago, the competition becomes even deadlier, and he knows he can't trust the girl who snuck into the competition this year...but Cyra might not survive his ruthlessness either in a game where only the lion's heart can win.

All wishes require sacrifice, and someone is going to pay the price for the Stourbridge.

Available now!
Learn more about The Stealing Steam Series at
lionsandlampsinfo.kmrobinsonbooks.com

ALONG CAME A SPIDER: THE FIRST PREQUEL NOVELETTE TO THE LEGENDS CHRONICLES

Little Hacker Muffet
sat on her tuffet
destroying her cords and Way.
Along came a hacker named Spider,
who sat down beside her
and frightened his opponent away.

When Fet, one of the most skilled hackers in the Legends, discovers her best friend and leader of her group has been abducted and held for ransom, she must escape unnoticed and find Peep before it's too late.

When Spider, a new recruit training to join her hacker ring, slips out with her and claims to have a plan to save her friend, Fet is forced to bring him along. As she discovers he's not who he claims to be, she faces grave danger and learns just how deadly a spider bite can be.

Now available!
Learn more about The Legends Chronicles at
acasinfo.kmrobinsonbooks.com

VIRTUALLY SLEEPING BEAUTY

She may be doing battle in the virtual world, but in the real world, they can't wake her up…

All Rora wants is to help people as class president, give her time to local charities, and quietly earn her way to the top level of the virtual reality system that the entire country uses without anyone noticing she's the second best player in the game.

All Royce wants to do is level up as a knight inside the gaming system, slay dragons, and eventually play his way to controlling the palace as he takes the crown away from the reigning queen.

When his Aunt Perry calls him, hysterically screaming that her goddaughter, Rora, has been inside for more than the four hours the game allows, Royce rushes over to help.

Entering the game, Royce soon discovers that Rora is trapped inside the system after an encounter with an evil magician who can change forms inside the game and control the virtual world. If he and his friend can't help her beat the game, she might not be able to wake up in the real world at all.

When virtual knights and princesses meet to slay dragons and defeat evil rulers, there's nothing stopping them from suffering real-world consequences too.

To wake her up, he must enter the game and help her beat it.

Now available!
Learn more about Virtually Sleeping Beauty at
vsbinfo.kmrobinsonbooks.com

THE REVOLUTION OF JACK FROST

No one inside the snow globe knows that Morozoko Industries is controlling their weather, testing them to form a stronger race that can survive the fall out from the bombs being dropped in the outside world—all they know is that they must survive the harsh Winter that lasts a month and use the few days of Spring, Summer, and Fall to gather enough supplies to survive.

When the seasons start shifting, Genesis and Jack know something is going on. As their team begins to find technology that they don't have access to inside their snow globe of a world, it begins to look more and more like one of their own is working against them.

. . .

Genesis soon discovers Morozoko Industries, but when a foreign enemy tries to destroy their weather program to make sure their destructive life-altering bombs succeed in destroying the outside world, only one person can shut down the machine that is spinning out of control and save the lives of everyone inside the bunker—Jack.

Now available!
Learn more about The Revolution of Jack Frost at
jackfrostinfo.kmrobinsonbooks.com

THE SINKING

The sea with wants to silence her, but not for the reason you think.

When a quirky older woman pawns a fancy seashell necklace at her mother's antique shop on the pier, Cara doesn't think much about the story the woman spins about the wearer turning into a mermaid.

On her way home, she accidentally drops the necklace into the ocean and is swept out to sea where she meets Quay--a merman who volunteers to take her to his mother, the sea queen, to help her get her legs back.

. . .

Cara soon learns that it's Quay's eighteen birthday--a day that has been a curse for his family--and is meant to be one for her too. Now she must fight to survive the sea with Quay at her side.

Fans of The Little Mermaid will love this twisted take on the beloved story.

Now available!
Learn more about The Sinking at
thesinkinginfo.kmrobinsonbooks.com

CINDRILL

CINDERELLA IS AN ASSASSIN OUT TO MURDER THE PRINCE...
but he's hunting her too.

The nanobots Cindrill's master gives her to use as a mask allow her to slip into the ball wearing a face that isn't hers, but when the assassination attempt goes sideways, Prince Davin doesn't understand why her face changes when he injures her, slicing her foot open around a unique pair of shoes as she runs away.

When Cindrill runs into the prince the next day without her nanobot mask on, he doesn't recognize her, but immediately decides her skills will be useful on his hunt for the would-be-assassin woman who nearly killed his father and his fiancée the night before.

Both are tasked with the job of murdering the other, but things don't quite go as they had planned when Cindrill's master and Davian's fiancée interfere as the two try to decide whether or not to kill the other.

It's hard to recognize a woman when she uses technology to change her appearance, but Cindrill is going to use that to her full advantage as she destroys the prince. ***Will either survive?***

Now available!

Learn more about Cindrill at
cindrillinfo.kmrobinsonbooks.com

THE GOOSE GIRL AND THE ARTTIFICIAL

WHAT WOULD YOU DO IF YOUR ARTIFICIALLY INTELLIGENT handmaiden stole your identity?

Threatened by her Artificial, Arta, Princess Goselyn is forced to switch places and pretend she isn't human when she reaches Prince Corinth to negotiate a treaty they both need to be able to take their respective crowns one day. If she doesn't comply, her Artificial, controlled by her evil cousin, will not only kill Goselyn's mother, but Prince Corinth and his father as well.

Can the quiet princess outsmart a machine created to be more intelligent than she is, all while surviving the other

Artificials and robots working against her in the foreign palace, or will Corinth and his father find out and destroy her chance to save them all?

382

Now available!

Learn more about The Goose Girl and the Artificial at goosegirlinfo.kmrobinsonbooks.com

SUGARCOATED

Hansel and Gretel's witch…wasn't.

Annika's job is to create a cake to match the candy-colored rooftops, nightly firework shows, and daily parades ending in unexpected executions for the mad king's ball, but her true mission is to sneak a thirteen-year-old assassin into the palace using her gift of illusions.

Hansel's job is to protect his little sister, Gretel, once she assassinates King Levin and ends the destruction in Candestrachen, using his power over light to rescue the young girl from the chaos her influence over life and death will create.

.   .   .

When the entire forest reconstructs itself under Gretel's command while trying to save herself from a king's guard, Hansel and Annika must put their feelings aside and ensure their plan holds true—even if it means one of them has to sacrifice themselves to protect the mission.

Her illusions were meant to save her....but not everyone will survive the assassination attempt.

Learn more about Sugarcoated at
sugarcoatedinfo.kmrobinsonbooks.com

BLOOD IS SILENT

RED RIDING HOOD IS A CIRCUS AERIALIST AND THE WOLF IS ready to cage her.

Sienna has grown up working for the circus, dangling off her signature red silks every night. Her grandmother has been known to wander off to train new acts for their boss, but when Sienna tries to find her to bring her back to the show, she doesn't expect the dashing and dangerous Elijah to join her.

When they finally find Grandma Ida has been transformed deep in the heart of the woods, Sienna will stop at nothing to save her—but the wolf has her right where he wants her, and she won't be able to escape his claws.

She was told not to go into the woods alone.

Now available!

Learn more about Blood Is Silent at
bloodissilentinfo.kmrobinsonbooks.com